tri

or

trat

JAMES I MORROW

The Book Guild Ltd

First published in Great Britain in 2021 by
The Book Guild Ltd
9 Priory Business Park
Wistow Road, Kibworth
Leicestershire, LE8 0RX
Freephone: 0800 999 2982
www.bookguild.co.uk
Email: info@bookguild.co.uk
Twitter: @bookguild

Typeset in 12pt Adobe Jenson Pro

Printed and bound in the UK by TJ Boks Limited, Padstow, Cornwall

ISBN 978 1 91355 123 0

British Library Cataloguing in Publication Data.

A catalogue record for this book is available from the British Library.

First do no harm
Hippocrates (460 – 375 bc)

preface

The World Health Organization (WHO) defines counterfeit drugs as those that have been 'deliberately and fraudulently mislabelled with respect to identity or source'. The *British Medical Journal* and the *Lancet* have both highlighted the growing threat posed by fake or counterfeit agents. In a congressional hearing, representatives of the United States Food and Drug Administration (FDA) told members that such medicines may contain cheap and potentially dangerous contaminants and had already been linked to the deaths of a number of patients in the US. It was also pointed out that the counterfeit drug trade has become increasingly difficult to combat with supplies, often emanating from countries without regulatory controls, now flooding the marketplace. In some countries it has been alleged that around ten to thirty per cent of medicines might actually turn out to be fake. A recent editorial (March 2016) in the *British Medical Journal* titled 'Can anyone stop the illegal sale of medicines online?' highlighted that some of the most commonly purchased fake drugs were those for erectile dysfunction and accounted for £11 million of the £12.2 million worth of illegal drugs seized from April to December alone.

chapter one

George winced; his arm was starting to hurt again. The steel bracelet was cutting into his wrist. He turned to look up and over his left shoulder where his arms were pulled sharply backwards and fastened tightly to the bedstead. He tried, awkwardly, to shift position, to get a better look at the handcuff's fastenings, but there seemed no way to relax their hold. He bent his knees up and pushed his heels hard into the mattress in another attempt to push himself further up the bed, to ease some of the pressure on his arms.

As he struggled, he glanced down, with some disgust, at the naked vulnerability of his own body. Beyond the wispy, greying chest hair, his stomach rose like a small rounded hillock from just below the diaphragm and stretched the blotchy abdominal skin. His midriff, he recognised, had seen better days and now reflected his more relaxed middle years; it lifted and fell in time with his gasping breaths. He puffed and panted his way through the exertions, limited to simply trying to get more comfortable. He caught a particularly unflattering view of himself in the full-length wardrobe mirror, felt a sudden surge of embarrassment and looked away quickly, preferring to confine his gaze to the rest of the bedroom.

Its plainly painted walls were dimly lit, illuminated only by the incandescent glow from the French widows, the curtains drawn but billowing slightly in the breeze. Noises from distant late-night revellers drifted in periodically.

He wished she'd hurry up.

He tried to console himself by thinking positively. He wasn't in that bad shape; he was, after all, fifty-nine years of age. Most of his friends were much less fit than him. He continued to make an effort: he didn't smoke, he drank less than he used to – though that, he had to admit, was as much to do with capacity as to any definite health decision – he did take long hill walks, even the occasional jog. These activities, he was convinced, kept him at a level of fitness which, if not on a par with his younger days, was at least one which he could maintain. Though he had to admit, if only to himself, that perhaps the exercise might be a little more beneficial if he didn't always insist on a couple of beers in the local pub afterwards.

There was a clattering in the bathroom as if something had been knocked over.

His shoulders started to ache again, but there was something else, an unfamiliar feeling lower down; he raised his head and spied the swollen glans of his penis starting to rise above the mound of his belly in proud expectation. George smiled, if a little embarrassed.

He wished she'd hurry up.

No, despite his current and unfamiliar predicament, George felt that he was one lucky old bastard and he knew know it. He had a good (okay, a bit boring but relatively secure) job, a company car (so it's a Ford) and a guaranteed pension (well, as guaranteed as any pension scheme is these days). The children were grown up, educated, actually in employment and one even married off. So, all in all, he postulated he was one fortunate, if fat, old middle-aged company accountant, with what life he had still ahead of him his to enjoy, and boy, was he going to try and enjoy it!

'Thinking of enjoyment, what on earth is she up to?'

The bathroom door opened and he blinked as light streamed into the room.

He could just make out her dark silhouette as she eased herself through the partially opened door. She turned out the light and moved into the bedroom. He squinted to see her more clearly.

She is so beautiful, he thought silently.

Her smile flashed at him as she sidled around the bed. He watched her intently, taking in every detail. Her blonde hair was cut short and bobbed as she moved. Now he understood why she took so long in the bathroom. She was wearing a dark red bustier, her breasts pushed firmly upwards by the tight lacing; lacing which ended in a tantalising bow in the valley between those soft, welcoming mounds; a lacy G-string, then a line of flesh above black lace-topped stockings completed the vision.

'Are you ready for me, handsome?'

He felt as if he was about to explode.

She stood beside the bed and fiddled with the bow that held the bustier together. She tugged softly at one end of the lace, at the same time climbing onto to the bed and lowering herself astride his chest.

'I can't quite manage this, can you help me?' She purred seductively, leaning ever so slightly forward so that the ribbon dangled tentatively, gently brushing against his cheek.

He strained hard against the shackles, shifting, trying to grip the ribbon in his teeth. She rocked slowly but deliberately so that the ribbon avoided any of his attempts to grasp it. Back and forth it went. He twisted and turned, biting, snatching at nothing but air.

He slumped back, sighing, seemingly defeated.

She leant further forward and kissed his cheek. 'So close and yet so far?' She whispered softly in his ear. He could smell her perfume, musky and sensual.

He sensed the ribbon's end brush his lower lip. He struck, biting hard, gripping it firmly in his teeth.

She pulled back as if startled by the suddenness of the movement. The ribbon pulled, trying to break free. But his bite was solid.

For a moment, there was an impasse. Neither the bow nor he would give. Then, almost imperceptibly, he started to win the private tug of war. The bow dissolved and came free.

He let go to admire his handy (or more correctly, dental) work.

The top of the bustier relaxed, revealing a little more of her breasts.

'Who's a clever boy then?'

He felt her thighs tighten either side of him as she straightened up.

'Would you like me to take this off then?' as she fiddled with the ribbon, loosening it more.

He nodded enthusiastically, like a schoolboy, unable to speak.

She slowly lowered the bustier and tugged it free. He watched her every movement intently. Her breasts bounced as she moves. She leant forward, pushing them hard against his chest. He sensed the small, hard buttons of her nipples pressing into his flesh. She kissed him. Her lips were moist; he could taste the lip gloss. He felt her tongue enter his mouth. He caressed it with his own. She engulfed him in her arms, almost squeezing the breath out of him. Then she released him again and raised herself up. He strained to kiss her breasts, sucking greedily at each nipple in turn. He could feel each tighten and firm, responding to the rhythmic movements, as he moved slowly from one to the other.

She broke free again, sweeping the hair back from her face as she straightened and pushed herself further down the bed.

'Now what have we here then?' She laughed. 'Well, hellooo, big boy.' He suddenly realised that she was looking at his penis, now bulging in anticipation, standing straight and true. 'Where have you been hiding? I haven't seen you for a while.'

He quivered momentarily in embarrassment. But it was only momentarily as she grasped it and rhythmically stroked the stem. Then she lowered herself and took it in her mouth, and he could feel the warm moistness of her lips as she devoured him.

Consummate pleasure seemed to engulf his whole being. He closed his eyes; his head fell back onto the pillow and he moaned involuntarily.

She stopped.

'Not so fast,' she said, as he realised that she was up again; now she was removing the G-string.

Then she was on top of him again. She put him inside her. She rocked back and forth on top of him. Slowly at first, but building. Her hands pressed hard on his chest, her nails digging in to the flesh.

Her pelvis pounded against his. He responded, thrusting rhythmically into her.

He tried to concentrate. He didn't want to come too quickly. It had been so long; he wanted this to go on forever.

'I love you, Mrs Baker,' he moaned.

'I love you too, Mr Baker,' she replied breathlessly.

George had always known that he was going to marry Jane. Right from that first moment. He had been sixteen years of age and she'd appeared at a friend's birthday party. It was one of those teenage parties where his parents had reluctantly gone out and agreed to let him have a few pals round. Of course there had been smuggled booze and the party was going great guns. A heady mixture of glam rock and heavy metal, considered hip in those days, boomed from the hi-fi. Sometime during the evening Colin Turner had appeared at the door. Colin was at school with George and his friends, but he hadn't been invited. He had another friend and Jane in tow. George had been about to tell Colin to bog off when Jane flashed him a smile and his heart had missed a beat.

'No problem. Come on in…' he had heard himself say.

The whole of rest of the evening had been spent trying to chat to Jane, finally seizing his opportunity when Colin had gone to the toilet.

'Fancy a drink…?'

'I didn't bring any.'

'Don't worry, I've got tons. Sit down…?'

To his surprise (George hadn't previously been that successful with the opposite sex), she did, and they had snuggled down on the sofa. Even then George hadn't felt entirely at ease. 'Err, what about Colin… sorry, your boyfriend?'

'Oh, he's not my boyfriend. A group of us from our road just hang out together and he said there was a party and would we like to go. I didn't know we'd be gate-crashing.' She'd looked a little embarrassed, he remembered, but his heart had missed another beat.

When Colin got back, it was clear from the look on his face that even if he hadn't been her boyfriend, he had certainly had ambitions. But George was bigger, stronger, played for the school rugby team and, most importantly, had more mates present than Colin, who was… well, just a bit creepy. So Colin had eventually slumped off and spent the rest of the evening stealing other people's drinks and finally ended up being thrown out, having been discovered, face down, in a pile of vomit in the bathroom.

The fact that Colin been blown out and jealous had simply added to the pleasure of that evening. But only marginally; the main pleasure had, quite simply, been Jane's company. The night had flown and they'd kept their own company for most of it.

But then the party was over and she had got up to leave. George mumbled with embarrassment, 'Err, can I walk you home?'

God! he recalled She had lived bloody miles away, and it was mid-winter. Still, he hadn't noticed the cold, at least, on the way to her house. Not with her slim arm around his waist and his arm across her shoulders. He had kissed her goodnight as he left her at her front door, and he could remember that kiss from forty years ago as if it had been yesterday.

Jane Baker née Irvine was, is and always would be the love of George Baker's life and nothing could ever change that.

Now here she was, as beautiful as ever, her head thrown back, writhing on top of him. She moaned, 'I'm coming, I'm coming.'

He thrusted, harder, deeper into her. Her pelvis gyrated above his. He could sense her pleasure, and that gave him a further surge of energy. His back arched, pushing his head firmly into the pillow. He could feel his penis swelling within her and the gratifying pulsation sweeping through his body towards it.

He exploded inside her.

'Oh, yesss!' she shouted. He was suddenly aware of the dampness of her thighs almost squeezing the life out of him.

The joy was beyond compare. He'd almost forgotten that feeling. A sensation beyond all others. One that only sex coupled with true love could impart.

Suddenly it changed.

A warm, numb feeling spread quickly down his body, like a dental anaesthetic but more all-encompassing. Sudden fear replaced pleasure. His face contorted. The numbness was replaced by an unpleasant burning sensation sweeping through his entire right side, from his head down his body, and felt as if it was shooting out of his fingertips and toes.

His body spasmed.

He struggled to open his eyes, but he seemed to be looking through a mist. He could see Jane, but her face had changed.

She was looking down at him.

She was not smiling.

She looked scared.

He felt her hands holding his head.

She was shouting.

He could hear the noise. But it didn't make sense. Her mouth seemed to be making words, but he could hear no words, only the noise.

He tried to say something to comfort her. But the words wouldn't come.

Then he could no longer see Jane, just a bright light, like a large star crashing towards him.

Then nothing more.

He heard nothing.

A soothing blackness engulfed him and he relaxed into it.

chapter two

'Are you carrying anything sharp on board the aircraft, Mr McNally?'

'Nothing sharper than my wit,' he replied, smiling smugly.

The British Airways girl at the check-in desk raised her head and fixed him with a contemptuous stare. Slowly and deliberately, she looked him up and down, taking in the Hugo Boss suit, the expensive white shirt and the Armani tie.

'And just how sharp would that be then, Sir?'

'Sorry, just a quotation from Oscar Wilde.' It was obvious she thought he was just another smug smartass.

'Really. I'm sure I haven't heard that one before, Sir.'

Raymond bit his lip. British Airways, 'The world's favourite airline'? *How did they get that handle?* he thought to himself, and this was business class as well. *Never mind*, he consoled himself. This was going to be a good day and no bolshie check-in girl was going to spoil it for him. He flashed her the brightest of smiles, giving her a glimpse of his recently and expensively whitened teeth. She checked his ticket and issued a boarding pass with feigned good grace, and he headed off to the executive lounge.

Just a coffee, no alcohol – not yet, anyway, he mused. He

9

could treat himself to a celebratory drink on the way back. All being well, that was. He could feel the nerves starting to kick in. He said to himself that he shouldn't really be nervous, but he was. The final hurdle. *It should only be a formality*, he told himself. A meeting with the head man and then all those years of hard slog would pay off. He settled down with the free copy of the *Daily Telegraph*. Trying to distract himself from his inner turmoil, he immersed himself in the ongoing saga of some minor government minister's alleged philandering with a model half his age. Stupid idiot. Not for doing it but for getting caught doing it. He for one couldn't criticise, despite his strong Protestant work ethic, he'd made the most of his thirty-two years. Work hard, play hard – that had always been his motto. That MP should have kicked his overly ambitious wife into touch a long time ago. Too demanding. Too high maintenance. Too full of her own importance. And, of course, it had been her that had gone to press to expose him. Call him old-fashioned, but he himself had always preferred the more shy, retiring types. Only room for one ego in the life of Raymond McNally, high-flying pharmaceutical executive and soon-to-be international jet-setter.

The flight to Basel was uneventful; for its duration he had swopped the *Daily Telegraph* for a folder that had previously been forwarded to him by UMBRA Pharmaceuticals and contained all the important details of Erexat, its formulation, production details and its sales predictions – all details that he needed at his fingertips for the forthcoming interview.

At the airport the waiting limo, with typical Swiss efficiency, picked him up promptly once he had cleared immigration. He climbed into the back seat and they set off towards the city.

Basel is a pocket-sized city at the crossroads of three countries. The town centre is essentially inaccessible to cars, being steep and cobbled, unchanged from medieval times.

The limo passed through the GrossBasel (Great Basel) which lies on the south bank of the Rhine. As the car climbed up the more accessible roads to the Munster terraces, Raymond spotted the coloured prayer flags, indicating the arrival of one of the many ferries which cross to KleinBasel (Little Basel), on the city's trendier north bank.

The city certainly appeared to be full of life. He could see trams plying their way through the crowded streets. He noted the many rooftop gardens, most of which would be invisible from the streets below. Looking beyond, on towards France, the headquarters of many of Basel's, and indeed the world's, pharmaceutical laboratories and headquarters crept into view.

They arrived at the UMBRA Pharmaceutical headquarters with thirty minutes to spare before the appointed hour. To kill time and settle any last nerves, he decided to take a short stroll around the complex, soaking up the midday sun. The green, well-watered grass and leafy trees imparted a park-like atmosphere, softening the grey concrete boxes that housed the offices and suites from which one of the world's largest pharmaceutical corporations was administered. He glanced around with growing satisfaction. After all, this was to be his home, in the business sense at least, for the foreseeable future.

On entering the building, there was a security screening area to pass through. The security guard that had taken his details then promptly disappeared into an inner office. The door of the office was ajar and as Raymond walked by he could see the guard making a phone call.

A little time passed as Raymond sat beside the reception desk in the large, modern atrium. Finally the recipient of the phone call, Dieter Heinz, the CEO of UMBRA, whom Raymond recognised from company magazine shots, emerged from a door at the far end of the atrium and greeted Raymond with sophisticated ease, which belied the formality of the occasion. He was a man in his early sixties with thick grey hair and matching beard; his forced smile exaggerated a few of the facial lines that betrayed his years at the top of his profession.

'You had a pleasant trip?' He spoke fluent English, but Raymond thought it was with a slight American tinge, presumably acquired during his early years at one of the top US business schools.

'Not too bad.' He winced slightly at the sound of his own voice, in the realisation that, in his anxiety at meeting the CEO for the first time, he'd reverted to a Northern Irish expression, something he thought he'd managed to absolve himself of after all his years in London.

Dieter Heinz didn't seem to notice and they made small talk as Raymond was ushered through the door from which Dieter Heinz had emerged, then down a corridor and into an elevator. They exited on the twelfth floor and made their way to the CEO's private office. There he indicated Raymond sit down in one of the largest and deepest leather armchairs he had ever seen. Dieter Heinz lowered himself into a matching sofa across the room and then leant forward, fixing his guest with vibrant blue eyes. Raymond, however, noted the steeliness behind the friendly façade.

'So, Mr McNally, you want to be our next international product manager?'

Raymond was a little taken aback by this opening gambit. After all, he had thought that he'd already been as good as appointed. He'd been through the internal trawl, survived the shortlisting, the referencing and waltzed through the initial interview only to come of age in the testing final interview. Raymond knew that he had easily beaten off the opposition and here he was – in his mind, at least, if not in Dieter Heinz's – simply to be confirmed in that position.

Momentarily, he struggled to find a suitable reply. He had

just regathered himself and started to speak when there was a soft knock on the door and an expensively dressed secretary eased her way in bearing a silver tray. Raymond flashed her one of his impeccable smiles, grateful for the interruption.

'Some canapés, Mr McNally? You must be hungry after your journey.'

Ah, ahh. Raymond saw his game, or at least he thought he did. *Trial by canapés.* In the old days it used to be called 'trial by sherry' – a tried and tested management selection technique. Raymond knew all about this from his training days at the London Business School. Of course, in these more politically correct days, alcohol may no longer be entirely considered to be appropriate, but the theory is the same: subject the prospective employee to an apparently informal gathering, make him relax, drop his guard and see how he or she would behave in a social setting while at the same time probing their suitability for the position.

There was no way Raymond was relaxing in any shape or form until this contract was signed, sealed and delivered.

Accepting a small morsel, he turned back to his inquisitor. 'Well, Sir.' Raymond thought that Dieter Heinz would appreciate the formality, reasoning that the Swiss usually did. 'As you know, I've been with this company for nearly ten years now and have been the product manager for Erexat in the UK for the last three. I think I do know the product and the business as well as anybody. I do hope that you'll agree that my work for UMBRA has been of the highest quality.'

'I am fully aware of your CV, Mr McNally.' Dieter relaxed back in his seat and crossed his legs. 'But it is a very major position within the company that is on offer. One that carries with it, shall we say, a heavy burden of responsibility.'

Raymond felt a small bead of sweat trickle down the back of his neck. Dieter Heinz was not a man to be easily impressed. Raymond leant forward again, clasping his hands in front of him, and he could feel the dampness of his palms as he became even more aware of the intensity in the ice-blue eyes which flashed from the impeccably tanned face.

'Erexat remains one of our flagship products. One cannot underestimate its importance to our company. There may be difficult times ahead. You are cognisant, of course, that there are existing competitors and of the rumours other pharmaceutical houses intend to launch further rival products?'

'Yes, but…' The trickle of sweat was now a stream.

Dieter Heinz silenced him with a raised finger. 'The potential effect on our market share is enormous. We need somebody with a variety of skills, not just financial, but with marketing and social skills not only to maintain our customer base but to expand it in the face of what is likely to be fierce competition.'

'I think I am up to the challenge, Mr Heinz.' Raymond now adopted a stern, business-like expression, oozing sincerity. Sincerity, Raymond knew, was undoubtedly the secret of success – once you learnt to fake sincerity you could go anywhere.

'I have to tell you, Mr McNally, that our board of directors do harbour certain concerns about your ability to fulfil this demanding role.'

Raymond shifted uncomfortably in his seat, his expression crumbling. 'What sort of concerns?' he mumbled.

'Well, you are rather young, are you not, for such an elevated position? Somebody who was a little unkind might say that you are perhaps somewhat lacking in experience in the worldwide marketplace?'

There was an undeniable coolness in his expression.

'Then,' he continued, 'there is also the matter of stability.'

'Stability? I don't understand.'

'The post in question requires the successful applicant to relocate in order to be based here in head office.'

'I understood that from the terms and conditions. I can't see any problem there.' Raymond could again feel the dampness of his palms as he gripped the armrest of the sofa.

'Basel is a quiet place, Mr McNally. Very family-orientated. You are not currently in a relationship, Mr McNally? No partner in tow?'

'I am separated from my wife, that's true, but—'

The finger stretched again. 'In the past the board have witnessed a number of ambitious young men and young women coming here. Initially all seems to go well, but then they go – how do the Americans phrase it? …Stir-crazy. Not to put too fine a point on it, Mr McNally, with difficult times ahead, we need stability. We need to be cautious; we need somebody who will settle here, be happy here and be with us for years, not just weeks or months. We don't want somebody who will up sticks and leave if a better offer comes along.'

'I can assure you, Mr Heinz, nothing is further from my mind.'

'At the moment, maybe. But, as I say, Basel may lack a certain appeal after a while.'

Raymond could feel his face flush. But before he could offer any further defence, the older man continued. 'That is why the board, after due consideration, has decided not to fully ratify the offer of the position to you.'

This was not what he had expected, not at all. His mouth opened to speak, but before he could utter a word, Dieter Heinz uncrossed his legs and leant even further forward.

'However, while not prepared at this point to formally appoint you, we are prepared to offer you the position on a temporary basis. Shall we say, as a trial, Mr McNally. Perhaps for, let us say, six months in the first instance. Then we shall meet again to assess your performance and re-evaluate our respective positions.'

Raymond was dumbfounded. Of course, he realised immediately just what was on offer: all the responsibility, all the grief, but none of the perks. Or at least, no chance to enjoy any of the perks, because they'd expect him to work his butt off in the hope of expanding the firm's portfolio just so he could stay put.

'Pay and conditions as previously agreed, of course. Do you accept our proposal?'

He stretched out his hand.

Raymond knew he had no choice; he shook the older man's hand in reluctant agreement. To do otherwise would have been, as he fully realised, professional suicide. The company had him in a corner, up a blind alley, up the creek without a paddle, essentially with no other real option but to accept the offer on the table.

They rose, and Dieter Heinz escorted him towards the office door.

'I look forward to working with you, Raymond.'

He in turn noted the twinkle in his new boss's eye as he was wished a pleasant flight home.

'Fucking old bastard has stitched me up,' Raymond said to himself as he exited Dieter Heinz's office and the door had closed behind him.

He had thought that nobody had heard the expletive, but he hadn't noticed the secretary, who had earlier brought in the canapés, sitting behind her desk.

She lifted her head and smiled sweetly at him. 'That's why he is where he is today, Mr McNally.'

chapter three

Large fluorescent squares were rushing by above his head. His head was pounding. He knew that he was flat on his back, but the whole world seemed to be moving around him. He could hear the clanking of wheels as he bumped along.

If this is heaven, it certainly isn't as the clergy have portrayed it, he thought.

Then the movement stopped and all was quiet. He stared intently at a single fluorescent tube in the centre of a peeling white ceiling.

Suddenly, from somewhere beyond his feet, a curtain swished and a young man, a stranger to him, entered the small cubicle. George struggled to make sense of it all. The young man was wearing an open-necked shirt and bore a harassed expression, but he moved easily around the small room. George groaned through the discomfort and the fug that seemed to engulf him. He forced himself to focus on the young man, hoping that in doing so things would become clearer. He quickly noticed that the young man had a pen and torch sticking out of his top pocket and some sort of a badge clipped to his shirt. A blue tube with metal ends hung loosely around his neck. He was holding a clipboard in one hand and he seemed to be reading it intensely.

George tried to speak. He desperately wanted to find out what was going on. He knew what he wanted to say and he thought that he could hear his voice. But there were no words. Just some unintelligible noise.

The young man looked up from the clipboard. 'Take it easy, old man.' He rested his hand gently on his patient's shoulder. 'You're in hospital, the A&E of Guy's Hospital to be exact. Apparently, you've had some sort of turn. I just need to have a good look at you, to see what's happened, okay?'

He was trying to be reassuring, and in truth his voice had a calming quality, but it did little to dispel George's growing feeling of panic. George tried to pull himself up on the trolley. But his movements seemed strangely uncoordinated, weak and ineffectual.

'Hey, hey. Whoa there. Just take it easy. Give me a chance and I'll have you sorted out in a minute or two.'

George slumped back down, exhausted by his efforts and frustrated by his lack of ability.

'That's better,' the doctor said, pulling out the torch and shining it into each of George's eyes in turn. Then he lifted the blue tube thing off his neck, placed one end on George's chest and listened through the earpieces at the other end. Then, with the earpieces still firmly attached to his ears, he wrapped a broad black band around George's arm and pumped it up. George could feel the pressure squeezing his arm. As the pressure relaxed, he heard the doctor mutter, 'Mmm, mmm.'

George tried to speak again, to tell him who he is, ask him what is going on. But there was the same result. Only a frightened, 'Yo, yo, yo,' emerged from his lips. He couldn't understand what is happening. He seemed to be on some foreign planet, but of his own making. Somehow, he had become an alien, one who couldn't communicate with those around him, seemingly trapped within his own body, unable to escape.

'Okay,' the young man said, 'your blood pressure's up. Now listen carefully. I want you to do some things for me. Alright?'

George looked blankly up at him. No point in trying to reply.

'Close your eyes.'

George closed his eyes.

'Very good. Now open them.'

George opened his eyes. The nightmare was still there.

'Now I want you to lift up your arms.'

George lifted up his arms. *That's odd*, he thought. He could see his left arm rising and he could feel his left arm rising, but he couldn't see or feel any movement on his right. In fact, when he thought about it, all he could feel on his entire right side was a sort of warm, tingling sensation, a bit like some sort of anaesthetic that hadn't quite worn off. But an anaesthetic shouldn't affect him like this, should it? He sensed another bout of panic coming on.

The young man seemed to sense the turmoil. 'Relax. We're nearly done.' He prodded George with a pin, asking him, 'Can you feel this? And that?'

George nodded in response to the pricks on his left side, but on the right, nothing – a bemused expression. He could see the needle hit the skin but felt no pain, no discomfort, nothing. Next the young doctor reached for a long, plastic hammer-like device from a tray sitting on a small trolley in the corner of the room. He hit George's elbows and knees with it. Then he wrote something onto his clipboard. George watched him intently. He couldn't take his eyes off him. He felt that he'd lose it completely if he did.

'Right. Finally,' the doctor said, picking up the clipboard again. 'I want to test your speech.'

George nodded.

'What's this?' he said, holding up the pen from his pocket.

What sort of stupid game is this? George thought, regaining some of his wits.

'Yo, yo, yo...' he replied.

'And this?' The doctor held up the torch.

'*Yo, yo, yo...!* George screamed.

chapter four

Raymond pushed the door open and eased his way into the austere yet modern boardroom. Everyone else appeared to have arrived, or at least every chair was taken – well, every chair but one: his, at the head of the long, rectangular table. Beside this seat, just a little back from the table, sat a rather a young woman, writing pad on her lap, pen poised to take notes during the meeting. Raymond eased himself into the rather hard upright seat. The sun glinting through the blinds caught him unawares and momentarily blinded him.

'Sun in your eyes?' quizzed the attentive secretary, rising to adjust the blind.

'Yes, and thanks.' He nodded a little self-consciously as the sunlight diminished and he squinted around the room.

Every face along the table turned and looked at him expectantly as the secretary regained her seat and Raymond regained his composure.

'Thank you, gentlemen… and, err, ladies, for meeting with me today. As you know by now, I have been appointed international product manager for our new drug Erexat – or, to give it its generic or chemical name, which obviously we hope you won't, radafinil.'

There was some muffled laughter around the room as the other members of the committee picked up on the reference to generic prescribing, the bane of the pharmaceutical industry, whereby other drug companies could copy, manufacture and sell more cheaply a successful product by simply labelling it with its proper chemical name rather than the brand name given by the parent company.

'We all, I'm sure, have high hopes for this new agent, which, if you'll pardon the pun, is part of a growing market for sexual wellbeing and longevity.'

'I think there were at least two puns in there,' whispered the man to his right.

'Mmm…' Raymond fixed him with a hard stare. 'Anyway, perhaps, as I'm the new boy, we could go around the table for introductions and job titles.' He turned to the whisperer.

'I'm Frank Kinney, your second in command. I was the locum product manager, but now I'm back to assistant product manager.'

'No hard feelings, I hope.'

'No, none at all, I prefer to be in the background – you attract less flack that way,' Frank said, oozing sincerity through what seemed to be clenched teeth.

Raymond anticipated some further animosity from this quarter at least.

Carrying on around the table, Raymond got to meet his team, though he admitted to himself it was hard at the moment to grasp everyone's exact role. He was sure that this would come later as he became more familiar with each individual.

'First on the agenda then.' Raymond grasped the opportunity to assert his position. 'Global sales figures?'

A tall, bespectacled man with heavily greased-back hair of the blackest hue that Raymond had ever seen rose to his feet at the far end of the table. Piercing blue eyes fixed Raymond through the steel spectacles.

'George…?' Raymond thought he recalled from the formal introductions round.

'Nearly,' the tall man answered; Raymond noted a lilting Swiss accent. 'Gregor… Gregor Reuber, Sales Manager.'

'Thanks, Gregor, my apologies.'

A PowerPoint presentation on the flat-screen television in the corner of the room lit up and everyone present shifted position in order to see more clearly.

Gregor turned to the screen and addressed it directly, seemingly ignoring the rest of his audience within the boardroom.

A series of statistics, tables and figures followed as Gregor spoke and pointed a laser pen at individual figures or graphs.

Many in the room nodded wisely, but others seemed to simply stare off into the middle distance.

'So…' Raymond interrupted. 'What's the bottom line?'

Gregor turned from the screen, shuffled his feet and fixed Raymond with a withering look. 'I was just coming to that, if you could just bear with me.'

He turned back to the screen, flicked his hand-held remote control and moved the laser point back onto the new slide. 'As you can clearly see,' and he appeared to stress the word 'clearly', probably for Raymond's sake, 'there has been an exponential growth in sales, particularly in the last six months. Initially there was a slow start, after product licensing and subsequent launch, but our drug now seems to be widely accepted and, more importantly prescribed, such that we are rapidly gaining ground on our competitors. If we continue to grow at the current rate, then I would anticipate we could be the number-one drug treatment for erectile dysfunction in the UK and later, hopefully, the world by the end of this, or beginning of next year at the latest.'

There was a small round of applause.

Frank leant over to Raymond, put his hand up to his face to shield his mouth from the others and whispered, 'Well, old boy, you seem to have come on board just at the right time.'

'Thanks, Gregor,' congratulated Raymond, turning to the presenter and pointedly ignoring Frank for the time being. 'Very encouraging, very encouraging indeed. Now, any financial projections? …Trevor?'

Trevor (Raymond congratulated himself on this time getting the name right) was the company financial advisor seconded to the Erexat project. To be fair, it wasn't that hard to spot that Trevor was an accountant. He wore a pinstripe suit, white shirt, sensible tie and his shoes were polished to within an inch of their life. Trevor remained seated but turned towards Raymond at the head of the table.

'Yes, it is as Gregor has said. Sales are up and encouraging. A word of caution, though, as with any pharmaceutical agent for human consumption, there are huge development and production costs because of the many regulatory bodies and safety measures that must be taken. Many prototypes and products fall by the wayside in the early development stages or, worse, if they reach clinical trials. The company has to bear these costs within the profit from the small percentage of agents that do make it.'

'Well, at least Erexat has made it,' interrupted Frank.

'Yes, but…'

'But, what?' asked Raymond, a little perturbed.

'Well,' Trevor continued, 'apart from the costs of other drugs that didn't make it, as I mentioned, Erexat itself has already taken the best part of ten years to achieve worldwide licensing.'

'Why so long?' asked Raymond.

'Perhaps Sarah would be best placed to answer that one,' offered Trevor.

Sarah was a tall, slim and well-toned woman, who Raymond guessed was in her late thirties. She was bespectacled, wearing designer glasses, and she sported an open-necked blouse and knee-length skirt, again of designer make. She stood in marked contrast to the other participants, the majority of whom were male and attired more formally, and certainly less fashionably. Sarah's collar-length dark brown hair was cut in a strikingly hard yet fashionable cut, and her slightly tanned visage made her an attractive woman. *But*, thought Raymond, *probably only in a strictly business-like way*. Dr Sarah Stephenson had introduced herself earlier during the round table introductions as the company's medical advisor.

'Mmm… yes, how long have you got?' she asked.

Raymond pondered. Did she mean how long to explain the intricacies of drug development or how long did he expect to be in post? He preferred the former and didn't really detect any ill will on her part.

'Okay, it is well recognised that any drug making it to the marketplace these days will take ten to fifteen years in development.'

'An expensive process,' added the accountant.

'Yes, indeed,' continued Sarah, 'and there are a number of stages of research. Even after the development in the laboratory and animal studies, there are a number of further regulatory human studies that have to be carried out.'

As she spoke, Raymond thought he could detect a slight Scottish brogue, but one worn down by years of working within the European medical industry.

'Phase one, the drug is tested on a small number of, usually healthy, volunteers to see how it works in the body, how it is metabolised or dealt with and whether there are any obvious side effects.

'Phase two, the drug has to be further tested on a larger sample of people, usually several hundred, with the problem it is to be used for, to see if it shows evidence of effectiveness.

'Phase three, information has to be gathered from large numbers – usually measured in thousands – often by combining a number of the above trials from various sites and wider afield to see how well the drug works and how safe it is.

'Phase four, where we are now, happens after the drug has attained a licence to be prescribed and consists of monitoring by the regulatory bodies and ourselves to see if there are any unexpected side effects or if it causes problems within certain groups of people.

'But in these respects, Erexat is no different in this respect from any other agent.'

Trevor turned to Raymond. 'All in all, the production cost to get to this stage of development has been $3.4 million, or at current exchange rates about £2.4 million. All of which we have to recoup before we see any profit.'

Raymond whistled.

'Also,' interposed Sarah, rising to the task, 'the patent on radafinil – or, as we prefer to call it, Erexat – is valid for only twenty years. Given the length of time from conception through development and licensing, we have ten years of continuing patent, but it has now been licensed and out there for nearly two years already. After gearing up production and then launching the drug, with, as we heard from Gregor, the inevitable slow start, we are left with just over eight years to market and sell the drug in order to recoup our losses, and then hopefully make a profit, before any other company can step in and make and sell it under its generic name, radafinil. Okay, so they can't call it Erexat, but so what? The big push generally in the health community now is generic prescribing. Basically they are saying it's the same drug at half the price, as there are no research and development costs, so why use the more expensive original?'

There were murmurings around the table.

'However, we all know that generics aren't exactly identical to the original drug, because the regulatory bodies do allow some leeway. But that makes no difference to prescribers or dispensers or, indeed, to the patient... Unless, of course, something goes wrong.'

'Right,' Raymond piped up, 'so we have just over eight more years to get the drug out there and sell as many units as possible before we get hit with competition, and if I understand you correctly, once the competition comes along in the form of a generic – or even a number of generics, if lots of companies see the potential – we are potentially going to be fighting a losing battle.'

'Precisely,' said Dr Stephenson as she sat down.

'Okay, let's hear from marketing then.'

The only other woman in the room rose to her feet and made her way to the foot of the table where the PowerPoint projector and screen stood.

'Thanks for that.' Jacqueline Becker stood stiffly up, a Germanic woman in her fifties who had introduced herself as not only marketing director for Erexat but who, as she had proudly asserted, also sat on the scientific advisory board of UMBRA.

Again a series of slides were to follow, though these at least were more colourful and interesting than Gregor's.

'As we heard, we now have a worldwide product licence, sales are on the up, but we have a way to go. Because of the nature of the product, advertising is always going to be restricted. Although the rules do vary from country to country, erectile dysfunction is a difficult one to address. It is not as if we can show limp cocks followed by a gross erection on the TV.'

Many of the men present bowed their heads, shuffled their feet and tried to avoid Ms Becker's eyeline.

'We have been working on a number of possibilities for a universal campaign and slogan, though,' she continued.

Turning towards the screen, a number of images flashed up. The common theme was confident, attractive women and shy, bashful and embarrassed men. The clear implication was that the men were embarrassed by their lack of potency.

'I can see where you're coming from,' injected Raymond, 'and have you a slogan to accompany the images?'

'We thought of "Don't hide it. Get it out there,"' stated Jacqueline.

Raymond spluttered, choking on his glass of water.

There were some stifled giggles from around the table.

'It is meant to convey the problem that is too often hidden and not discussed,' continued Jacqueline Becker, unfazed and unsmiling.

'Mmm... I'm not really sure that it is an entirely appropriate strapline for a drug to harden one's reserve, if you'll excuse the pun.'

Raymond's intervention appeared to lighten the atmosphere and produced murmurings of consensus.

'We do have other ideas,' retorted Jacqueline, 'but maybe the committee could offer some thoughts?'

'Maybe we should sleep on it,' offered Raymond.

'That's another good one.' Frank Kinney smirked to general laughter.

'Okay, okay.' Raymond stretched out both arms and raised his hands, trying to regain control. 'We need to take our time and consider this carefully. We are at a point where we have the production capacity and sales are increasing, but we really need to get this drug out there – sorry, Jacqueline. But Jacqueline is actually correct. Now that we are getting to the end of the phase four trials, we need the public as well as the medical community to be aware of this drug and its potential benefit. It seems probable that there are likely to be tens or hundreds of thousands, if not millions, of men who would benefit from it and keep on benefitting from it.'

Raymond relaxed. 'I am correct, Dr Stephenson, in saying that we are now at the end of the official drug surveillance period?'

'Yes, but there will always be ongoing monitoring for potential or as yet unrecognised or even longer-term side effects, as is the case with any drug. Most, if not all, countries, Mr McNally, now have these ongoing regulatory mechanisms. You are no doubt familiar with, for example, the UK's "yellow card" scheme, whereby any doctor who becomes aware of any unexpected effect of any drug fills in a pre-printed yellow card and returns it to the Committee on Safety Medicines, or the CSM. The CSM then logs and files these reports, and if something very serious, or even if something less serious but happening frequently, is flagged up, warnings are issued and the drug can be restricted or even withdrawn.'

'Of course, of course, but again, am I correct in saying that no serious side effects associated with Erexat have come to light?'

'Absolutely correct, none to date.'

'Then on that happy note, perhaps we can conclude this meeting.'

Raymond breathed a silent sigh of relief.

chapter five

The screen flickered in the darkened room. The curtains were drawn, shutting out the last of the sun's evening rays.

'Harry, Harry. What are you doing up there?' His mother's shouting voice from the bottom of the stairs broke through his concentration. 'Your tea's ready.'

He heard her steps on the stairs and he tried quickly to shut the computer down.

Too late. Her head appeared around the door. She looked disapprovingly firstly at the computer screen and then at her son.

'Harry Boyle, you need to get out more. You cannot, you just cannot, spend all day and all night up here on that bloody machine. Alright, I accept that it is hard to get a proper job these days, especially with your... your... disability.'

'It's called epilepsy, Mother.'

'I know what it's called,' she snapped. 'Even more reason not to be sitting here in the dark staring at that computer screen. It is common knowledge that flickering lights or sitting too close to computer screens could set off a fit.'

'That's called photosensitive epilepsy, Mother, and you know the consultant told you that I didn't have that sort of epilepsy. It's quite uncommon, in point of fact, despite what people think. And anyway, if I was going to take a fit because of the computer, do you not think it would have happened long before now?'

His mother sighed and withdrew, retreating back downstairs; she had learnt that it was pointless trying to get Harry away from his computer. Before following her, Harry sat and stared at the now-blank screen. He pushed his glasses back up his nose and eased his long, unkempt, curly dark hair back from his face, contemplating his lot.

She was right, of course, he did spend most of his time up here in his bedroom. It could all have been so different. Harry had been smart at school, nearly always top of the class, destined for a fruitful academic or business future, but then, at the age of sixteen, the epilepsy had appeared. At first his teachers thought he was just daydreaming. He would stop and just stare into the distance, then he would have lost the track of what he was being taught. The number of times that he'd been chastised by the teachers was innumerable. But then he had a full-blown fit; it happened during morning assembly. Of course, it had to be in assembly – the maximum possible audience. He knew something was going to happen. He felt strange, a feeling he'd felt before, but he couldn't describe it. Then he'd fallen over unconscious. He was told that he'd stopped breathing, gone blue and then shaken all over, but only for a minute or so. When it stopped, he passed into a deep sleep, barely rousable. Finally, he came around and found that he was in the school medical room. He was sore all over, especially on his tongue, which he'd bitten quite badly.

He was immediately carted off by ambulance to the local hospital. There followed a series of tests, then medication. Happily things seemed to settle and it had been years since he had had any further seizures. However, he was banned from the sports that he had so enjoyed; the teachers seemed wary of him, always checking that he was alright. The fact that he was alright didn't stop his so-called mates making fun of him, making his life intolerable; he became known as 'shaky' or 'fit boy', and they avoided him as much as they could. On the rare occasion that he was invited to the home of his remaining friends, their parents, who should have known better, regarded him with caution and suspicion. Harry had spent increasing time locked away in his room, often, at least initially, with tears streaming down his face. Somehow he felt he was to blame; he'd obviously done something wrong, but he couldn't figure out what. His parents had been supportive, his mum especially, but eventually the strain of constantly reassuring and caring for him, at least that's how he interpreted it, became too much for his parents' own relationship and his dad had left, never to return. Harry did see him, but increasingly fleetingly, as their father/son relationship also faltered. So it was his mum who had been left to look after Harry alone. Indeed, it seemed that whilst Harry had been initially dependent on her, later she seemed to rely on his company more and more.

Harry's schoolwork suffered, and the once-prime university candidate became reclusive and withdrawn. He dropped out of school halfway through his A levels, never to return or to continue with his studies. His response was to retreat to the comfort of his own company, his only contact with the outside world being through the internet, a place where his problems diminished, didn't seem relevant and he could have a life worth pursuing.

He pulled on his loose, long, woolly round-necked pullover, switched off the computer at the plug and, with a last glance back at his old friend with the now-blank screen, he rose, walked across the room and, closing the door behind him, made his way downstairs.

chapter six

He was on his own again.

An eternity seemed to pass, then he heard voices. One seemed familiar. Through the clamour he could hear Jane's voice above the others. But it sounded different than he'd heard it before. She sounded frightened, bewildered. She was trying to find him.

The curtain was pulled aside and in came the young doctor, closely followed by Jane. She looked pale, apprehensive, scared.

'George, I've got your wife here. I want to explain what's happened to you and where we go from here, okay?'

'Yo, yo, yo.' George gestured with his left arm for Jane to come closer. He needed her comfort, her support. She did, and he hugged her as strongly as he could one-handedly. His right arm still wouldn't respond.

He could feel her tears on his shoulder.

As George released her, the doctor stepped forward. 'Now, Mr and Mrs Baker, I'm sure you want to know what's going on.'

George looked at Jane. Jane nodded tearfully. 'Please...' she sobbed.

'There is no easy way to say this.' The doctor looked at

Jane. Tears rolled down her cheeks. 'It looks like George has had some form of a stroke.'

'A stroke?' wailed Jane. 'What do you mean, a stroke?'

'A stroke happens when a part of the brain is starved of oxygen, usually because of a clot in one of the arteries supplying blood and oxygen to the brain; sometimes it can also be caused by a bleed within the brain itself. As the brain controls all our bodily functions, if a part is damaged, then the area controlled by it doesn't function. That's why George can't, at least at the moment, move his arm and his leg or speak. As George can't move his right side, this suggests a left-sided insult to the brain. The suddenness of the onset is typical of a stroke. But he needs a scan, a CT scan, to try and prove what I'm saying. The scan's already been ordered, we are just waiting for the call to bring him down.'

'He will get better, though, won't he?' pleaded Jane.

'In some cases the effects are very transitory and get completely better very quickly. We call these TIAs – sorry, transient ischaemic attacks – we usually regard them as simply a warning.'

'Is that what's happened here?' Jane said with plaintive hope in her voice.

'It is too early to be sure either way, but to be brutally honest, I don't think so. I suspect, and I hope I am wrong, that whatever has done this has already caused some damage, in which case any recovery is going to be much slower.'

Jane went even paler and just held her hands to her mouth, unable to speak.

At that moment, a nurse popped her head around the curtain and said that radiology was looking for George for his scan.

George was wheeled away, Jane clinging to his hand. She was prised away from him and asked to sit down in a corridor leading to the CT scanner. George was then transferred from the trolley to what appeared to be a stretcher, but one that was attached to the large machine shaped like a huge metallic doughnut which sat in the centre of the otherwise-bare room. Once on board and strapped down, the stretcher slid slowly into the large hole in the centre of the machine. His head enclosed, the machine whirred, and he was moved mechanically back and forth, just inches at a time at regular intervals, before emerging back into the relative illumination of the small room once again. George had closed his eyes and just tried to shut it all out.

Following the scan, George went through the formalities of being finally admitted to the medical unit. Afterwards, as he lay in the relative comfort of the hospital bed, a drip was hooked up to his right arm with a tube leading to a plastic bag containing what the doctor had referred to as thrombolysis or, in layman's terms, a clot-busting drug. The junior doctor who had attached the drip had tried to explain everything slowly and carefully to George and Jane at what he understatedly had said was a difficult time. He told them that the CT scan had confirmed that George had indeed suffered a stroke and in his case it was caused by a clot (or, as he called it, a thrombus) not a bleed. This clot had blocked one of the main arteries supplying the brain and the scan had further shown an area of damage to the brain itself caused by the blockage of the blood supply. The drip attached to his arm was to administer a drug which, the doctor hoped, would break down this clot, reopen the artery and so reduce the size of the area of damage.

'Why can't he speak?' asked Jane.

George also looked expectantly at the doctor.

'The damage is on the left side of the brain,' explained the young doctor. 'The left side of the brain controls the right side of the body; that's why George's right arm and leg are weak.'

'But what about his speech?' persisted Jane.

'I was just coming to that. George is right-handed, yes?'

'Yes,' confirmed Jane. George also nodded in agreement.

'Well, in right-handed people, the left side of the brain is what we call dominant; the speech centre is always located on the dominant side. So George's speech centre has also been affected by the left-sided stroke. One small blessing is that George's reception – sorry, understanding of speech – hasn't been affected. Isn't that right, George?'

George nodded in agreement.

Jane wept silently, dabbing the tears away with a handkerchief. 'What now?' she sobbed.

'Well, once the drip is through, we will reassess George. Then he will be kept here in our acute stoke unit for a couple of days before transferring to the rehabilitation unit, depending on his progress, obviously.'

*

The days passed slowly for George. There had been some useful return of function in his right leg, and with the help of the rehabilitation unit staff he could now stand unaided and even walk a few paces between the parallel bars in their gym as long as he steadied himself with his left arm. His right arm still hung largely uselessly by his side, though as the time passed he started to feel a little movement around his shoulder and elbow. His speech had not returned, except now he could say 'yes' and 'no', usually, but not always, appropriately.

Jane had told him that the consultant wanted to see them both that morning, and now they waited patiently at George's bedside.

The consultant, a prim young lady in, George guessed, her early forties – too young, at least in his opinion, to be a consultant

– arrived somewhat breathlessly at their bedside, apologising profusely for being late. The outpatient clinic had run on, she explained. 'Anyway, I am Dr Hilary Wilson, George's consultant here in the rehabilitation unit. Thank you for coming in, Mrs Baker, I thought it best to see both of you together.'

Dr Wilson pulled out a stool from under the bed and sat down. She adjusted her knee-length skirt, flattening it down, and adjusted her blouse, which was of a fawn-coloured light material which only seemed to highlight her pale, slightly chubby arms. Her face also seemed a little too chubby for her body and made her look slightly comical. But her expression was of extreme seriousness.

'As you are aware, George has had a stroke, but he seems to be making good progress here in the unit.'

'But why can't he speak or move his arm yet?' asked Jane.

The consultant referred to the bundle of notes she had carefully balanced on her knees. 'You must be patient – recovery after a stroke is always slow. According to the physio's and the speech therapist's reports, which I have here,' she shuffled the bundle once again, 'George is, in fact, doing as well as expected. It is just a question of time and, as I said, patience.'

'I didn't mean to criticise. We are, both of us, very grateful for what you are all doing.'

'Thank you, Mrs Baker – may I call you Jane? Why I asked to come in was to clarify and tie up a few loose ends.'

'Loose ends?'

'Yes. Although we know that George has had a stroke, we don't know why.'

'Why?'

'To be fair, very often we never find a cause – it turns out to be just one of those things. But usually there are what we term risk factors.'

'Yes, yes…' George interrupted.

'Mmm, yes,' continued Hilary Wilson. 'But in George's case, we just can't identify any. That's where I thought you could help.'

'Anything we can do,' replied Jane.

'Did George ever suffer from high blood pressure or anybody suggest that his cholesterol was high?'

'No, in fact George had a medical at work just a few months ago, something to do with health insurance. He had blood tests and everything – isn't that right, George?'

'Yes, yes...'

'Mmm, those examinations are indeed usually fairly rigorous. If something had turned up, I'm sure you'd know about it.' She glanced at the pile of notes again, pulling out one particular page. 'I see here that his BP was a bit up on admission, but that's probably understandable given the circumstances, and it has always been within normal limits here on the ward. Any history of strokes or heart disease in George's family?'

'No, none that I'm aware of. George's parents lived till their mid-eighties and were as fit as fleas. Your brother, his older brother, is still alive, and as far as we know has none of the things you mentioned wrong with him.'

George nodded.

'Sometimes an injury, even a very mild one to the neck, can result in a weakness in one of the arteries and that can cause a stroke. No history of a recent such injury, a whiplash car injury, for example?'

'No, no, definitely not.' Jane looked increasingly puzzled by the questioning.

'Yes, we also couldn't see any evidence of an arterial tear on the scans. It is a mystery, isn't it?'

Dr Wilson rose to leave. 'Mmmm... one last thought. What were you actually doing at the time of the stroke?'

George pulled himself up the bed, turned and looked guiltily at Jane, who was visibly blushing and shuffling in her chair.

chapter seven

Raymond was sitting behind his desk. There was a knock at the door.

'Come in,' he shouted, raising his head from the paperwork that was so engrossing him.

Ruth, his newly appointed secretary, popped her head around the door and flashed a friendly smile at him. 'Sorry to disturb, Mr McNally, but there's a gentleman here to see you.'

'Who is it? And what does he want?' replied Raymond curtly, annoyed at being distracted from his labours.

'He says he is from our audit department and that he has some important information for you.'

'Important information?' Raymond replied with a sceptical look. 'You'd better show him in then.'

As Raymond rose from behind the desk, a small, bespectacled man in a tweed jacket, chinos above a pair of brogues, strode purposefully in. 'Mr McNally?' he enquired.

'The one and only,' replied Raymond, extending his hand.

'My name's Jim, Jim Westin.' He noted Raymond's quizzical expression. 'I'm head of our audit division,' he said with a seemingly false modesty.

'And what can I do for audit?' asked Raymond.

'It's just that we have been alerted to some rather worrying reports regarding your product, Mr McNally.'

'Raymond. Please.' And, somewhat bemusedly, 'Worrying reports?'

'Mmmm, yes.' He took the seat on the opposite side of the desk without being invited to do so.

'Coffee? Tea?' enquired Raymond.

'No thanks, straight to business.'

Ruth withdrew quietly and closed the door behind her.

Jim Westin leant forward, elbows on the desk. 'We, we in the audit department have recently been made aware through clinical monitoring that a few unexpected side effects attributed to Erexat have come to light.'

'Unexpected side effects?' Raymond's attention was now focused and his antennae up. 'What sort of side effects?'

'Well.' He sat back and stretched his fingers till they cracked, something Raymond had always found intensely irritating. But given the potential gravity of what Jim Westin was trying to convey, he was prepared to overlook it this once.

'Yes, and a bit concerning at that.'

'Concerning?' He now had Raymond's undivided attention.

'Concerning, in that we have been notified of some really potentially serious and unexpected results associated with the use of your drug.' He seemed to emphasise the 'your' in the sentence, before adding, 'I'm even talking about, in some cases, death.'

'Death?' Raymond paled; his whole life seemed to flash before him. His one big chance and now this, something that could destroy him, and, as an afterthought, the firm he worked for. 'Oh my God! What do you mean, death?'

'Extinction of life, fallen off the mortal coil, *morte*.' The man from the audit division almost seemed to smirk.

'I know what death is.' Raymond, now recovered from the initial shock, was now becoming somewhat irritated with this rather supercilious little man. 'What I mean is, what has this to do with Erexat?'

'The reports we have received,' continued Jim Westin, 'are from a variety of sources and, indeed, from a number of different countries, but put together, they paint a rather worrying picture.'

'Ummm…?' Raymond folded his arms across his chest in a defensive posture.

'Some of the reports have come through the international regulatory authorities, others from individual physicians and even patients' relatives. But unfortunately, as I see it, there is a common link to the problems reported.'

'Common link? What do you mean?' Raymond almost shouted, becoming increasingly agitated.

'Yes, firstly and obviously, all the effects have occurred in close temporal proximity to the ingestion of Erexat, and secondly, all appear to affect the cardiovascular system, for example strokes, myocardial infarction – sorry, heart attacks – sudden death.'

'What does this mean for Erexat?'

'At the moment it's only a pointer. After all, the drug's main audience is middle-aged and older men – in other words, those most at risk of these things anyway. Particularly in the context of unaccustomed exercise.'

Raymond was sure he saw the beginnings of that smirk again, but it was aborted presumably on noting Raymond's fixed gaze upon him.

'So it could just be chance,' he continued. 'But we do need to flag it up. However, on the bright side…'

'There's a bright side?'

'Happily, because the problems are so geographically

spread, the regulatory authorities in the individual countries haven't, as yet at least, put two and two together.'

'And if they do?'

'Well then, they may well suspend or even revoke Erexat's product licence.'

'Meaning we couldn't sell it.'

"Fraid so. At best they may just severely restrict its use. For example, only allow it to be prescribed to fit young men not at risk of cardiovascular disease.'

'In other words, fit young men that actually don't need any help getting an erection.'

'Mmmm, I hadn't thought of that, but yes. I suppose even if that, the best-case scenario was the final result, then it might still be the end of Erexat.'

'What can we do?' Raymond almost pleaded.

'I don't really know. I'm not a clinician or indeed a pharmacist; all I can do is monitor the situation. But if many more reports do come in I'll have no option but to formally alert the regulatory authorities myself. Not to do so would be negligent and only expose the company to widespread criticism, with resultant possible serious consequences to its reputation, not just regarding Erexat but with likely knock-on effects to the global sales of all our other products. A serious state of affairs entirely.'

'Okay, we need to think rationally about this,' Raymond stated, recovering some of his former composure. 'How can we investigate this? Prove if there is a causal link? And then try and rectify it?'

'All I can think of is that I will send you the reports that we have in the department and then you or your team can follow them up and see where it leads.'

'That would be helpful, thanks.' Though thankful was the last thing he actually felt.

'I'll get on it.' Jim Westin rose to his feet and let himself out of the office without a backward glance.

Raymond felt as if the world had just crashed in on him.

chapter eight

Raymond sat at his desk, head in hands. Seemingly, the weight of the world was on his shoulders.

There was a gentle knock at the door and Ruth popped her head round, if somewhat warily. She had detected his low mood as he had ushered Jim Westin out of his office.

'Coffee, Mr McNally?'

He'd asked her to call him Raymond, but she still preferred the more differential form of address.

'To be honest, Ruth, I think I need something stronger, but coffee will be fine, thanks.'

She looked at him quizzically as she withdrew to fetch the requested beverage.

She returned a few minutes later with the mug of black coffee, no sugar, the way she knew he liked it.

Raymond looked up from his musings. 'Ruth, can you get me the files and reports that Jim – sorry, Jim Westin – was telling me about and then set up a meeting with Brian Thompson from the pharmacy department, Sarah Stephenson from the medical department and Michelle Dubois from public relations. Oh… and Frank Kinney. Let's say, for first thing tomorrow morning, nine o'clock, my office.' Then almost as an afterthought, 'Tell them it's important.'

*

It was with a heavy heart and a troubled mind that Raymond set off home that evening. He had gathered what information he could and now carried under his arm the files that had just come down from the audit department. There was to be a busy evening ahead.

Distracted as he was by the day's events, he initially turned left but quickly realised his mistake and did a U-turn, much to the distaste and the honking of horns of following vehicles. Maybe Dieter Heinz was right; it was at times like this that he missed the stability of a partner and a home life most. He pined for the modest townhouse that he had once shared with Claire; to return home to her welcoming arms, for her to sit him down and massage his shoulders as he unburdened himself of the frustrations of the day behind.

He and Claire had been an item from their days at university. Because she was bright, she'd been fast-tracked through school, and when they met in a student pub she was the youngest student in her first year at university whilst he was a mature student at business school six years further down the educational road. At the time the age gap had seemed a big deal; even though realistically there was only seven years between them, it was just that at their young years that difference represented a significant proportion of their actual ages.

After dating for a few months, Claire had finally persuaded Raymond to meet her parents. From that first meeting Raymond had always thought that Claire's parents were a bit wary of this older boy dating their one and only daughter.

Increasingly, though, as time passed and their relationship developed, the discrepancy in their ages, if not actually shrinking in numerical terms, became an irrelevance and a lesser fraction of their time on earth. Even Claire's parents had reluctantly come to accept their relationship.

Claire had given up everything for him, now he recognised that, but it was too late. She had eventually got fed up sitting at home, waiting for his return. As Raymond's career flourished and he became increasingly engrossed by it, Claire became increasingly lonely. She felt second best behind his career and his work colleagues. The things that interested her were no longer of any interest to him, or at least, he had no time for them. In the early days of their married life she had been content to curl up on the sofa in the evening and listen to his tales of corporate finance and his deliberations wheeling and dealing; over time, however, these stories had become, in her mind at least, repetitive, if not frankly boring. Worse still, as he had risen through the ranks, he had succumbed to an increasing workload, returning home later and later, their evening time together becoming increasingly curtailed. When he did return home, he preferred to simply doze off in front of the television.

Claire tried to occupy herself by joining a gym, taking up tennis and forming a book club with a circle of friends. She did enjoy her nights with the girls of the book club, though any discussion of the book of the month was of secondary importance to a surfeit of wine and revelations regarding absent friends or discussion and complaints about their other halves.

As Raymond's career really started to take off and he moved up the cooperate ladder, further sacrifices had to made, in particular they had to up sticks and move to different parts of the country in order for Raymond to fulfil his commitments to any new position. So Claire repeatedly lost any new friends far quicker than she had taken to make them.

The inevitability of their separation was written loud, visible to anybody – to anybody but Raymond, apparently. He had to admit, he shouldn't have been as shocked and surprised that when one evening, on his customary late return, Claire had announced that she was leaving. She assured him that no one else was involved. It was just that her life as it was, was not worth living. She had already packed her bags and loaded them into her car and was just awaiting his arrival to say goodbye.

He remembered sitting on the stairs, staring at the front door that she had exited through and shut firmly behind her.

Raymond had tried to keep in touch, perhaps even hoping to re-kindle their relationship, but to no avail. As time had passed, they drifted further and further apart. As he drove, he thought that in fact it was about two years since they had last spoken. He had heard that she was now working as a PA to a tax advisor and was dating a bank official. *Someone probably a lot more reliable than me*, thought Raymond, with a hint of loss but no real bitterness.

When he did get back to his rented apartment – situated, as it was, in a newly fashionable area on the eighth floor of a tower block, not quite the penthouse but nevertheless affording spectacular views over the city – he tossed the not-inconsiderable pile of files and notes onto the sofa and headed into the galley kitchen to fix himself an espresso. A double he thought might be required.

Then, cup in hand, he settled down beside the pile of paperwork and started to work his way through it.

There were seven reports of so-called potential adverse reactions to Erexat. Scribbled on these were some appended notes, presumably from the firm's medical advisors. The reports emanated from different sources; two had come down through regulatory authorities. These, he concluded, probably required the more serious attention. The others were largely from individual medical practitioners. These latter files might just turn out to be simple enquires regarding the possibility of a link between the drug and an unexpected reaction.

Reviewing them, one could be dismissed straight away. Apparently the subject had experienced a sudden severe disabling headache during intercourse. He had attended his local A&E, was examined and even scanned with nothing found, and more importantly, there did not appear to be any longer-term effects. Except, Raymond thought, a probable wariness of sexual intercourse in the future.

One of the company's medical advisors had written an attached note: *'Typical of "Thunderclap" headache. A not uncommon and well-recognised symptom. Typically occurs at time of climax and, although frightening, not of any serious import. Unlikely to be related to drug.'*

There were, however, three sudden deaths, occurring at the time of, or shortly after, intercourse. One had occurred in France, another in Germany and the last in the UK. All had been attributed to a cerebrovascular or cardiac event, but post-mortem results were awaited.

These were clearly more worrying; there had always been a worry that this class of drug, of which Erexat was one, might have some effects on blood pressure or heart function. But before these reports these worries had, so far at least, proven unfounded.

The last report came through the 'Yellow card' system from he UK. This, a,method of reporting had proven itself very effective in the past in identifying side effects of a medicine. Many of the side effects reported had not previously been detected, or even suspected, during clinical trials. This was usually because once the drug was licenced, it would then be prescribed to much larger numbers of people than were ever included in any trial but also, and perhaps more importantly, to groups of patients that had not been included or were formally excluded from the trials, usually for sound ethical reasons, i.e. pregnant women, elderly or infirm.

This report, passed on from the CSM to the company, detailed the case of a previously well fifty-nine-year-old man who had suffered a sudden a devastating stroke during intercourse. He had been admitted to hospital, had made a partial recovery but remained disabled. He had reportedly taken Erexat to help achieve erection.

Mmmm… thought Raymond. *Worrying.*

He was heading towards a sleepless night.

chapter nine

As Raymond entered his office the following morning, he found the three of the four people he had requested to attend already there. The codicil he'd asked Ruth to add – '*Tell them it's important*' – had obviously had the desired effect at least on these three.

Sarah Stephenson, the company's medical advisor who had given the presentation at the earlier board meeting, sat cross-legged on the sofa in the corner of the room, whilst the other, who he assumed was Brian Thompson, the company's chief pharmacist, hovered nervously around the desk. They turned as Raymond entered his office. Of the latter two, Sarah he knew was Scottish whilst Brian was English. Both he knew were qualified professionals who had had separate careers within in their individual health systems. Both had been successful in their own right. Brian had been a lecturer in pharmacy and therapeutics in a red-brick university in the north of England. Sarah had continued in hospital practice and risen swiftly to the grade of registrar in general medicine as part of a large regional centre. Both had become disillusioned with the healthcare system and therefore left – or, in the eyes of many of their colleagues, sold out to the devil by going to work for the pharmaceutical industry. The advantages were obvious: the workload was considerably less demanding and the financial rewards considerably better, but Raymond suspected they both still hankered for the cut and thrust of proper medical practice.

Frank Kinney, the third attendee, was the company man. Ostensibly his number two, but, having been superseded, he didn't seem a man who would take it on the chin. He lounged back on the sofa at the back wall of the office, legs crossed but in a relaxed sort of a way, his ankle resting on his knee such that his legs were widely splayed. He seemed to have sensed there was trouble ahead for Raymond; he probably had company spies still loyal to him. Raymond thought he could detect a slight smirk on his face. *Probably my imagination*, he told himself, but Frank did not appear to be sharing any of Raymond's discomfiture.

Brian Thompson was of medium height, a little rotund with a round, smiling face and ruddy cheeks. This contrasted with Sarah's somewhat more aloof presentation. On this occasion she appeared even more business-like than their previous meeting; she wore a sharp grey business suit with a skirt that just covered her knees and a jacket that was tightly buttoned across her chest. As they rose to greet Raymond, he noted that Sarah was at least six inches taller than her colleague. Sarah smiled charmingly at Raymond and nodded, causing some stray strands of hair to fall over her face.

'Michelle not here yet?' Raymond asked.

His other more punctual guests glanced disparagingly at each other. 'Not yet.' It was Sarah Stephenson who replied and Raymond could detect a note of frustration in her voice. She was, he concluded, not a lady to be kept waiting.

As they sat down again there was a kerfuffle at the door and in burst a somewhat bedraggled female. Her short brown hair was tousled, her cheeks were red with the exertion of running up the stairs and her blouse was buttoned unevenly.

'Hi, I'm Michelle Dubois, from public relations. Sorry I'm late.' She gasped through uneven breaths. 'The bloody car wouldn't start.'

Her expletive sounded out of place given the formality of the meeting. Raymond also doubted the veracity of her excuse. All employees of the company, at least those of the ranks that those present held, were provided with company cars. Usually top-of-the-range BMWs, Fords or other generally mechanically sound vehicles. They were also regularly maintained and serviced by local garages paid to do so as part of the loan agreement. *No,* he mused, *public relations is a messy business.* Dealing with the press and public, having to attend and even sponsor charity events, nights out and free dinners entertaining clients. No, he suspected that Michelle's tardiness was just as likely to have been an event the day before that had run on into the small hours. Raymond was not one to judge, but first impressions suggested that Michelle was a little unusual in the field of public relations but was probably quite a sociable person and therefore probably well suited to her role in the company.

Raymond had met both Sarah Stephenson and Frank Kinney before. He was aware of their individual roles within the company. But to acquaint himself more fully, he suggested a short formal round of introductions.

'Ladies first,' offered Brian.

Sarah Stephenson was first to offer her details.

Michelle appeared be still a little out of breath.

'I am currently one of the company's medical advisor, with special reference to Erexat.'

The 'one of' and 'currently' suggested to Raymond as-yet-unfulfilled ambitions.

'I have been responsible for the initial trialling of Erexat on volunteers and subsequently on small groups of individual patients.' After that short dissertation, she stopped and glanced around her.

Michelle Dubois was next to offer her CV. 'I head up our PR department, at least with respect to Erexat.'

Raymond detected a hint of a slight American twang in the background; he was a little bemused by her accent, as clearly Michelle was of French descent.

'To date, at least, the advertising and reception for Erexat has been very positive.' Raymond detected a little wariness in her voice; she was fully aware that this group would not have been gathered together unless something, and possibly something negative, had happened.

Frank lounged even further back into the sofa. 'I think you all know me. I am "currently" Raymond's number two on the Erexat project.' Another 'currently' probably with the same underlying meaning.

Brian was last to speak. 'In my former life, I was a clinical lecturer in pharmacology at Newcastle University. I was particularly involved in many aspects of drug development there. Subsequently I was head-hunted by UMBRA to head up part of their pharmaceutical division, working closely with Sarah on the Erexat project.' He glanced over at Sarah Stephenson, who nodded. 'Essentially I have a number of roles within the company. Firstly, I supervise our laboratories on the development of new agents, then, if we identify a potential product, I co-ordinate pre-clinical trials, usually involving animal testing, and finally I advise the directors on the agent's progress and readiness for actual clinical trials involving human subjects, as well as advising on potential medical developments in other areas and alternative treatments to our own product range, and finally, as I suspect I'm here for, I advise on the medical appropriateness of our own medicines and comment on any difficulties or side effects that might have occurred.'

'You guess right, Brian,' interjected Raymond. 'An issue, or in point of fact, several issues have arisen that have caused me some concern and made me summon you all here this morning.'

'Concern?' said Michelle and Sarah simultaneously.

Frank leant forward, his attention secured.

'Yes,' Raymond continued. 'We have received some reports of serious side effects which have occurred around the time of usage of Erexat. Happily, if that is the right word, and I suspect it is not, there are only a small number to date and they come from a number of different areas, so the regulatory authorities haven't reacted as yet, except to just pass the reports on to us. However, taken together it wouldn't be hard to raise a case to restrict its use or even suspend Erexat's licence altogether. Also, and perhaps even more importantly from your point of view, Michelle, the press haven't got hold of any of the details yet. If they did, it could be very damaging to the firm whether or not there was anything in these reports.

'I have got us together to examine these individual reports, hopefully exonerate Erexat, but if not then to investigate further and take whatever remedial actions are necessary. Primarily that's your areas of expertise, I think.' He looked towards Brian and Sarah.

'Your role, Michelle, is to monitor any media interest and to try to stall them until we have a complete picture of what is actually going on here. Okay?'

'And me?' queried Frank. 'This is all very new. There were no such problems when I was heading up the project.'

Helpful, thought Raymond.

'I hope you will support and aid me to get through this, what is hopefully only a temporary glitch.'

'Of course, of course.' But his face couldn't hide the pleasure he was feeling at Raymond's predicament.

Raymond gave each of them a copy of the reports received that Ruth had diligently copied and dropped in while their discussion was going on.

The four rose and filed one by one out of the office, Raymond accompanied them to the door, requested the long-since-offered cup of coffee and then slunk back behind his desk.

chapter ten

Raymond was musing leaning over his desk, his head propped up on one hand, when there was a gentle knock on the door.

Ruth opened it a little and peered round. 'Another coffee?'

'Mmm, thanks, Ruth, but no thanks, I haven't even drunk the last one you gave me. I am a little preoccupied at the moment.'

'Penny for them, then.'

'Sorry, what?' He looked up bemusedly.

'Penny for your thoughts. You've been in here for hours after the others left, and I hadn't heard anything, so I reckoned something was up.'

'Understatement, I'm afraid.'

'Anything I can do to help?'

'Not sure.' But then he had a thought. 'Actually, maybe there is. You know Jim Westin?' Then he added, somewhat needlessly, as Ruth had ushered him in to the meeting, 'From the audit department.'

'Of course.'

'Sorry, stupid question, of course you do. Anyway, could you get hold of him and see if he can get the authority to release some of the personal details from the reports that he says have come in?'

'Personal details?' She looked at him quizzically.

'Yes, names, addresses, ages and effects reported.'

'I'll do my best.' And she turned to leave.

Then, as he rose from his desk to open the door for her, he added as an afterthought, '…And tell him that I do realise that this is not an easy task, nor is it an entirely ethical one, but emphasise the importance. Tell him to pull a few strings, call in some favours – whatever he has to do, do it. I need those details, and I need them now.'

Ruth glanced sideways at him, a questioning look on her face, but she didn't delay and left to carry out his bidding.

Raymond walked back slowly, his head hanging, and sat down once more behind his desk to mull things over.

His career, he now realised, hung in the balance. He was the head man; the buck stopped with him. He had been appointed, even if only on a trial basis, to oversee the success of the company's new drug, a drug that had the potential to earn millions, to become the flagship of the company and with Raymond McNally being propelled to greater things. Now everything was in doubt. If the drug failed, he failed, simple as that.

The drugs progress he knew depended on firstly it working but secondly it being safe. It was this latter point that now was clearly in doubt. If this got out, it could finish the drug before it really even had a chance to start and with it, his own future.

He needed more details; he needed to know what was going on. Was there a problem or wasn't there? If there was, he had no choice he had to fess up to take the consequences and try to salvage what he could.

The phone rang.

'Hello, Jim.' He knew who it would be before he even spoke.

'Look, Raymond, I realise what you are after and why you want the info. but authorities just don't release that kind of information to the public.'

'We're not the public.' Raymond was not going to capitulate on his demand. 'We are the manufacturer. We could – and I stress, could – be responsible here. We need to investigate this properly.'

'I know, but—'

'No buts. Just do what you can, contact the people that gave you the feedback in the first place and stress that we as a company have a responsibility to follow this up. Pull in favours, ask Sarah, she might have some medical contacts, even bribe somebody, I don't care, just get me some inside information.'

'I just don't know—'

Raymond hung up and slouched back over his desk.

chapter eleven

Much to his mother's disgust, Harry had gone back up to his room as soon as he could after eating his dinner. Even during the meal he was his usual, at least in recent years, withdrawn and uncommunicative self. His mother had, albeit reluctantly, grown to accept this, contenting herself with the thought that it appeared that many of his age group also tended to lack social or verbal communication skills and, like her son, tended to spend large parts of the day, and probably the night, with their minds focused on some electronic device or other.

What she had never really got used to was the way that when he sat down at the table he would stare at his cutlery, examining it from a number of different angles before re-arranging it so that the knife and fork were exactly parallel and at similar distance from the table's edge and also equidistant from the dessert spoon. 'Autistic spectrum tendencies,' her GP had called them some years ago when she had described these habits to her; apparently they were often found in association with epilepsy or were possibly related to an issue when the brain was momentarily starved of oxygen, for example during pregnancy or birth, causing a small but definite amount of brain damage. This explanation only left her with further feelings of self-doubt and even guilt. This was despite the fact that she knew, and it had been explained to her many times, it was no fault of hers. Not in any way could she be held responsible for Harry's subsequent development. But she could never quite dismiss the idea that somehow she had let him down.

After the meal and alone again in his bedroom, he switched on the computer and waited for the screen icons to unfold, then he pressed the internet button and immersed himself in the revelations of the outside world, or at least the electronic world that was of interest to Harry Boyle.

As Harry's mother cleared the dishes, she simply assumed that Harry was playing internet games, which she did worry about, but he hadn't seemed to be influenced in any way, except for the overriding preoccupation, so she had let it go. In reality this had been the case in the past. But now Harry had moved on; he had become a self-taught expert in infiltrating or getting behind the on-screen presentations, and he often amused himself, if not the people that had set up the sites, by trying to disrupt their function.

Once he had broken into a site, his obsessive nature usually drove him to further explore and exploit it. On many of the major servers he had actually been able to obtain other users' screennames and passwords, and in some cases their names, addresses and even, on occasion, bank details.

At times Harry's breach of internet security was detected, more often than not by the other user, as Harry often ordered the legitimate user unwanted items or even embarrassing articles that they themselves would never have contemplated buying. Then passwords would change or subscriptions to that server would be withdrawn. Harry presumed that his targets would report to the server that their files had been infiltrated, but what surprised him most was that very little then seemed to happen. The first few times that he had become convinced that he'd been detected he had panicked; he had shut his computer down for days, finally only daring to open it up for brief periods to see if some security message was waiting for him. When the doorbell rang, he jumped, expecting the police to raid the house and seize all his equipment. But no, nothing. He couldn't understand it. At least he couldn't until he came across an article on the news which outlined a report that in excess of five hundred million users of Yahoo had had their personal details hacked and the firm had not reported it for two years!

Five hundred million users... two years! The only rational explanation could be that those in charge of the servers didn't want anyone to know of its weakness, in the security sense at least. In comparison, Harry's individual forays were small fry indeed, much less likely to attract untoward attention and much less likely than the alleged state-sponsored hackers who perpetrated the Yahoo breach, to trouble the server hierarchy.

So what next?

Harry surfed the net. He was searching for something interesting, something to challenge his mind. He googled various subjects to see if his interest could be drawn. Finally, glancing over his shoulder, just to make sure his mother hadn't entered the room, he searched 'sex'. Harry was a young male, after all, but while he had the interest, he lacked any real experience. That, of course, didn't curb the theoretical desires.

Various aspects of sexual practices flashed up on the screen; he scrolled through them, alighting on a variety of sexual manuals, behaviours and even transmitted diseases. None of these really grabbed his attention. Then he alighted on 'sexual dysfunction'. *Perhaps a little closer to home*, he mused.

Top of the list was a variety of aids and appliances, but these held little interested to him. Then he came across medications and tablets that purported to improve function.

Mmmm, interesting, he thought, especially as there appeared to be a huge market for these agents which were available online.

He opened a few of the sites and scrolled through them until he stumbled on one that reported to sell a new 'wonder drug', one that claimed to be the best and the safest drug for erectile dysfunction, and more interestingly, claimed to be the only site from which to obtain it.

Harry started investigating. After only a relatively short time he was able to get behind the screen and determine the number of orders, where they were being bought and even many of the identities of the purchasers.

Then suddenly his screen went blank.

'What the…?'

Nothing like this had happened before.

Then the screen flickered back to life. He reached for the mouse, but the cursor wouldn't respond. Rather it set off, almost with a mind of its own.

'Christ! A virus of some sort.'

But as the cursor alighted on some of his personal files and even started to open them, he realised it was worse, much worse. Somebody had taken control of his computer and was trying either to disable it or, worse, track him down.

Panicking, the only thing he could think of doing was to shut the computer down and quickly. Even that proved difficult, as the computer seemed to be resisting its demise, and it kept restarting despite a number of attempts to disable it. He disconnected it from the electric, but it automatically switched to battery power. In desperation, he flicked the laptop over and pulled out its internal battery. The screen went blank.

Harry slumped back in his chair, visibly shaken. *What the hell was that?* he thought.

Recovering his composure, he started to rationalise what had just happened. The only thing he could think of was some sort of security system, but not one he had ever come across before. Certainly one of some sophistication.

One that scared the hell out of him.

He breathed a sigh of relief that he had seemed to get away with it by disabling his computer so quickly.

But had he?

That program had been opening his personal files. How much information had it gleaned and downloaded to its own server? Could it have traced him, even in the short time that he had been exposed? He knew from his own experience that anything was possible. Computers had huge potential and, worse still, could achieve incredible speeds of information-gathering.

Harry shivered at the thought.

chapter twelve

Raymond, still with the weight of the world heavy on his shoulders, waited patiently for some news from Jim or Sarah. He tapped the desk repeatedly in agitation. Finally, unable to contain himself any longer, he buzzed through to his secretary and asked her to ring Jim Westin to see if there had been any progress.

A little while later, there was a soft knock on his door.

'Come in,' shouted Raymond, looking up from his desk.

It was Sarah Stephenson; as she strode in, Raymond noted a file tucked under one arm.

'Yes?' he said, a bit more aggressively than he had intended.

'I've got something for you. Jim Westin and I have managed to pull in a few favours and have managed to get some limited inside information.'

Raymond now could barely contain his impatience. 'Tell me what you've got.'

She laid the file on his desk. 'As I said, it is, at least so far, quite limited, but it might help.' She opened the file and spread the paperwork across his desk.

'To date, we have managed to pull only limited clinical information and only on a few of those affected, but hopefully we can get some more detail later and perhaps even some leads on some others that have been reported.'

Examining the paperwork, it seemed that Jim Westin had been as good as his word. He had obtained the information that Raymond had requested, or at least some of it. The public bodies, like the CSM, had generally proven themselves most resistant to releasing any confidential patient details to enquiring pharmaceutical companies. However, Jim in a previous life had worked with, and even trained, some of the people that now headed up departments within these information-gathering authorities, and with Sarah's help as a qualified physician they had, albeit reluctantly, acceded to some of his requests.

Using his contacts, Jim had gathered a few snippets of information regarding people allegedly (and he had used the word advisedly) adversely affected by Erexat. Some countries had been a little more forthcoming than others, but at least he had something to feed back to Raymond.

'Jim thought it best that I went through what we have got with you, as I can understand the medical speak better than him,' Sarah explained.

'Okay, hit me with it.'

'A few of the patient details you asked for. The list is by no means complete, but it's a start. I have clinical details on some of the people that have died and others that have suffered some sort of side effect but recovered. As Jim had suggested, they do come from a number of different countries and some details are more complete than others, mainly down to the different ways they collect the information and to how much they were willing to share.'

Raymond reached forward to examine the paperwork more closely, but before he could lift any of them, Sarah Stephenson unexpectedly stepped forward and covered them with her hands. 'Okay, I will let you see them, but you must be aware these are confidential; we are not, and I emphasise *not*, supposed to have them. I do not want this all coming back to me. Is that understood?'

'Loud and clear,' Raymond sublimated.

There were quite a few reports, from a number of countries, in a number of languages. Although Raymond did have a fair grasp of many languages (a pre-requisite for his job), some of the technical or medical terms certainly did throw him. He was glad Sarah was there to interpret.

They sorted the bundles into groups. Those where the effect reported was relatively minor or, on Sarah's suggestion, where it was in fact very unlikely to have actually been associated with the drug. Then into the more interesting pile of those where a connection might indeed possibly exist and the effect had had a more serious outcome. The latter pile was then sub-divided into two groups: dead or alive.

By now the number of reports had risen to twelve reported deaths and seven serious side effects, but in some the information was very limited indeed. Most related to heart attacks or strokes. Admittedly, these were the sort of effects that the company would have been concerned about, as the drug did act on the vascular system. Earlier testing on animals and then on human volunteers seemed to vindicate the drug with respect to any association with obvious circulatory, blood pressure or other changes. However, Raymond himself was only too aware of the limitations of such testing. Animals did not always metabolise or utilise the drug in the same way that humans did, and the testing on humans that was performed was, in general, carried out on healthy young men, usually medical or other students who could supplement their grants with the payments received from hiring out their body for experimentation.

Young fit men could not be said, however, to accurately reflect Erexat's target audience. Erexat was aimed at older, or at best middle-aged, men with a failing libido. Just the population group that were intrinsically most at risk of cardiovascular disease, of which strokes and heart attacks were by far the most common manifestations. On top of that, one had to factor in the unaccustomed activity, again a recognised risk factor in precipitating a circulatory complication.

Raymond reviewed the reports. Happily, he noted, the disparity of the sources meant that it was unlikely that any single authority would have received sufficient numbers of reports to raise a red flag and alert them to a probable or even possible link to Erexat, which in turn could lead to, in the worst scenario, a suspension of the drug's licence. Even, at best, if such a link was postulated, the authorities could impose a lesser form of restriction on its use. But, as Raymond postulated, what would that restriction be? The only logical one would be to ban the prescription of Erexat to middle-aged or elderly men with a history of possible heart or circulatory problems. Essentially that would rule out the vast majority of Erexat's potential target audience and even with the small, still eligible population of younger men, most doctors would likely become very wary of using an agent with a potential for such serious side effects. Essentially, Raymond concluded, that would undoubtedly herald the early demise of Erexat, and with it his newly acquired position within the company.

Raymond knew that he had to take matters in hand. He really had only limited options. He needed to investigate these claims as quickly and as thoroughly as possible, and certainly before the regulatory authorities put two and two together.

Hopefully there would be nothing in the claims, just coincidence, and Erexat would be vindicated; after all, the authorities would themselves recognise that they always did receive the majority of adverse effect reports within the first few weeks and months immediately after a drug was released onto the market, as doctors and others tended to view new drugs with caution and report any event, where unlikely or not, as a possible side effect. Later, as a drug became more mainstream, its true adverse effect profile, and all drugs have side effects, would become well known, and the reports to the authorities would eventually dry up.

Conversely, if there was indeed a link between these problems and the drug, then he could try and hush them up for as long as possible. This might maintain his and the company's profit margins for a sufficient time to, at least, hopefully overturn the deficit incurred in formulating, trialling and manufacturing the drug, and even, perhaps, allow time to look again at the formulations to see if the drug could, in some way, be modified to reduce risk. But, there would be a lot of uncertainty with that strategy, and it certainly was not entirely ethical. Raymond did have a conscience, even though it didn't always shine through.

So, no, Raymond concluded that the company would have to come clean as early as possible by highlighting any such problems and making the prescribers and the clients aware. Then at least they could portray themselves as a responsible manufacturer. Raymond didn't really want to contemplate this latter scenario, as his job would be on the line, but he did recognise that this strategy would, at least, be the honourable thing to do.

Raymond took the two bundles and set the one in which the clients had died to one side. He and Sarah could have a look at them later. Sarah said she could probably obtain the post-mortem reports. And she was certain that there would have been post-mortems, unless the death was predictable in some way, but the fact that these deaths had given rise to regulatory reporting meant it was likely that the deaths had occurred unexpectedly or was unusual, and in most countries, post-mortems were considered mandatory in such cases.

The second smaller bundle contained the reports of some serious illnesses occurring in conjunction with the ingestion of Erexat. Again the reports emanated from a variety of sources.

Raymond's eyes alighted on one report partial obscured by some of the others. The reason he noticed it was that the patient's address emanated from London. The report was from a consultant neurologist in a major teaching hospital less than ten miles from where he himself used to live.

Raymond extracted the report and examined it more carefully. There wasn't a lot of detail but what was there made interesting reading.

A fifty-nine-year-old male with no previous medical history had suffered a stroke whilst making love to his wife. According to his wife it was the first time in many months that they had engaged in such activity. During intercourse he had collapsed and been taken by ambulance to hospital, where it was diagnosed that he had suffered a stroke. The stroke had affected his right arm and leg and also his speech. The doctors had administered thrombolysis therapy (which Sarah explained to Raymond), and it seemed that he had made, at least, a partial recovery.

It was a few days later that his wife had discovered the Erexat tablets hidden in a drawer beside the bed. She had given some of them over to the medical staff, who then in turn reported the event to the CSM.

'Do you think you could get hold of the medical notes, Sarah? It might help our understanding and suggest a way forward.'

Sarah looked dubious. 'Mmmm, I can try, but there still is the patient confidentiality issue.'

'Also what do you think would be the chances of talking to this man and his wife? That might really cast some light on the true sequence of events.'

'Now look, Raymond, that is probably a step too far. We don't even know his identity or address; these adverse event reports are always anonymised.'

'Hence getting the notes. We know the reporting physician's name and the hospital he was treated in.'

'I really don't know.' Sarah's dubious look had now evolved into one of set opposition.

'Look, I don't want the details just to vindicate the drug. If there is a problem, then we should hold our hands up and admit there is a problem. This poor guy has had a stroke, for Christ's sake; he deserves to know what's happened to him and probably even some compensation for it.'

'Alright, I'll do my best. But I'm not happy and I suspect our lawyers won't be either if you start waving compensation offers around willy-nilly.' With that, Sarah Stephenson turned on her heel and left the office.

Raymond sat down at his desk and rifled through the reports that she'd left behind.

chapter thirteen

Michael 'Slab' McBride stood over the grave of his beloved son. He stood virtually alone surveying the artificial grass sheet that covered the burial pit.

The majority of the funeral cortege had already left to attend the wake that was so customary in that part of Scotland. An unaccustomed tear welled up at the corner of one eye as he looked at the temporary covering over the burial place. He quickly wiped the tear away, not wishing to demonstrate any form of weakness. Though in truth it was unlikely any of the others still remaining at the graveside would have noticed or, indeed, given Slab's reputation, dared to say anything anyway.

His wife gripped him by the arm and he put it around her waist.

'It's a terrible thing, to have to bury one of your own, and so young,' she sobbed.

Slab said nothing. He just continued to stare down at his son's final resting place.

He gritted his teeth and silently swore to himself that he would find out precisely what had happened, why his son had died at the age of only nineteen, and if anyone was responsible, he would make sure that they would pay.

This would be no idle threat, even if he made it only to himself. Slab McBride was a 'community worker' in in the East End of Glasgow, one of the roughest areas of the city, though the term 'community worker' was a self-styled handle. In reality Slab had a reputation as a hard man, a gang land leader. He had gained his present standing initially through threats and in some cases actual violence, progressing inexorably on to other areas of activity, principally drug dealing, protection rackets and reputedly armed robberies. In truth, he and his companions were little more than an organised group of thugs and racketeers, though no one was likely to say this to their face.

Slab continued to hold his gaze on the hole which was his son's resting place. The nickname 'Slab' had nothing to do with the word 'slob', though in actual fact his appearance would not have differed much from the traditional view of such a character. The grey skies overhead only served to highlight his bulky stature, his bald shaved head and paunch, but his strong, heavily tattooed, muscular upper body and arms denied the comparison.

Locally, Slab had a fearsome reputation, built up carefully over time. It was even rumoured, though never proven, that in earlier days he had been responsible for the death or the disabling of a number of individuals, some by his own hand, later others by those who now followed his orders.

Slab had also been linked to numerous other crimes and was well known to the local constabulary. To date, however, apart from one short sojourn at Her Majesty's pleasure, Slab had avoided the clutches of the law. It was, however, common knowledge that Slab had acquired his nickname through what had become his preferred method of doling out punishments to those he deemed had crossed him. He would have the transgressor pinned down by two of his associates and then he would hurl a breeze block or other large slab of concrete down onto each of the victim's legs in turn, shattering both the tibia and fibula below the knee. In most cases his victims had been young men often from within the community in which Slab lived and was simply carried out as a punishment and to assert his own position within that locality. Following such a punishment, the recipients, even after surgery and a prolonged hospital stay, would thereafter walk with a pronounced limp, in many cases for the rest of their lives. This, Slab deemed, served as a warning to others not to cross Slab McBride. Slab ruled his locality with an iron fist, and nobody, but nobody, was going to threaten that.

He turned and, supporting his wife with his arm around her waist, he led her out of the graveyard and towards the waiting car.

*

Back at his house, the wake was in full flow. Too much drink had already been taken, but most of the guests had the sense to act soberly in front of Slab himself. His closest companions in turn had put their arms around his shoulder or shaken his hand and expressed their commiserations.

Slab wended his way through the melee and took up position in his favourite armchair beside the wood-burning stove in the living room. His wife brought him a beer, still in the can, and then disappeared back into the kitchen where her sisters had gathered. He simply sat, staring into space, gripping the beer can in his right hand resting on the chair's arm.

After a while he rose and motioned to Frankie O'Reilly to come over.

Frankie pushed his way through the crowd and Slab leaned forward to talk directly into Frankie's ear. 'Meet you upstairs. My bedroom. Five minutes, and bring Billy with you.'

Five minutes later and the three of them had extracted themselves from the party and now sat in Slab's front bedroom. Frankie and Billy perched on the side of the bed, cans of beer still in hand, looking somewhat uncomfortable. Slab moved over towards the window and sat down on the small stool beside his wife's dressing table. Slab's considerable bulk only enhanced the menacing look on his face. Frankie and Billy shifted in their positions, becoming even more uncomfortable as Slab fixed them in a hard stare.

'Okay,' he said, 'here's the deal. Jimmy was only nineteen, too young to die.' He wiped another tear from the corner of his eye. 'The cops say it was a heart attack brought on by a drug overdose. I don't believe it. Yes, I know Jimmy took the odd illegal substance, but he knew what he was doing; he wouldn't have overdone it, he knew better. So I want to know. If it was an overdose. Of what and how it happened. Start with who was there when he died and then, and most importantly, find out who supplied the drugs. Okay?'

Frankie and Billy nodded dumbly. They knew this wasn't a polite request from a grieving father; this was an order.

They filed out of the bedroom, risking a sideways glance at each other as Slab stood immobile, looking out of the front window over the street beyond.

chapter fourteen

After everyone had left, Raymond studied the files individually and somewhat more carefully than when he and Sarah had gone through them; at that time, it had been largely to allow her to explain some of the more obscure of the medical terms contained within them.

He studied one report in particular, the one that had caught his eye for the simple reason the subject of the report lived near to, or at least not that far away from, Raymond's own apartment in London. An apartment which he still owned even after his move to Basel.

The report on the distinctive yellow form of the CSM had given the patient's name and address and it reported that he had suffered a cerebrovascular accident, or, as Sarah had explained, a stroke, during intercourse after taking an Erexat tablet.

Raymond read on; there were certainly some pre-existing risk factors: his age, his blood pressure, being a little overweight, for example. A candidate for a stroke or heart attack anyway, with or without the Erexat, and with the unaccustomed exercise.

But, it had been reported as a potential drug adverse

effect and so would been taken seriously by the authorities and investigated as such. Raymond viewed it with seriousness as well. He realised that he needed to try and ascertain the full facts so that he would have answers when the CSM came calling.

He rang the GP whose name appeared on the report. He explained the purpose of the call to the practice receptionist and was put through to the doctor after a few minutes, allowing the GP to finish dealing with another patient.

'Dr Brown speaking.'

'Hello, Dr Brown.' Raymond explained who he was and that he had discussed the case with his own medical advisors.'

'And the purpose of the call is…?' The doctor sounded a little defensive.

'I wanted to see if there was any way I could meet with Mr Baker or his relatives to see exactly what happened and if there is indeed a link to our product. If there is, then I would like in some way to compensate the family, as well as obviously trying to iron out any potential for similar problems in the future with other recipients.' Raymond tried to appeal to the doctor's loyalty to his own patient as well as the greater good.

'This is most irregular, Mr McNally.'

'I know, I do realise that, but I just want to help in whatever way I can.'

'Mmmm… So what exactly do you want me to do?'

'All I want you to do is to contact the family and find if they would agree to meet with me.'

There was a long pause. Raymond could hear Dr Brown putting the phone down on the desk and the scratching of his chair on the floor as he leant back to consider the request.

At least he hasn't dismissed me out of hand, thought Raymond.

After a few minutes the doctor came back on the line.

'Okay,' he sounded sceptical, 'I'll give them a call and see what they say.'

'Thank you so much, Dr Brown – and don't worry, I will be tactful, really, I only want to help.'

'I'm not promising anything, mind.'

'Of course not.'

'Give me your number and I'll ring you back.'

Raymond gave the GP his office and mobile numbers and hung up. He gave a sigh of relief, even if he didn't really feel it. The family may well refuse to see him, and even if they did, what was he going to say?

After what seemed like an age, his mobile rang.

'Mr McNally?' Raymond immediately recognised the doctor's voice. 'They have said yes.' Another pause, then, 'I have their telephone number here. I think you already have their address.'

Raymond copied the telephone number onto a post-it on his desk.

'Be very respectful, Mr McNally. They have, as you are aware, suffered a grievous trauma. It is my understanding that Mr Baker has only just been discharged from hospital and is being cared for by his wife whilst we try to put a package of measures in place for formal home care.'

'It goes without saying. Thank you again, Dr Brown.'

The GP hung up.

He considered his options. Obviously having gone so far he should contact the family, they were expecting his call, but he was apprehensive. What sort of reception could he expect? Raymond took a deep breath and dialled the number that the GP had given him.

The phone was answered almost immediately.

Mrs Baker had sounded frosty, offhand, but a meeting was set up. It was to be at the Baker's own home in two days' time;

he reassured the family that he would be alone and that there would be no platitudes, simply a fact-finding mission and an offer of whatever help he and his firm could offer.

chapter fifteen

It was only by the next day that Harry's curiosity finally overcame his apprehension. Twenty-four hours had probably been the longest that he'd been parted from his beloved computer in the last three years.

Tentatively, he plugged it in and pressed the on button. The screen flickered to life. His usual screensaver popped up.

'So far, so good.' He breathed a sigh of relief. *Here we go, in for a penny in for a pound*, he thought. He opened the internet.

Nothing unusual.

He checked his emails; he did a brief Google search for nothing in particular, just to make sure everything worked.

Having satisfied himself all was working satisfactorily, he convinced himself that he must have imagined the whole previous scenario with the computer developing a mind of its own.

Finally he plucked up the courage and decided to investigate the website that he'd logged in to on that evening.

He opened the site; it seemed harmless enough. It, at least superficially, looked legit. It seemed simply to be a sellers' site, peddling mainly medicines to the public. He looked at the products and wrote some of them down, noting the prices, planning to investigate further later. Then, typing furiously, he started to probe deeper into the site itself. This is when the problems had arisen previously.

Nothing untoward so far.

The site seemed to be UK-based. Then, following a lead in the site itself, he located the origins of the site, or at least the developers of it and their details.

Then, all of a sudden, his computer screen went blank. He had hit some very unusual security system again clearly.

After his last experience he shut the computer down immediately and breathed a sigh of relief.

chapter sixteen

It wasn't long before Frankie and Billy reported back.

They sat in Slab's front room to explain that Jimmy McBride had died in a small terrace house just off Clyde Street in the East End of Glasgow. Apparently there had been some sort of a party and no one had noticed that Jimmy had gone upstairs and hadn't returned. The partygoers were all spaced out by all accounts. It wasn't till the next morning that his body was discovered, already cold, in one of the upstairs bedrooms.

Slab was silent for a moment. He lit a cigarette and thought quietly to himself.

'Do you know who found him?'

Billy confirmed they did and that they had the names of some of the others present at the party.

Slab paced up and down the small room. Then he stopped and leant forward, bending at the waist until his face was right in Billy's. Billy could smell the nicotine and stale alcohol on Slab's breath.

'Bring them in. I want to talk to them.'

'Okay, anything you say, Slab.' Billy tried to back away a little but was prevented by the arm of the sofa behind him. 'Where do you want them?'

'Not here, obviously.' He thought for a moment. 'You know the row of run-down houses on the road just off McIntosh Street?'

Billy nodded.

'At least two of them are definitely empty – we can use one of those. Bring them there about seven o'clock. I'll meet you there.'

Billy and Frankie again nodded their affirmation and slunk quietly out.

*

The sky behind the terrace houses looked dark and foreboding as Slab turned off the larger road into the small cul-de-sac. There were lights on in only two of the houses' front rooms. He drove slowly past the lit rooms and on down to the darker end of the road. He gripped the steering wheel tightly between his fingers and gritted his teeth as he rolled to a halt outside number 23.

Earlier in the afternoon he had received a call from Frankie saying that they had caught up with two of Jimmy's so-called friends and had 'invited' them here for a 'tête-à-tête'.

Slab exited the car and strode up to the front door. The paint was peeling and the bell no longer worked. He knocked. To all intents and purposes the house appeared deserted. Certainly there did not appear to be any lights on despite the growing darkness in the street. However, he noted that the curtains were tightly drawn in all of the front rooms so there may yet be activity beyond. As if to confirm his thoughts, the front door was opened quickly and Frankie's head appeared in the aperture. Both Slab and Frankie almost simultaneously glanced left and right, surveying the street to ensure nobody witnessed their coming and goings.

'You got them?' Slab growled.

'Just the one,' announced Frankie. '...so far,' he quickly added, observing Slab's menacing expression. 'The others had heard we were looking for them and have gone to ground. But if you still need them after talking to this guy, we've put the word out. It'll not be long before we track them down.'

'Okay, where is he? Have you brought him here as I told you?' Slab still didn't look pleased at Frankie's efforts so far.

'He's in the front room. Billy's keeping an eye on him. Name's Michael, Michael McCloud. He's quite posh, actually.'

'Posh? Posh? What the hell do you mean?' roared Slab.

Frankie shrank back at the outburst. 'Mmm… I mean, he's not really one of us. Lives with his parents on the west side. Went to the academy.'

The academy was the Glasgow Academy, a public school in Kelvinbridge, a nice part of Glasgow and not really a school that Slab or any of his associates would have been affiliated with.

'So what was Jimmy doing hanging out with him then?'

'You're better asking him that yourself, Slab. We've sort of… well, softened him up a bit. I think he's quite amenable to talk.'

'Right, let's go.' Slab pushed past Frankie into what had previously been the main sitting room of the house. Now it was in semi-darkness; a small candle in the corner of the room was the only illumination. An old fireplace partially removed dominated the wall opposite the doorway, wallpaper hung from the walls, and, as Slab had noted from outside, the curtains had been pinned up and tightly shut against the outside world.

In the centre of the room, seated on a rickety kitchen chair, sat Michael McCloud. His hands were tied behind his back and his feet were secured to the legs of the chair. His head hung forward, blood dripping from his mouth. His eyes were closed; he appeared unconscious.

Slab glared at Billy. 'He better be fit to answer my questions. What have you been doing to him?'

'Nothing, not much. Just a few preliminaries, that's all.' Billy, however, backed off at Slab's enquiry.

Slab stepped forward till he stood directly in front of the seated hostage. With his left hand he pulled the bleeding visage up so he could look him in the face. 'Okay, mister, I want to know what exactly happened to Jimmy.'

'Jimmy?' His voice was low and it took him some effort to squeeze out the reply, but Slab could still detect the hint of an upper-class Glaswegian accent.

'Yes, pretty boy, Jimmy. My son. You were with him when he died. I want to know exactly, and I mean exactly, what happened to him and who was responsible.'

'Your son?' Michael McCloud groaned, possibly for the first time realising the full extent of the trouble he was in. 'I don't know,' he pleaded. 'It was an accident, some sort of freak accident, he just died.' He paused momentarily, then added, 'We just found him, that's all.'

'So, tell me.' Slab bent down so that his face almost touched that of the hostage. He could see the tears welling up in Michael McCloud's eyes.

'We were just having a party, that's all.'

'Who's we?'

'Me and some old school pals.' He paused for thought, then added, 'And some girls. It was just a piece of fun, that's all.' The tears had congealed into a stream running down his cheeks.

Slab hit him hard with his free right hand, striking him on his left cheek and knocking the chair and its occupant to the floor.

Frankie and Billy stepped forward and between them manhandled the chair back to vertical again.

'Let's start again,' Slab snarled.

'Okay, okay, please don't hit me again.'

'Speak.'

Michael McCloud explained as best he could through the throbbing of his face and his aching limbs, that he and some friends had arranged a party. One of them knew Jimmy slightly and knew he could get them some drugs to help the party go with a swing.

Mmmm, Slab thought, *probably nicked from me.*

'Anyway,' Michael McCloud continued, 'Jimmy arrived early. He, as promised, brought some 'E', some skank and something he said that if the girls were up for it would be some fun.'

Slab looked a little confused by that comment; he didn't know what Michael had meant by that. But he remained quiet at the moment, biding his time.

'Jimmy insisted on staying – we didn't really want him to. He wasn't really one of us.'

Slab bit his lip.

Realising what he'd said, Michael tried to explain. 'I mean, we didn't really know him. He was just a passing acquaintance of one of my mates.'

Slab pulled back a little.

'He insisted saying that we weren't getting the merchandise until we agreed. The party was all set up, so we had no choice.'

'And?' Slab bent forward again into the young man's face.

Michael McCloud could smell the tobacco on Slab's breath he was so close. He tried to lean back but couldn't escape because of the bonds.

'So, he stayed. I didn't really notice him – that is, until he disappeared.'

'Disappeared?'

'Yeah, apparently he copped off with one of the girls and had taken her upstairs. The next we knew she had come running down the stairs screaming that he had collapsed. We all rushed up, but it was too late. It was obvious he was already dead.'

Slab took a deep breath and sat down on a chair opposite the hostage, whose head lowered once more.

After a moment Slab looked pale. 'Anything else?' he said quietly.

'Well…'

'Well, what?'

'The girl he was with…'

'Yes?' Slab was interested again.

'Well, she said that he took something, a pill, a small blue one, not one of the ones he'd sold to us, after they had got into bed. It was just after this that he had complained of a pain in his chest and then passed out. She couldn't get him round. That's when she came down and got us.'

Slab looked confused. 'What was this pill?' He didn't recognise the description as a pill from his own hoard.

'I don't know. Beth, the girl he was with, thought it might be some sort of Viagra. The packet was still sitting on the bedside table. But we didn't hang about. We just called the ambulance and legged it.'

'So you don't know what this other pill actually was?'

'No, but you could find out.'

'Find out. How?'

'On my way out I grabbed the packet and took it with me.'

'You what? Where is it now?'

'It's at home, hidden in my bedroom. In my bedside cabinet.'

Slab got up and walked around the room. He turned to

Frankie and Billy. 'Untie him, let him go, but go with him back to his house, get those fucking tablets and bring them to me. Understand? We'll find out what this tablet was and where it came from and then we'll sort this. Okay?'

'Yes, boss,' they chorused.

'And, you.' He turned to Michael, who was slowly and stiffly rising to his feet as Slab's accomplices untied him. 'You, I don't want to see ever again. You get my drift?'

'I do, I do.' The tears continued to roll down Michael McCloud's red and swollen face as he slunk out of the room between Frankie and Billy.

chapter seventeen

Raymond had made his arrangements to visit George Baker. His flight to Heathrow was uneventful, though he couldn't really settle or get comfortable, despite the business-class seat that Ruth had booked for him. His mind was full of misgivings as to how he should approach the meeting with the Bakers, what exactly he would or could say to them.

It was mid-morning as he left the airport and hailed a cab.

His inner turmoil persisted though his journey, which in reality was only a short taxi ride to the Baker's house.

He barely noticed as the taxi pulled up outside the sixties-style semi, in a row of similar houses, so engrossed was he with his own thoughts.

'Number 32, guv?' the driver announced.

'What?'

'It was number 32, wasn't it? If so, we're here. That'll be £37.50, guv.'

'Okay, mmm, would you mind waiting? Keep the meter running, I shouldn't be long.'

He alighted the taxi and stood for a moment, surveying the house and the street. The Baker's house was identical to most of the houses on the road. Red-brick construction. It had a bay window on the ground floor and first storey, in which series of rectangular windows made up the bay. Supporting the ground-floor windows was the red brickwork that made up the rest of the house, but the upper bay window sat on a semi-circle of brick of a greyer hue. The triangle above the upper bay window was outlined and then crossed by strips of wood which formed the shape of a large downward-facing arrow. *A mock-Tutor wood design typical of the era*, thought Raymond. Against a white background, the triangle of planks were painted blue, a colour which matched that of the front door, towards which Raymond strode after his momentary pause.

There was a brass knocker just below the letter box, which in turn was situated below a rectangular window that filled the upper part of the door. However, it was the bell situated on the framework of the door that Raymond reached for.

The door was opened on the first ring by a woman, who, on first impression, looked haggard and drawn. She was, Raymond knew from the reports he'd read, in her mid-fifties, but now she looked older.

'Yes?' She peered around the partially open door.

'Mrs Baker?' said Raymond, nodding slightly in deference.

'Yes,' adding, 'Oh, you must be that chap from the drug company that I talked to.'

'That's right. Raymond McNally, we talked on the phone.'

'Right, you better come in then.'

Raymond thought he detected a coolness in her voice.

She led him down the short hallway and turned right into the front room. The room was small and cluttered. A sofa and two armchairs dominated the available space; a television flickered in the corner.

Mrs Baker reached for the TV remote which had been sitting on the arm of one of the chairs and extinguished the mid-morning chat show.

'As you know, Mrs Baker, I've come to—'

He didn't get to finish the sentence; she interrupted him. 'Oh, I know what you've come for. You're here to say that George's condition is nothing to do with you or your company.'

'No, no, Mrs Baker, honestly. I'm here because I want to understand.'

'Understand? Understand what?' Her voice had become quite hostile towards him.

'To understand what happened to George, err... your husband.' He had adopted as quiet and conciliatory a tone as he could. 'Why it happened and is there anything we could have done to prevent it.'

She ushered him to sit down on the sofa while she chose one of the armchairs.

'Well, you know the circumstances. I'm not going into that,' she said quite abruptly.

'No, no, of course not.'

'It was only later after he collapsed and had been taken to hospital that I found your tablets. They were in the bedside cabinet. There was one missing – obviously he'd taken it. I handed some of the tablets in to the doctors at the hospital so that they could investigate.'

'He collapsed quite suddenly? There was no warning?'

'Nothing – one minute he was fine. The next he was just lying there, couldn't move, couldn't talk.' She started to sob.

Raymond offered a handkerchief which he had retrieved from his trouser pocket.

She waved it away, preferring a crumpled tissue which had been tucked down the side of the armchair on which she sat.

After a few moments to allow her to regain her composure, Raymond asked in as soft a tone as he could summon, in order not to distress her any further, 'I believe it was a stroke?'

She nodded, still mopping the tears from her face.

Raymond persisted, 'Had he ever had any problems like this before?'

'No, never. Nothing.'

'Nor any heart or blood pressure problems?'

'Nothing.' She was almost shouting at him now. 'He was as fit as a flea, my George. Until this.' She sobbed uncontrollably.

Raymond sat back in the sofa and remained quiet in order to give her space and time to allow her to recover her composure again.

After several minutes he plucked up the courage to ask if he might see and speak to George himself.

She sat quietly now, not say anything; at least she seemed to be considering the request.

'Well, alright. But you won't be able to get any sense out of him, you know. His speech was affected. Nowadays I can sort of know what he's trying to say, but strangers, well, they don't understand at all. He's upstairs. Still in bed. I can't get him up myself. The district nurse usually calls and we use a hoist thing to get him into the wheelchair. But she's late today.'

Raymond looked at his watch – it was nearly twelve o'clock. *Late indeed*, he thought.

'She's often late these days; sometimes she doesn't make it at all. She's so busy, see. God bless her, she does her best. I don't know what I'd do without her.'

'Maybe that is something my company can help you with, Mrs Baker,' Raymond offered.

She seemed to shrug the offer off and led him out into the hallway and up the stairs. As they approached the front bedroom, she turned to him and whispered into his ear, 'Don't you go upsetting him, you hear?'

'No, no, of course not.'

The curtains were open; the windows overlooked the

small yet cluttered street beyond – car parking was clearly at a premium in this part of town.

George Baker was sitting propped up in bed by two pillows. His face was twisted and his right arm, which lay on top of the bedsheets, was bent at the elbow and at the wrist, the fingers curled into a claw. He raised it in greeting as he twisted himself to see the new arrivals; it was obvious, though, to Raymond that the limb had only limited function.

Raymond noted a wheelchair on the far side of the bed, and a commode tucked into the recess beside the bay window.

'Hello, Mr Baker, my name's Raymond, Raymond McNally. I'm from the drug company. I think your wife told you that I might be coming?'

George Baker looked quizzically at his wife and then at Raymond himself.

'O... K...' The letters came slowly and with difficulty as George tried to reply.

Jane stepped forward, sat on the edge of the bed, and reached for and held the twisted hand, stroking it gently with her other hand.

'He's got a lot better, since... since... it happened. He can stand by himself at least for a few minutes, if he holds on to something. And he understands what I say, but his speech, while improving –' she turned to her husband, stroking his hand more vigorously, 'isn't it, darling? – is still quite limited, I'm afraid.'

George Baker seemed to nod in response, though it was difficult to be certain.

'I just wanted... I just wanted...' Raymond was floundering a bit, seeing for the first time the extent of George Baker's disability. 'I just wanted to come and see you for myself and offer whatever help and support we can. Not, you understand, that anyone can know with any certainty that our drug has been responsible for your... difficulties.'

Jane Baker's face hardened.

Raymond bit his lip, realising that what he had said had, in all certainty, come across as cruel and heartless, and was being interpreted as a legalistic-sounding 'no admission of liability' statement. Too late he realised that this was neither the time nor the place for that kind of sentiment. He immediately wished he could retract the words.

Jane Baker rose to her feet and, fixing him in a hard stare, announced, 'I think it's time for you to leave, Mr McNally.'

Raymond momentarily stood his ground. He wanted to apologise, make things better again. But, almost immediately, he concluded that ship had sailed.

'Now, Mr McNally.'

Raymond detected a firm determination in her voice.

As he turned to leave, Jane Baker bent down, opened a cabinet drawer beside her and retrieved a package of some sort.

As Raymond turned to look, she threw the package at him. It struck him on his left cheek and fell to the floor.

'And you can take your filthy pills with you. These are the rest of them, the ones I didn't hand over, the ones apparently nobody can prove did this to my George.' She spat out the words, mocking those of Raymond himself.

Raymond bent down and retrieved the small cardboard package from the floor where it had fallen. Some of the contents had become dislodged so he pushed the silver tinfoil wrapping that contained the tablets back into place. He slid the packet into his jacket pocket.

'I'm so sorry, Mrs Baker, Mr Baker. Really, I meant no offence. I just wanted to understand, and my offer of help stands.' He proffered his business card. He had to hold it out for several minutes whilst Jane Baker made up her mind whether to take it or not.

Finally she snatched it from him and set it down on the bedside table.

'Right, time to go, Mr McNally.'

Raymond offered his farewells to George and followed Jane Baker back down the stairs.

No more words were spoken. She opened the front door, and Raymond nodded and left.

He was glad he'd asked the taxi to wait, and there it sat, two doors down, in one of the few available spaces in which to park on the little street.

'Airport, please,' he muttered as he clambered on board.

Sitting once again in the back seat, Raymond felt full of regret.

Regret at the way that he had handled things, regret at upsetting the Bakers, but mostly an overwhelming feeling of sadness and responsibility for the broken and incapacitated state of George Baker himself. As he mused over things, he reached into his jacket pocket, fumbled around and then retrieved the small box of pills that Jane Baker had thrown at him.

'EREXAT' was emblazoned across the front of the box, and a green stripe, along with his company's logo, appeared on both the back and front of the container. He examined it a little more closely, then he pulled out the tinfoil strip and burst out a tablet from it. Clutching the small, round, blue tablet between forefinger and thumb, he held it up to the taxi's window.

'That's strange,' he said to himself.

He spent the rest of the taxi ride to the airport in silence, buried in his own thoughts.

chapter eighteen

The sky was cloudless, the sea turquoise and translucent, and only a slight breeze disturbed the tranquillity of the scene. The small day cruiser sat alone in the expanse of ocean, the nearest land only a distant shadow on the horizon. The small boat bobbed in the slight swell encouraged by the breeze. Rohit Khanna stood on the small deck at the boat's stern and surveyed the scene. His two colleagues, Aarav Batra and Rahul Chaudhary, sat quietly in the small open cabin, not talking, only smoking cigarettes.

The peaceful scene was intermittently disturbed by the sound of irregular splashing coming from the water behind the deck on which Rohit stood. There was a man in the water; his head bobbed up and down only just above the waterline. Each time the struggling man approached the boat, Rohit leant over the guard rail and pushed him back using a boat hook that he had picked up from the deck and now held in his right hand.

More and more desperate the swimmer became as he treaded water frantically. He had only his legs to keep him afloat, as his arms were securely tied behind his back.

'Tell me what I want to know,' Rohit hissed at the struggling man.

'Go to hell,' he replied, only to submerge under the waves with the distraction of speaking.

'Four minutes, not bad. The record for treading water, in my experience, is around ten or thereabouts. So you better think about it, Amit.'

Amit did not reply; he simply kept Rohit determinately fixed in his gaze. Aarav and Rahul looked up from their seated position but made no attempt to intervene.

Rohit Khanna in response swung the boat hook around and, placing it squarely on the swimmer's shoulder, he applied pressure and pushed him down under the water.

Amit's head re-emerged, panting and blowing, water streaming from his eyes and mouth.

'Five minutes. Halfway. Come on, Amit, speak. Who are you working for and what have you told them?'

'I didn't do anything!' spluttered Amit, clearly now struggling to keep his head above water.

'You were seen talking to that policewoman, the young pretty detective that's been giving Mr Patel such a hard time recently. So what were you talking about?'

Amit tried to reply, but each time he opened his mouth water rushed in and he choked. His face was red with the effort; he was finding it harder and harder to stay afloat.

Taking his silence as more defiance, Rohit Khanna pointed the boat hook at his victim and, with menace in his voice, said, 'Okay, have it your own way then, Mr Saagar. Appropriate name by the way, Saagar – means ocean, doesn't it?'

With that he pushed the boat hook towards Amit's neck and on making contact pushed him down with all his force so that his head disappeared beneath the ocean's waves. There he held it. Bubbles came to the surface; still he maintained the downward force.

Aarav and Rahul appeared at the cabin's entrance and stood unmoved, watching proceedings.

Eventually the bubbling ceased and, after a few more minutes, Rohit released his grip on the boat hook.

The lifeless body of Amit Saagar floated to the surface.

Throwing the boat hook at Rahul, he turned away and ordered them to get it on board.

Rahul and Aarav rushed forward to do as they were bid. Firstly they secured the hook of the boat hook in Amit's clothing and pulled him towards the boat's edge, then, grabbing his arms and legs, they hauled the lifeless corpse aboard and dropped it on the deck.

'Untie his hands and throw him back in,' shouted Rohit from the cabin where he had retreated to smoke one of Rahul's cigarettes.

'Won't they see the marks on his wrists anyway?' asked Aarav sheepishly.

'The fish and the crabs will probably get to him first before he's found way out here; they'll eat the flesh and destroy the evidence. Even if that doesn't happen, it'll just serve as more of a warning that Mr Patel does not tolerate informers.'

Rahul and Aarav removed the bindings and then, with Rahul lifting the arms and Aarav the legs, they manhandled him over the boat's edge and dropped Amit Saagar's body back into the water. There it floated, partially submerged, face down, arms and legs outstretched; they stood motionless on the deck and watched as it slowly drifted away.

'Start the engine and let's get out of here,' Rohit barked.

chapter nineteen

Raymond had returned to Basel and was sitting in his office. He buzzed through to his secretary and asked her to request Brian Thompson and Sarah Stephenson to come and see him ASAP.

When they arrived, Raymond rose from his seated position behind his desk; he ushered them to sit down and stood in front of them, leaning on his desk. He leant further back and fumbled in his trouser pocket to find the tablets that Jane Baker had 'given' him.

He gripped them tightly in his fist and then, theatrically slowly opening his fingers, showed the tablets in his outstretched palm for Brian and Sarah to see.

Both looked quizzically at the pills.

'What are these?' Brian asked.

'Erexat, apparently,' replied Raymond.

Sarah Stephenson glanced at Brian, and, in turn, Brian looked up to engage Raymond's gaze and spoke. 'But they don't look right.'

'My thoughts exactly,' replied Raymond, turning the pills over in his palm. He handed one each to Brian and Sarah.

'So where did you get them?' asked Sarah.

'I "got" them from the wife of the man who had the stroke.'

'You went to see him?' Sarah said with surprise.

Raymond nodded.

'But was that not a bit… unethical?'

'I just wanted to see if there was anything we… or the firm, could do to help. Especially if Erexat was actually to blame. Anyway, as I was leaving the wife "gave" me these. She said that her husband, unbeknown to her, had got hold of them and taken one just before he became ill.'

'So how did he get them?' Brian asked.

'In the UK, Erexat is a prescription-only medicine, so if he got them, he must have got them through his GP. That's what I want you, Sarah, to find out. Can you contact him or her and then, doctor to doctor, see if a prescription was issued and why, and tactfully see if there were any contraindications that should have prevented the prescription being issued in the first place. Then, Brian, if the script was issued correctly, I want you to check with the chemist where the prescription was cashed, and to find out the exact source of these tablets. Is that okay?'

Sarah Stephenson and Brian Thompson nodded their reluctant affirmation and got up to leave.

'Actually, just one more thing.'

They stopped and turned to face Raymond again.

'Brian.' He tossed a tablet across to him. Brian caught it in one hand. 'Can you get this analysed, just to make sure it is what it says it is?'

'Sure, boss, will do.'

As they filed out of the office, Raymond returned to his chair behind the desk and sat, head supported by his arms, and again looked at the small silver-foiled packet and the remaining tablets within. He turned it over and over in his hand. The more he looked at it, the more he was convinced that it was wrong, somehow, just wrong.

*

It was a couple of days later that Sarah Stephenson reported back.

'I contacted the GP. He was a bit reluctant at first. Doctors are very wary of releasing sensitive clinical details, but with a bit of persuasion, coupled with the fact that I am medically qualified and therefore should know the rules, he eventually agreed to check his records and get back to me.'

'And…?' Raymond sat bolt upright at his desk.

'Neither he nor any of his partners prescribed Erexat to Mr Baker.'

'Mmmm… the plot thickens. So where did Baker get them from?'

After a moment's pause, Sarah Stephenson came back. 'It's possible one of his friends with a similar problem gave them to him, or he went to another doctor.'

'Surely the GP should know if another doctor were to prescribe something to one of his patients? Wouldn't they write and tell him, if only as a matter of courtesy?' Raymond snapped.

'Of course you're right. But you never know. There are a few rogue doctors out there, and that still leaves the possibility that a friend gave them to him.'

'I don't suppose we will ever find out the answer to that one. George Baker currently can't speak because of the stroke, and if a friend did give them to him and then heard what happened, he's unlikely to tell us or George Baker's wife.'

Then, after a short pause for thought, he added, 'Let's just wait and see what Brian comes up with from the analysis of the tablets.'

*

It was a few more days before Brian came back to Raymond.

Raymond had barely time to say 'hello' on answering the phone when Brian announced, 'You were right. There's something funny going on with the tablet you gave me.'

'Something funny? What do you mean?' Raymond's interest was piqued; he leant forward on his desk.

'Well…' Brian shuffled his feet. 'The basic formulae of the radafinil is there, but there are other elements… ingredients, if you like, that shouldn't be there.'

'You mean that there has been some mistake in the manufacturing process?'

Raymond's demeanour shrank. If there was a mistake in manufacture at his end, that was the end of Erexat. Even if they managed to fix the problem, the drug's reputation would be in tatters. Doctors would be unlikely to ever prescribe it again, fearful of causing injury to one of their patients. And… if Erexat went down the tubes, so did his career.

'That's certainly one possible explanation. Look, Raymond, leave it with me. I'll need to do a bit more work on this and then I'll get back to you, okay?'

'Okay.' Raymond slowly replaced the receiver and sank back into his chair.

As Raymond sat, head in hands, his secretary put her head around the door. She had overheard a bit of the conversation and sensed Raymond's despair.

'Anything I can do, Mr McNally?'

'I think I need a stiff drink, but for the moment a coffee will suffice, thanks.'

As she set the coffee down in front of him, he barely looked up, engrossed as he was in his own thoughts.

The secretary turned to leave but then turned back. She spoke, a little reluctantly, as she hadn't really wanted to interrupt his thoughts. 'I'm sure you've got more on your mind, Mr McNally, but one of the company secretaries picked up this email this morning and her boss said she should pass it on to you. It's probably nothing important, but, you know…' Her voice trailed off.

Without looking up, he held out his hand for the email and she passed it to him and then turned and left.

For next hour or so Raymond did nothing; he simply sat, bent over, staring down at the desktop.

Finally he reached for the coffee, but, taking a mouthful, he quickly spat it back into the cup. Stone cold – he'd left it too long.

So, with nothing better to do, he turned over the sheet of A4 that she'd given him and looked at the email.

He read it and reread it over and over again, open-mouthed.

It was short and to the point.

Somebody's selling your drug illegally on the internet.
I think I've traced them.
Harry Boyle

Raymond sat and thought for a few minutes. Then he opened up his computer and googled Erexat. After a few moments, up came a number of hits; most were from UMBRA themselves and promised technical data, prescribing details and warnings of possible adverse effects. But further down there it was a site offering to sell the drug; he opened the site and scrolled through it. It purported to sell Erexat directly to the public without any medical screening procedure. When he reached the price for a dozen tablets, he stopped and gasped. It was far too cheap. This couldn't be correct. It was less than half the price UMBRA sold them for at wholesale prices to pharmacy suppliers.

'There is something very wrong here,' he said to himself. He jumped to his feet and rushed to the office door.

'Who sent this?' he asked, brandishing the email at his secretary.

'The sender's email address is there at the top. But according to anyone I've asked they've never heard of him or the address.'

'Email him back and tell him I need to talk to him right away.' Raymond couldn't control his agitation. 'In fact, tell him I want to see him here in Basel – we'll organise transport. If what he says is true, then we need to get our IT department and security on to this pronto.'

He went back into his office, thoughts racing through his mind.

He rang Brian Thompson.

The phone seemed to ring for an eternity. Finally it was answered by one of Brian's colleagues.

'Is Brian there? I need to speak to him, urgently.' He emphasised the last word. 'Tell him it's Raymond McNally.'

'Oh, Mr McNally? Oh right, I'll get him right away.'

After a few minutes' silence, Brian Thompson's voice came on the phone.

'Hi, Raymond, I was actually going to ring you. These tablets you gave me, there is indeed something very, very wrong with them.'

'I think I know what's wrong with them – can you meet me in my office, sometime this morning? I've a few calls to make first.'

'Er, okay,' answered Brian with more than a hint of curiosity in his voice. 'Give me about an hour to get cleared up here and I'll be straight over.'

Raymond hung up and then sat in silence, waiting for his secretary to tell him contact had been made with the mystery emailer and a meeting set up.

An age seemed to pass, though in reality it was probably only about thirty minutes. Finally his secretary knocked and then tentatively put her head round the door.

'Well…?' Raymond couldn't contain his anticipation. 'Did you get hold of that Harry Boyle chap?'

'He says he can't come.'

'What? Why not?' Raymond barked.

'He says his mother won't let him.'

chapter twenty

S lab McBride looked at the small foil wrapper in his hand; there were five pockets still unopened and one empty shell where the tablet had been removed. He turned the wrapper over and over in his hand, taking in every detail.

'Erexat' it said in bold lettering, and below, 'manufactured by UMBRA Pharmaceuticals'.

He remained deep in thought for a few moments more. This, he was sure, was the tablet that had killed his son.

There was no other rational explanation.

He remained silent and withdrawn as he took the small package over to where he kept his laptop. Then he opened it up and googled Erexat.

Up came a list of details.

He scrolled down them.

The drug, he learnt, was for erectile dysfunction, something like Viagra. Slab knew that many people without erectile dysfunction used Viagra for sex games and to heighten sexual activity. He guessed this was why Jimmy had used it.

But it had killed him.

Somebody was going to pay, reasoned Slab.

He next googled UMBRA Pharmaceuticals.

Headquarters in Basel, but offices in most countries, including the UK. It produced a raft of drugs for nefarious uses. He searched Erexat on their website.

Up popped various details about the drug itself: its description, its uses and its possible side effects. Delving deeper into the history of the company and the drug itself, he found out that it was fairly new, only recently launched and, more importantly, he found the personnel involved with its production and distribution. One name kept appearing: Raymond McNally.

Here, Slab determined, was the individual ultimately responsible for his son's death. He was the one in charge of producing and selling a drug that was patently unsafe.

In his mind, this Raymond McNally was going to pay.

But how to get hold of him?

Slab was used to face-to-face encounters, not a chain of worthless correspondence.

No, this had to be direct.

From the website he was able to get a telephone number and email address for Mr McNally himself. Now he just had to think of a way of tricking him into a face-to-face meeting.

*

By the next morning, following a restless night, he finally thought he had hatched a plan so that he could meet directly with Raymond McNally and tell him exactly what he thought of him and his company.

In fact, so pleased was he with his plan that for the first time since Jimmy had passed away he actually smiled as he opened up his laptop. Firstly he created a new email address for himself, then he checked the email address that had been given on the firm's website for Raymond McNally – r.mcnally@umbra.com – then he carefully composed an email to him, making sure to engage spellcheck. Spelling was not one of Slab's greatest assets.

> *Dear Mr McNally,*
> *I am a local distributor of a range of pharmaceutical agents with many years' experience and I have a number of contacts in the distribution industry here in the UK. I would be most interested in setting up a meeting with you at your convenience in order to discuss your recent product, Erexat, and how my firm might be of assistance to you in its distribution in the UK.,*
> *Terry Johnson*
> *CEO McBride Pharmaceuticals*

'Well,' he said to himself as he reclined back in his chair, feeling slightly smug. 'Not a word of a lie.' Slab had, indeed, many years' experience of drug distribution; it was just that it was not entirely legal distribution, but no need to mention that. He was quite proud of the false name and title that he had given himself.

*

There was no reply for several days, and Slab began to despair that they had seen through his ruse or been suspicious and researched McBride Pharmaceuticals and not found any such firm. He wished that he'd been a bit cleverer and put down the name of a legit firm. But then his phone pinged.

An incoming email.

He opened it and read it out to himself.

> *Dear Mr Johnson,*
> *Mr McNally apologies for not replying sooner; this was due to pressure of work.*

He would be delighted to meet with you. In point of fact he is just about to travel to the UK on a business matter and perhaps he could meet with you then.
Ruth Davies
Secretary to Raymond McNally

'Right on,' exhaled Slab. 'Gotcha.'

Now it just remained to set up a meeting, somewhere Slab could get Raymond McNally on his own and impress him with his point of view on his so-called drug.

He carefully typed in a reply to the secretary's email.

Dear Ruth,
What are his travel plans? I'm based in Glasgow but could arrange to meet somewhere else if it suited.
Best wishes,
Terry

He thought he could risk first-name terms.

It wasn't until later in the day that a reply came through.

Dear Mr Johnson,
Mr McNally is travelling to London next week. He has some urgent business there and is on quite a tight schedule. He says, though, if you could come down one evening, he'd be happy to meet with you, perhaps in his hotel?
Ruth Davies
Secretary to Raymond McNally

Slab thought about it. If he could get him alone outside or even in his hotel room, then that would give him his chance. London was a bit of a nuisance, but if it had to be there, so be it. He knew some people there; he'd give them a ring and see if they could put him up for a day or two.

> *Dear Ruth,*
> *Not a problem.*
> *Where's he staying and when would be the best time to meet up?*
> *Terry*

Again there was a delay. *Presumably*, thought Slab, *as the secretary checked with her boss.* Then the phone pinged again:

> *Dear Mr Johnson,*
> *Mr McNally is going to be in London next week for three days, the 24th to the 27th. He is staying in the Intercontinental Hotel, beside the O2 arena and would be happy to meet you for dinner on the 26th. He may be busy the other days.*
> *I hope that suits.*
> *Ruth*

I can do that, thought Slab, though 'dinner' wasn't really on the menu. He confirmed the meeting and sat back and smiled to himself.

He would have preferred that the meeting was on his home turf, but, he had realised, that was unlikely right from the outset. Nevertheless, he was happy to have the opportunity and started to make arrangements to get down to London for the appointed day and hour.

chapter twenty-one

Raymond had reasoned that if Mohammed wouldn't come to the mountain, then the mountain would have to go to Mohammed.

Further communication with Harry – or, more correctly, Harry's mother – had revealed that Harry was indeed just a teenager, albeit only for the next year or so, who lived with his mother in Kingston, South London.

In telephone conversations with Harry's mother, Raymond got the distinct impression that she was somewhat protective, if not a tad over-protective, of her son. He didn't fully understand why. Nevertheless, she had seemed reasonably amicable, apart from mentions of Harry's apparent proficiency on the internet, of which she clearly disapproved. Eventually, and after much persuasion, she had agreed for her son to meet with Raymond, but only in her presence. But, no, they would not come to Switzerland. Not under any circumstances. However, she would allow Raymond to visit them at their home.

'So be it,' Raymond had finally agreed.

So it was he found himself, feeling tired and exhausted after the flight and now in the back of yet another taxi on the way to the London hotel that Ruth had booked for him.

His phone pinged.

An incoming email.

He opened the phone to an email from Ruth.

She had set up the meeting with the distributor that they had been in communication with.

Dinner, his hotel, tomorrow night.

He transferred the information to the phone's diary. He couldn't say that he was pleased by this distraction, but still, this was his job and attracting distributors was just a part of it. So he had felt obliged to go through with the meeting.

*

The taxi pulled up outside a small semi-detached house in a short cul-de-sac.

'This is it,' announced the driver, turning in his seat to face Raymond. 'That'll be thirty-six pounds, please.'

Raymond got out, took in the small, unkempt garden at the front of the house, the partially broken-down gate and the peeling paintwork on the windows. He spotted a twitch of the curtains on one of the windows on the ground floor and thought he saw the face of a woman peering out at him; she seemed to stare directly at him before quickly disappearing out of sight.

'There you go, keep the change.' He proffered two twenty-pound notes to the driver. 'But, oh, can I have a receipt?' *Company business, after all,* he thought.

The taxi manoeuvred around at the end of the short street and then sped off. Raymond watched it go and then turned and eased himself through the dilapidated garden gate and ambled up the short path towards the house.

He had just raised his hand to ring the bell when the door was opened by a small, neat lady in an apron.

She struggled to untie the apron's strings and then held out her hand for a handshake.

'Mr McNally? Sorry, you'll have to excuse me, I was just doing a bit of baking. You got here a little quicker than I had expected.'

'The traffic was very light,' Raymond explained as he stepped through the doorway, allowing her to close the door behind him.

The hallway was narrow and he followed her down it, noting her short, slightly stooped stature. She turned right into the front room. In contrast to the exterior decay, the room was immaculate, tidy and tastefully furnished. It had the look of a room that wasn't used very often. *Probably reserved for special visitors*, Raymond thought. Still, he was pleased that he was being made feel welcome and honoured by being allowed into the 'special' room.

'You'll want to talk to Harry?' she said as he sat down on the sofa that she was indicating him to.

'Please. Thank you.'

'He's upstairs on that damn computer – sorry, excuse the language. But these days he seems to always be up there. What was it you wanted to see Harry about, anyway?'

'Well, actually, it's about that computer. He seems to have discovered something that could be very useful to our firm.'

'Oh…' Mrs Boyle looked sceptical. 'Well, don't you be getting his hopes up, he's… he's a delicate boy.'

'Delicate?' It was Raymond's turn to look quizzical.

'He suffers from epilepsy. The doctors say he shouldn't get worked up about things.'

'Mrs Boyle, I can reassure you, all I want to do is talk to Harry to find out what he has discovered. There really shouldn't be anything stressful in it.'

'If you promise. I'll call him down.'

'Actually, Mrs Boyle,' Raymond became serious, 'I'd like to see him with his computer, if that's okay? Perhaps you could just tell him I'm here and show me up to his room.'

Reluctantly, she turned and led him up the stairs. 'Harry, there's someone here to see you,' she shouted through the closed door of Harry's bedroom.

After a few seconds the door opened, but only partially.

In the gap between wall and door appeared a rather skinny young man with dishevelled hair and horn-rimmed glasses, which only partially disguised his somewhat bored expression. Raymond noted that the untidy appearance was completed by his wearing of a pullover that was patently too big for him atop a pair of faded jeans.

Harry pushed his glasses back on his nose. 'Mr McNally, I presume?'

'You presume right.' Raymond guessed that Harry didn't get many visitors, probably due to his own fixation with the internet coupled with his mother's obvious over-protectiveness.

Raymond stepped into the room. The curtains were only drawn back halfway, leaving the room in a semi-gloom. There was an unmade bed with sheets pulled roughly back, discarded clothes strewn about on the floor. On the back of one of the chairs, the impression of teenage habitation was completed by a slight smell of sweaty body odour in the air.

The state of the room was in marked contrast to the neatness of the rest of the house. Raymond concluded that Harry's mother was not granted access to Harry's private chamber very often.

As if to confirm this suspicion, Harry's mother started apologising and picking up some of the clothes while simultaneously trying to straighten some of the bedsheets.

'Mother. Please!' exploded Harry. 'Leave things alone. They are fine the way they are. Mr McNally wants to see me, not the house. I'm sure he doesn't care about the state of my room.' Then he turned towards Raymond and gestured in his direction, not, Raymond noted, directly engaging with him. 'Isn't that right?'

'Mmm, yes, don't you worry, Mrs Boyle,' Raymond mumbled, his voice lacking conviction. 'If Harry is happy with things as they are, then so am I.'

Harry's mother looked from one to other, a strong disapproving expression on her face. But despite her obvious reticence, she turned to leave. As she did so she only half shut the door behind her, leaving a gap between door and frame. Raymond listened to her footsteps slowly descending the stairs.

Harry moved past Raymond and shut the bedroom door more firmly.

Only then did he turn to face Raymond; it was probably the first direct eye contact Raymond had received from his host. It didn't last long. Harry shuffled his feet and pointed Raymond towards the chair that was still hung with some of the items of clothing that his mother hadn't had time to remove. Harry beat Raymond to the chair and, lifting the clothing, tossed it onto the bed before Raymond could sit down.

Raymond became aware of a definite lack of eye contact on Harry's side. *Probably shyness due to his self-imposed isolation*, thought Raymond. Though, in fairness, even given the short time since he'd met him, Harry did come across as a bit of an oddity, or at least that was Raymond's first impression of him.

'You got my email then?' mumbled Harry as he too sat down, this time directly in front of his computer and with his back to Raymond.

chapter twenty-two

Together they agreed that the website which Raymond had previously accessed through his Google search was the likely source of any illicit Erexat. Harry, at first, had been a little reluctant to probe further. He explained about his previous experience with it. Nevertheless, on Raymond's persuasion he had accessed deeper levels and demonstrated to Raymond the full extent of the site. It appeared to be linked to other website areas selling other agents including other medications but also among other things arms and militaria.

'Can you trace the source of these sites?' Raymond asked, his face only a few inches from the computer screen, trying to take in just what Harry had discovered.

'I can put in a tracker virus and see what comes up?' Harry replied.

'A tracker virus?' Raymond was intrigued.

'Yep, it's a virus that spreads down the lines of communication back to the source and I can track its progress. Only... Mmm.'

'Mmm, what?'

'Well,' Harry continued hesitantly. 'If I do so, it won't be long before they will realise I've done it.'

'And?'

'And… I think they've detected me before, probing around in their affairs. If they can trace the tracker back to me and realise it's me again, there could be repercussions.'

'What sort of repercussions?' Raymond queried.

'Mmmm… I don't really know. But you and I both suspect that this site is not kosher, yes?'

Raymond nodded.

'So these guys are criminals, right?'

Raymond shrugged his shoulders but nodded again.

'So what if they come after me? Or Mum?'

Raymond thought for a moment. 'Okay, Harry, I get your point. What if we do this from somewhere they won't know it's you, and where my firm and I can protect you and your mum from any harm until this is properly sorted out?'

Harry stopped deep in thought. 'So how are you going to do that?' he asked.

To be honest Raymond hadn't really thought this one through, so he hesitated, but then came up with an idea.

'Let's go back to plan A,' he said, a smile of satisfaction spreading over his face.

'Plan A?' questioned Harry, looking up from the computer screen, if only momentarily.

'Yes, Plan A. You come to Basel with me and we track the source through our firm's computers, then no one will know you are involved.'

'Okay, I'm in,' asserted Harry.

For first time since Raymond had entered Harry's domain, Raymond thought that he could actually detect a smile on Harry's face.

Now all he had to do was persuade Harry's mother.

chapter twenty-three

Raymond sat on the bed in his hotel room and pondered the day's developments. He remained unsure about involving Harry. He was, after all, at least to all intents and purposes, simply an insecure young man, and one with a disability. But undoubtedly, he possessed the skills and insights which might help Raymond solve his difficulties and bring some clarity to the issues.

He glanced down at his watch.

'Shit,' he exclaimed as he jumped to his feet. Ruth had emailed him the details of the client, Terry Johnson, the one he was supposed to meet. There was a meeting scheduled with him in half an hour's time in the hotel's restaurant. Raymond reasoned that, despite the exhaustion he felt from his travels and his meeting with Harry, and more so his mother, that this was a meeting he should attend. It sounded as if this Terry Johnson might be of some value to his department. There was, of course, the proviso regarding the current issues surrounding the drug. However, Raymond reasoned that is was unlikely, in the extreme, that this distributor had had any prior knowledge of these issues and Raymond, for one, was certainly not going to raise them.

He pulled off his shirt and undid his belt, letting his trousers slip to the floor. Stepping neatly out of them, he headed to the bathroom for a quick shower to freshen up.

He soaped himself and let the warm shower water sweep over him, removing the foam from his skin. He lifted his head and, closing his eyes, he allowed the water to stream down his face.

Just as he felt he was starting to relax, he thought he heard a knock at the door. But he wasn't sure; he stopped soaking and leant out of the shower cubicle whilst simultaneously reaching behind him to turn the water off.

He waited a few seconds in silence.

Sure enough, he heard it clearly now, another knock at his bedroom door. He called out, 'Hold on. In the shower. Give me a minute.'

Reaching for the towel and then the bathrobe, he silently cursed the interruption. He hadn't ordered anything and wasn't expecting anybody to come to his room. So, somewhat puzzled, he stepped out of the shower. Despite his attempts to dry himself, the lack of time resulted in drips of water following him across the bathroom and then the bedroom floor.

In his annoyance at the interruption and in his haste, he didn't check the spyhole in the door but simply pulled it roughly open.

'Yes? What is it?' he asked, not able to keep the annoyance out of his voice.

Standing in the doorway was the broadest man Raymond had ever seen. Not the tallest – Raymond was six foot and he had a good couple of inches over his visitor. But the visitor was broad and heavily muscled. He was wearing jeans and a grubby T-shirt, the arms of which were stretched over his muscular tattooed arms. His head was shaved and there was a short white scar under his left eye.

The stranger didn't say anything at first; he simply stood there with his arms folded across his chest and fixed Raymond in a malevolent stare.

Taken somewhat aback, Raymond tried again, this time in as polite terms as he could muster. 'What can I do for you?'

'Are you Raymond McNally?' the man asked.

Raymond immediately latched on to the way that the 'R' of Raymond had sounded. It was rolled and prolonged: 'Rrrr...' Clearly a Scottish accent and probably, Raymond reasoned, Glaswegian at that.

Somewhat reluctantly Raymond confirmed his identity, at which the stranger quickly sprang forward, quickly certainly for a man of his bulk; he pushed forward through the open door, dislodging Raymond's grip on the handle as Raymond was knocked backwards into the room.

'Good. We're in business then,' the man growled, glancing the room for any other unwelcome inhabitants.

Confused, Raymond tried to gather his thoughts. 'Are you Terry... Terry Johnson? the guy I have an appointment with?' Though not for a second did believe that this man could actually be the businessman he was expecting.

The intruder shoved Raymond backwards again and again until his legs hit an armchair and he was forcibly pushed down into it by a firm grip on his shoulder.

'Mmmm, you could say that. Yes.'

'What do you mean?'

'I just wanted to see you, so to find out where you were I set up a meeting calling myself Terry Johnson, and here we are.'

Raymond looked up from his seated position; he could feel himself cowering back into the cushions of the chair as the width of his assailant bent over him, his face lowered and glowering directly in the face.

'Okay, okay, hold on a minute.' Raymond was ashamed of the pleading tone his voice had adopted. 'There must be some mistake. I'm just a businessman, I don't have any cash or valuables on me.'

'I'm not after money.'

'Then what do you want?' He felt that he had regained a little of his composure.

'I want to talk to you.' There was a definite hint of menace in the voice now.

Raymond felt any of the composure that he had regained quickly draining away.

'Talk to me? I don't understand. What do you want to talk to me about?'

The man straightened up a little but kept his eyes fixed on Raymond's face. At first he said nothing.

Raymond had tried not to return the stare and his eyes flicked around the room, seeking anything or any way that he could escape this confrontation. The man's silence, though, prompted him to glance up at the man towering over him. He looked again. He thought that there was the hint of a tear in the corner of his attacker's eye.

Finally his assailant spoke. 'I want to talk about my son.'

'Your son? I don't understand?'

'Yes, my son. My son, Jimmy.'

'Jimmy? Jimmy? I'm sorry, you've lost me.'

'Jimmy McBride, my son, nineteen…'

'I don't know any Jimmy McBride.' Raymond's voice was filled with panic. 'There must be some mistake.'

Slab bent further over, his nose virtually touching Raymond's. 'No. You didn't know him.'

'Didn't?' pleaded Raymond. 'What do you mean, didn't?'

'Yes, didn't. Past tense. He's dead. And as far as I am concerned, you and your company killed him.'

'What? Sorry, there must be some mistake.'

'No mistake on my part, I can assure you. But a mistake on your part, yes. He was my only son, and your pill did it for him.'

The tear in the aggressor's eye now trickled down his cheek. His body shook a little, clearly moved by his own words, threatening and menacing to Raymond as they were. Simultaneously he backed off a little, allowing Raymond a little more freedom.

Raymond, whilst still shaken by the confrontation, seemed to understand where the big man was coming from, and this allowed him to speak with a little more confidence.

'Okay, I seem to get it. You are saying that one of our products has led to the death of your son? Which one? And how do you know?'

'The doctors told me. He had some sort of heart attack. He was only nineteen, for Christ's sake. How does a nineteen-year-old have a heart attack if something didn't cause it? The doctors said that it must have been your drug, the one you are responsible for, that brought on the attack.'

'The drug I'm responsible for? I don't understand.'

'Look.' Slab leant forward again. 'I looked it up – you are the boss man. So it's your responsibility.'

'Which drug are we talking about?' asked Raymond, but he thought he already knew the answer.

'It's called Erexat, it's something to do with sex, and it's your drug.' There was more than a hint of malice in his voice again.

'Okay, okay. Just back off and we can discuss this. I think I know what's happened here.'

Slab didn't move an inch. 'I'll back off when you admit you are to blame and I decide what to do about it.'

'Whoa, big fella. Give me a chance to explain.' Raymond

raised his hands in the air as if to surrender and tried to ease himself up in the seat.

'Explain away.'

'Right, I believe that there is indeed a problem with Erexat—'

'So you admit it then,' interrupted Slab.

'A problem, yes, but not of our... my making.'

'Stop trying to wriggle out of this—'

'I'm not doing anything of the sort. This is to do with counterfeit, sorry, fake' – Raymond worried that his assailant might not recognise words with more than one syllable, especially in his current agitated state – 'medicines. Drugs that are supposedly our drug, but actually aren't and might be harmful.'

'What do you mean?'

'Okay, I am here because we have detected some apparent serious side effects associated with Erexat.'

'Side effects?'

'Yes, mostly strokes and heart attacks, in other words like what your son had.'

'So explain.' Slab moved back, and then stood up, and whilst still towering over him, it did allow Raymond to adjust himself into a more comfortable position.

'Okay, just hear me out.'

Slab nodded his affirmation.

'We, sorry, the company, started to receive alerts regarding an increased incidence of cardiovascular, sorry, heart attacks and strokes, that kind of thing. Just recently, actually. We were worried, obviously, especially as none of our own tests predicted any such problems.'

'So?'

'So I took it upon myself to try to investigate these problems, and if they were down to the drug then to rectify them and compensate anyone who had suffered due to it.'

'And just how are you going to compensate me then?' Slab growled.

'Well, that's just it, you see. It wasn't our drug.'

"What…? I don't understand.' Slab leant forward menacingly again.

'Where did your son, sorry, Jimmy, get the drug?'

'I don't know, he bought it somewhere, I think.'

'Well, that's my point—'

'And your point is exactly what?' Slab did not look impressed by the explanation thus far.

'My point is Erexat, the real Erexat, made by our company, cannot be bought. It can only be obtained through a prescription from your GP. I don't think a nineteen-year-old would be prescribed a drug for erectile dysfunction by his GP, do you?'

'Erectile what?'

'Impotence or the like.'

'My Jimmy wasn't impotent. Far from it.' It looked as if Slab had taken Raymond's inference personally.

'Exactly, that's what I'm saying. We have found out that someone is selling a fake Erexat to all and sundry over the internet. Not only that, but the drug they are pushing is dangerous – it has killed or damaged people, like, I'm afraid, your Jimmy.'

The big man's shoulders visibly slumped. He turned away from Raymond and sat down on the edge of the bed.

Raymond heaved a sigh of relief.

chapter twenty-four

Back in Basel, Raymond was pacing up and down the length of his office, deep in thought. He contemplated his lucky escape from 'Terry Johnson', or, as he now knew, 'Slab' McBride, a hood from Glasgow. A dangerous man as may be, but one who had lost his son. Lost to a scam that involved Raymond, his firm and, of course, others who might be similarly affected, now and in the future.

In order to extricate himself from Slab's attentions, Raymond had agreed to keep Slab in the loop. Realistically, he did not relish the idea and would probably renege on his promise, but he would let him know if the culprits were identified and brought to justice – proper legal justice, not Slab's form of retribution. But, on the other hand, you never knew, if things turned nasty, having someone of Slab's persuasions on board might just come in handy.

A knock on the door.

Ruth poked her head around the door. 'All well?' Though she could sense that indeed all was not at ease with her boss.

'Developments,' he replied distractedly.

'Sarah Stephenson's here to see you.'

'Okay, show her in,' replied Raymond somewhat apprehensively. *Not more bad news, surely*, he thought.

The look on Sarah's face did nothing to dispel his anxiety.

'Has something happened?' he tentatively enquired.

"Fraid so. You better sit down. Things have got a bit worse,' she said as she lowered herself into the seat in front of Raymond's desk while he made his way around it to reclaim his own seat.

'Okay, shoot.'

Sarah Stephenson leant forward, as if about to impart something confidential, which of course it was, but there were only the two of them present.

'There's been another report,' she bluntly stated.

'Another one? What? Where?' Raymond blurted out, visibly shrinking in his seat.

'This one is a death.'

'Not another one?' replied Raymond.

Sarah looked at him quizzically; she didn't know of Raymond's meeting with Slab McBride and the death of Slab's son.

'Sorry, don't worry about it. Just my paranoia,' Raymond tried to explain. 'What happened? Where was it?'

'Suspected MI, sorry, myocardial infarction—'

'A what?' asked Raymond, puzzled by the medical terminology, or at least too tired and too shaken to think it out.

'Sorry, a heart attack. Happened shortly after taking the drug, and worse—'

'Worse, how can it get any worse?' Raymond sank his head into his hands and stared at the desktop.

'Well,' Sarah continued. 'This time apparently he had just taken the tablet, but his partner wasn't in the mood after all, so nothing happened, or at least nothing happened till he keeled over thirty minutes later.'

From Raymond's perspective, Sarah appeared to present a cold, uninvolved overview, probably one evolved from years of clinical practice where the physician had to maintain a degree of aloofness, if only to protect their own sanity.

'Where was this?'

'Well, the good news, if there is any good news, it was in France.'

'Why is that good news?' Raymond asked.

'Because this is the first report from France. Therefore the authorities there won't necessarily start to question the drug, simply accepting it as a one-off, and...' She paused and consulted the note that she had made for herself on receiving the notification of the death.

'And...?' Raymond's spirits had lifted a little as he looked up from the desk.

'Well, the subject...'

The subject, thought Raymond. Again, the apparent lack of identification with a fellow human being.

'The subject,' she continued, 'did have a history of heart trouble, angina, to be exact. So there is a strong likelihood that his death and the taking of Erexat was pure coincidence.'

'Even so,' replied Raymond, 'make a note of it. See if you can get any further details and let me know.'

*

For the rest of the morning Raymond busied himself in the mountain of paperwork that had built up since his visit to London.

He was just starting to unwind from the news that Sarah had imparted when his phone rang. It was his secretary, Ruth.

'Yes,' he answered somewhat impatiently, regretting it immediately. 'Sorry, just trying to work through things in here.'

'Brian Thompson from pharmacy is on the phone,' replied Ruth. *A little curtly*, thought Raymond. *But serves me right, I suppose*, he conceded.

'Thanks, Ruth, put him through.' This time he put on as much of a conciliatory tone as he could muster.

Brian's voice came through the earpiece. 'Raymond... Uh... Hi... Listen, there is something here you need to see. Can you come down to the lab and we can discuss it?'

It didn't seem that Brian was keen to discuss things further over the phone, so Raymond agreed and said he would be down in ten minutes.

*

The pharmacy lab was large and impersonal, a long, white space with rectangular windows along each wall, many of these windows housing extractor fans for the expulsion of any noxious gases or emissions. The interior of the room was dominated by long, wooden benches, each of which stretched nearly across the entire width of the room. All were cluttered with scientific articles, equipment and notebooks. Behind the clutter on the benches sat a number of laboratory staff, two to each bench. Although they varied in their ages, sex and ethnicity all were similarly attired. All wore white knee-length coats, white plastic gloves and their faces were largely obscured by large Perspex goggles.

Most of the staff remained oblivious to Raymond's arrival, engrossed as they were in their activities. Finally one of them looked up, stopped titrating a pale yellow fluid into a pipette, raised his googles and waved in Raymond's direction.

Rising from behind the desk, the technician walked in Raymond's direction, hand outstretched. It was only when he removed the googles completely that Raymond recognised that it was Brian Thompson himself.

They shook hands.

'Sorry to drag you down here, Raymond, but I thought we might get a bit more privacy in my domain rather than your own.'

'I see you like to keep your hand in,' Raymond observed, pointing to the bench from which his head of pharmacy had been working.

'Not really one for the office,' Brian explained. 'Though I do have an office – it's over here. Please.' He indicated for Raymond to go ahead into the cramped, airless office that was indeed Brian's own space. He thought he understood why Brian had described himself as not an office man.

The office was small and situated just off the main laboratory, windowless and nondescript. *Clearly an afterthought by the architect who designed the laboratory*, surmised Raymond.

Brian carefully, but firmly, closed the door of the office behind them. 'Don't want any prying ears,' he explained.

Brain squeezed around the solitary desk in the little room. There was really only just room for the desk, small though it was, and the two chairs, one either side of it. He sat down and indicated for Raymond to do likewise.

'Okay,' Brian said in a low voice. 'Down to business.'

Raymond leant forward, intrigued by the secretive way Brian was acting.

'You asked us to analyse those pills that you brought us. The ones from one of the victims. Yes?'

'That's correct,' affirmed Raymond.

'Well, you were right.'

'Right?' asked Raymond, intrigued.

'Yes,' opined the head of pharmacy. 'These are not our tablets.'

'Not ours?'

'No. Definitely not. Unless our colleagues in manufacture are completely stupid.' And then he half smiled and added,

'Actually, knowing them, mmmm…'

'I don't think so, Brian, do get on with it.' Raymond was becoming a bit irritated, anxious as he was to proceed.

'Right, sorry, not the time to be facetious, I suppose,' apologised Brian. He continued, 'Okay, the analysis proves that the active ingredient is indeed radafinil.' He paused for effect. 'But there are important differences.' Again he paused to allow Raymond to digest what he was saying.

'Important differences…?' Raymond tried to keep his voice under control.

'Yes, important differences.' Brian was clearly trying to spin out his moment in the sun as much as possible.

'Brian,' said Raymond firmly. 'Please spell it out, now.'

'Right. Okay. Here it is,' Brian continued, a little chastened. 'Our analysis proves that the active ingredient is indeed our own radafinil, but the fillers are different…'

'The fillers?' asked Raymond.

'Yes, the fillers. Fillers are those agents that are added to the drug to allow the molecules to coalesce and fill the drug out so it can be moulded into a pill-sized pill.'

'And…?' queried Raymond, now on the edge of his seat.

'Well, whoever made the pill you gave me to analyse put in something else as an added extra.'

'An added extra? Like what?'

'To be honest, we haven't got that far yet. But we're working on it.

Preliminary results do however suggest that it does seem to be an active substance not the inert filler we would normally expect.'

—five hundred … 'Oh my God,' exclaimed Raymond, falling back into his chair, raising his hands to his forehead in exasperation.

'This is not the first time something like this has happened, you know,' Brain added.

'Not the first...?' Raymond's voice trailed off.

'No... Do you remember a few years ago there was a lot of publicity surrounding some diet pills that contained caffeine in large quantities with the same results? Heart attacks, deaths and so on.'

'Caffeine? As in coffee?'

'Yes, but this is pure caffeine extract – each pill contained the equivalent of approximately five hundred cups of coffee. Caffeine, as you know, speeds up the heart and when combined with lactic acid, which, again, as you know, is produced during exercise. can result in kidney problems, but more importantly coagulation, sorry, clotting to you and I, in blood vessels. Clots, again, as you are fully aware, are the main cause of blockages in arteries and such blockages will result in strokes, heart attacks or, in extreme cases, sudden death.'

Finally recovering some of his composure, Raymond replied, 'Actually, I do remember something about that. Yes, it turned out to be a fake variant of a legitimate weight-loss tablet. So basically you're saying it's not our drug? Oh my God. So we are not to blame?'

'Well... it may not be quite as simple as that,' offered Brian.

'What...?' Raymond almost screamed. 'What do you mean? If we didn't manufacture this drug, if it's not ours, what's your problem?'

'Mmmm... As I said, the active ingredient is still radafinil. That is our compound, we hold the patent, and although radafinil itself may be safe, it's still in there and is the reason why people bought the drug in the first place.'

'Okay, okay, I see your point. But that still doesn't detract from the fact that UMBRA didn't make or approve these particular pills.'

'No, but that is not always the way the press, or indeed the public, may perceive it. If a radafinil compound is implicated with serious side effects, how many people are going to risk taking Erexat, knowing it contains radafinil?'

'But how? But how did the forgers get hold of the formula for radafinil anyway? We hold the patent and we control the manufacture and make-up of the compound, all of which has been a closely guarded secret. It had to be to prevent our rivals, our legitimate rivals, getting hold of it. How did the forgers get their hands on radafinil?'

'Ahhh, that, Raymond,' Brian answered., '...is the million-dollar question.'

chapter twenty-five

Raymond returned to his office and sat quietly, with his elbows resting on his desk supporting his head. Initially deep in thought, he quickly formulated a plan of action, or at least a plan of action of sorts.

He pressed the intercom button. 'Call a board meeting, please, Ruth,' he barked into the speaker. 'I need to see Sarah, Brian and Frank ASAP. Oh, and Michelle from public relations.' And then, as an afterthought, 'Thanks.'

It wasn't long before those summoned sat in Raymond's office around his conference table.

Turning to his pharmacist, he spoke, 'Okay, Brian, tell them what you told me this morning.'

Brian Thompson then related his findings to the assembled group, highlighting the discrepancy in the formulation of the counterfeit drug but also alluding to its similarities to Erexat. Finally he arrived at his own conclusions about the sequence of events.

'Basically as I see it, person or persons unknown got wind of the release of Erexat, somehow got hold of its formulation, copied it, but didn't quite get it all right. They added toxic substances that in turn have resulted in the side effects that we are hearing about.'

'But how are the public getting hold of it?' asked Sarah.

'Very simple,' said Raymond, leaning forward in his seat. 'Previously the counterfeit drugs trade was small scale, usually only located in small, discrete areas and overseen but local hoods. Nowadays, however, it's big business. The internet has seen to that. You just have to google what you want, prescription-only drugs included, and up they come, almost unlimited choice. Michelle, is this an area of your expertise?'

Michelle glanced up from the documents she had been reading. 'To a limited extent, I suppose,' she replied hesitantly. 'It's on the boundaries of PR, but we do sometimes use Google and other areas of social media as well as the more traditional routes to get our message out there.'

'So tell us what you do know.'

'Well, I have read articles in a number of mainstream newspapers just recently condemning Google for its policies of allowing, and in some cases even promoting, the sales of pharmaceutical agents, including so-called cures for AIDS and cancer, but also for more common things like diet pills, acne cures and sleeping pills.'

Some of the group whistled quietly in astonishment.

'And they get away with this?' asked Raymond incredulously.

'Well, I believe the Conservative Party has recently established a select committee to look into this area,' Brian chipped in. 'To try to limit this illicit trade, principally of prescription drugs. There have been a number of previous reports of many such agents being counterfeit and, indeed, frankly dangerous. Diet pills in particular have been cited in many of the newspapers and indeed from many more reputable sources.'

'So how do they do it?' asked Sarah.

'My understanding is that Google auctions advertising

space to any firm, even those selling bogus medicines. Companies pay Google so that their adverts appear first on searches such as websites purporting "Weight loss", "Cancer cure", etc. Companies bid to appear top of the search results and then pay Google each time their link is clicked on.' She smiled. 'Raymond had tipped me off that this discussion was on the agenda, so I did a bit of background digging.' Michelle turned to Raymond. 'So I googled diet pills, sex change hormones, sleeping pills, cancer drugs and, of course, sexual dysfunction. Here's the results.'

She reached behind her and then set a pile of computer printouts on the table. 'All of these agents were available to buy within minutes following a simple search, and involved minimal checks or health questions from online pharmacies. Nor did the majority of sites warn of potential side effects or verify the buyer's age, even those that did simply required a single box to be ticked, but of course access to a credit card was mandatory.'

'Doesn't Google have any morals? Can't they oversee the content of their website?' Sarah asked.

'Google, of course although the most used search engine in the world, apparently cannot remove websites from the internet, though it is capable of blocking webpages from appearing in its search results.'

'Can't anybody stop these people from selling these agents illegally?'

'It is certainly illegal to sell medication in most countries without a licence, or to sell prescription drugs without an actual prescription. My research has revealed that in the UK, at least, the MHRA, the Medicines and Healthcare Products Regulatory Authority, last year alone shut down nearly five thousand such websites and there have been prosecutions. But even it warned that it was impossible to control the vast number of unlicensed pharmacies selling these illegal drugs. Especially as many of the compounds emanate from third world counties like India, Pakistan, Mexico, etc. where regulation is much less strict. Even in many other more developed countries, bodies like the MHRA, which are capable of overseeing the sale of these agents, simply do not exist.'

Raymond visibly slumped in his seat. 'Is there nothing we can do to stop this?' he asked.

'Well, there have been some prosecutions, but only a small number, mainly due to the difficulties in tracking down the culprits. And usually only if the seller is found to be within the jurisdiction of a European or American judicial system. Even then the result has usually been a slap on the wrist in the form of a fine. Which, given the profits to be made, doesn't really deter the sellers.

'The biggest issue, as I said, is that the manufacturing of the "drugs" is often in less developed countries, where labour is cheap and controls are often non-existent. But, in fairness, some of these countries, when encouraged to do so, have been fairly ruthless in closing factories and imprisoning those responsible.'

'So what as a company can we do?' piped up Sarah.

Raymond, who had been listen intently to the conversation, sat forward, clasped his hands in front of him on the table and, with more enthusiasm than previously in the meeting, spoke. 'Okay, as I see it we have two, not mutually exclusive options.

'One is to get it out there that Erexat is a POM, that is, a prescription-only medicine. People must not, absolutely must not, buy it over the internet. They need to have it recommended and prescribed by a doctor in the first instance and then it can only be obtained through official and accredited outlets. To do otherwise may be harmful and even dangerous. Michelle, this is your area of PR expertise, I think?'

'Yes, boss,' she replied. 'I'll get working on the press releases right away.'

'Secondly,' Raymond continued, 'we need to track down the source or sources of the counterfeit Erexat and put a stop to it, preferably through the police and the court system.' And then he added under his breath, 'Or by whatever means possible.'

'And just how are we going to track the perpetrators, Raymond?' Sarah asked. 'Given that all we have so far is an internet website.'

'I think I know just the person,' said Raymond.

*

After the meeting and after everybody else had left, Frank Kinney, who had remained largely silent throughout, sat rigidly and stone-faced in his seat.

Raymond turned to him. 'You didn't have much to say, Frank?' It was a question rather than just an observation.

'Just a bit shocked, that's all. After all, Erexat was my baby, long before you arrived. I was there at its inception and all the preliminary groundwork, market research, etc. You only came in when it was ready to go.' There was a hint of malice in his voice. 'Now the whole project is threatened.'

'So what do you think we should do? I've given you my ideas.'

Frank seemed to pause for a moment. *Perhaps just for effect,* Raymond thought.

Then he fixed Raymond in the eye and said matter-of-factly, 'Put me in charge of trying to trace and stop the counterfeiters. Put me in charge of trying to save the drug's and the company's good name. I know the drug inside out, better than you or anybody else here. I know all the staff involved in the project, I have worked with them for years, whereas you have only just met them and then again only a few of them, not all of them by any means.'

Raymond was taken aback by Frank's clear and forthright attack.

'Yes, you're right, but I'm the one ultimately responsible now,' he countered. 'You, rightly, will be an invaluable resource in getting this mess sorted out, but I am not about to shirk my responsibilities in this problem. Work with me or step aside. I'm the one in charge now, not you.'

Frank coloured. He was clearly and visibly trying to restrain himself from another outburst. It took several minutes to compose himself; during that time they sat in silence face to face, neither wanting to be the first to blink.

Finally, controlled again, Frank spoke, slowly and deliberately. 'Alright, have it your own way and on your head be it. I need to consider my position, but as this mess has happened on your watch, I'll leave you to sort it.'

With that he got up, sending the chair that he'd been sitting on toppling backwards and landing noisily on the floor.

'If you do reconsider, Frank, my door is always open.'

Frank Kinney didn't reply. One final cold stare, then he spun on his heel, strode to the door and exited, slamming the door behind him.

'That went well,' Raymond said to no one but himself.

chapter twenty-six

Harry Boyle's mother was doing the washing up when the telephone rang. She quickly dried her hands on the tea towel and rushed to lift up the receiver.

'Hello?'

'Mrs Boyle?'

'Yes, speaking.' She spoke with feigned posh accent, realising it was not one of her friends calling.

'Mrs Boyle, it's Raymond McNally here,' adding unnecessarily, 'from UMBRA.'

'Yes, I know who you are,' affirmed Harry's mother. The accent was now replaced by one with a hint of distain.

'Could I talk to Harry?'

There was silence at the other end of the phone.

'Please. It's important.'

At last a response. 'I don't want you upsetting him or building his hopes up – he's a delicate child, not used to the world, you know.'

'Honestly, Mrs Boyle, that is the furthest thing from my mind. I want to offer him a job, that's all.'

'A job...? Harry?'

'Yes, really. Harry has certain skills that could prove invaluable to us.'

'Skills?' Harry's mother sounded incredulous.

'Really, I promise you. It is a proper job. His big chance. You can't deny him that.'

'Of course not. I would never deliberately hold him back,' Harry's mother snapped.

'Can I talk to him?' Raymond repeated.

'I'll fetch him.'

There followed a silence of several minutes, then some muffled conversation in the distance. Finally, the receiver was lifted and Harry Boyle's voice came on the line, if a little shakily. Harry was unaccustomed to receiving phone calls, let alone one from a senior business executive.

'Yes…?'

Raymond explained that he wanted Harry to join UMBRA, at least on a temporary contract, to help them track down the criminals that had set up the website that had served as their introduction to each other.

'I'd love to.' Harry brightened up. His mother, hearing this, scowled in the background. 'But, but I can't use my computer. They've hacked into it, so they'll be onto me immediately.'

'No, of course not, Harry. We wouldn't expect you to. No, you'll have the full IT resources of UMBRA at your disposal.'

'Oh my God!' exclaimed Harry. His mother's scowl deepened.

'The only problem is…'

'Yes…?' Harry couldn't contain his excitement.

'You will have to come to our headquarters, here in Basel.'

'Oh.' Harry hadn't travelled much despite his twenty-odd years, and even then it was always in his mother's company. 'No problem.' He tried to make it sound as if he was some sort of international traveller. 'Deal.'

Raymond wasn't fooled by Harry's attempt to sound confident. Now for the hard part. 'Can I speak to your mother?'

*

After a long debate Harry's mother finally agreed to let Harry travel to Basel. Initially she was insistent on accompanying him, something Raymond resisted. He knew that her presence would inhibit Harry's enthusiasm for tracking down the origins of a sex-related website. In the end Raymond's view prevailed, but only after he had offered to have Harry chaperoned all the way to Basel and given his assurances of monitoring Harry personally during his time in Basel, with updates on his progress and wellbeing conveyed back to her at regular intervals.

*

Two days later there was a knock on Harry's front door. His mother rushed to open it before Harry. Standing on the doorstep was a young woman, in her late teens or early twenties, Harry's mother surmised. She looked the young woman up and down. She was not the usual type of caller to the Boyle household, dressed casually as she was in a short leather jacket and faded jeans, which, the older woman noted with some disgust, were ripped at both knees.

'Yes?' she asked. 'Can I help you?' Harry's mother seemed to suspect that there was obviously some ulterior motive for this young women's arrival at her house.

'I've come to pick Harry up.' Although the English was perfect, there was a hint of a French accent.

'What?' Harry's mother exploded. 'I think you've come to wrong house.'

'No, I do not think so. Mr McNally gave me this address. I wrote it down. See?'

She proffered a small sheet of paper; Harry's mother snatched it from her.

Reading it, there was Harry's name and underneath their address and today's date.

'I'm Maria, from UMBRA. I work in the IT department in Basel. Mr McNally said that Harry was coming to work for us and that I was to come and to accompany him to our headquarters there.'

Mrs Boyle was now completely taken aback by this girl's appearance and her subsequent assertions. She gripped the doorframe as much for reassurance as support.

'But… but, you are so young.'

'So is Harry, I believe. Mr McNally thought that Harry would be more comfortable with someone his own age.'

'Well. Well, I just don't know, it's…' Before she could finish her sentence she heard Harry coming down the stairs.

'What's up, Mum?' he asked.

'Nothing. Just you go back to your bedroom while I sort this out.'

As she had turned to address Harry, Maria had slipped quietly past her into the hall and, hand outstretched, she greeted Harry before his mother could intervene.

'Hi, Harry, I'm Maria. I was just explaining to your mother that I work in IT for Mr McNally. He sent me to pick you up and take you back to Basel to work on the project that you and he discussed.'

Harry stood open-mouthed. He raised his hand to shake Maria's but remained rooted to the spot- as much in shock that this was actually happening. He was going to Switzerland. Not only that, he had an escort who was roughly the same age as him, although clearly more worldly wise and confident than he, but more importantly, she was gorgeous. He noted her long, dark hair which was dyed blonde at the ends and the perfect almond-skinned face which it framed.

Harry had once naively, in the confines of his lonely

bedroom, tried to break down female beauty to its lowest common denominator. His final theoretical formulation was that if a girl possessed just two physical features then she would be considered attractive to the majority of men. Harry, being Harry, had not come up with the usual physical features that most men think of first, but rather he had concluded that straight white teeth and a thin upper arm were the two factors that if present, everything else would follow. He had never really had the opportunity to test this theory, except from internet pictures. But here in his hallway stood this mysterious girl, hand outstretched in greeting... and he had been right all along!

As he shook her hand he noted her vibrant blue eyes which appeared to be smiling at him.

He felt her pulling her hand back, so engrossed was he that he had held on to her hand a little longer than was expected.

'Sorry,' he apologised. 'I'll just go and pack.' With that, he turned and bounded up the stairs.

Harry's mother stood frozen to the spot.

Maria smiled apologetically.

chapter twenty-seven

Detective Sergeant Amrita Banerjee stood before her boss's desk, hands clasped behind her back. The ceiling fan whirled aimlessly above, making little impact on the stifling heat in the office.

'I've just received a report of a body being fished out of the sea.' Chief Inspector Gupta intoned, glancing up from over the sheet of paper he held in both hands and fixing his subordinate with a withering stare.

Amrita Banerjee felt a trickle of sweat run down her back. 'A body?' she asked.

'Yes, and someone I think you might know.' The chief inspector's stare hardened.

'Might know? Sorry, you've lost me,' the young woman stammered.

'You've lost me, *Sir*.'

'Yes, of course, sorry, *Sir*.'

In truth she wasn't sorry; Amrita had never warmed to Chief Inspector Puli Gupta. When she had first joined the detective team in South Delhi, she had found him cold and unwelcoming. She had felt that despite these days of female equality, he retained some of the older and outdated misogynistic traits, and that he didn't really appreciate a young woman detective inspector being parachuted into his team at the orders of those above.

'I heard on the grapevine that you had questioned an individual about some drugs ring, a certain Amit Saagar? Is that correct?'

'Well, yes, Sir, it is. But—'

The chief inspector didn't let her finish her explanation. 'Well, strangely, I don't seem to have received any report of any such interview, and now this young man, or at least what is left of him, washes up on a beach.'

'Oh, goodness. What happened?' Amrita felt the trickle of sweat increasing and her knees starting to buckle.

'That's what I'd like to know, young lady,' Puli Gupta growled.

'I just, I just got a lead—'

'A lead?' The chief stood up and leant forward over his desk.

'Yes, Sir. A lead about some illegal drug factory. Amit, sorry, Mr Saagar, was my informant.'

'He was your informant? Why didn't you report this to me in the first place?' The chief inspector was visibly angry with his subordinate.

'I just thought—'

'Your duty, as you well know, is not to think; it is to report anything that might be important to those older and wiser than you in this department.'

'It was early days, I didn't know if there was anything in it or not.'

Puli Gupta stared hard at the now-trembling young lady in front of him. When she had first appeared under his command, he had thought of her simply as an attractive young woman with ambition, an ambition he had seen in so many before her, but an ambition, which in his experience, was seldom fulfilled. However, Amrita Banerjee had proven herself more forthright and more determined than any of the other aspiring young female detectives that had preceded her. He had found it hard to control and manipulate her the way he had with most of the rest of his team, whether male or female.

'Your job, I repeat, is to document and inform those you work with of any, *any*, new leads or evidence, no matter how trivial.'

Yes, Sir.' There remained some defiance in Amrita's voice, but not enough for the older man to detect or comment on.

'Right, now that we've cleared that up, do you want to tell me exactly what this Amit Saagar told you and what you'd done about it?' The chief relaxed back into his seat.

'Really, actually very little.'

'What do you mean very little?! The man's dead, for goodness' sake!'

'Sorry, sorry, Sir.' Amrita recoiled at the chief's outburst. 'We just met up once. I had known him from years ago. He was a friend of my cousin—'

'Get on with it!' the chief barked, becoming increasingly impatient.

'He was frightened about something. He knew I'd joined the police, so he rang me and we met up.'

'And...?'

'And, very little – he had been a trainee chemist and that he was offered a job. At first it seemed to be too good an opportunity to miss, so he signed up. But it wasn't long before he realised that things were not as they seemed. He suggested that the legitimate job was actually just a cover for some illegal drug-manufacturing group. Once he knew this, he just wanted out. But they threatened him, told him he couldn't leave or there'd be consequences.'

A tear ran down Amrita's cheek as she now knew what those consequences were to be.

'So how much information did you get from him about the operation?' Chief Inspector Gupta's tone was now more conciliatory.

'That's just it, Sir. Very little. Very little indeed. We had only had the one meeting and he was on edge the whole time, convinced he was being watched. So other than that, this operation existed somewhere in Delhi, he wasn't prepared to tell me any more until I could arrange safe passage for him and his family out of Delhi. I did tell DI Kapoor as, being new, I didn't know what options I had.' And then a thought came to her. 'Was DI Kapoor the grapevine that you heard this from, by any chance?'

'That, young lady, is none of your business. Now please leave and let me think about what you have done, and how to retrieve the situation.'

DS Banerjee turned and, suppressing her desire to confront the chief inspector, used her better judgement and simply left the office.

'And close the door,' Chief Inspector Gupta bellowed after her.

As the door closed, he lifted the phone and dialled a number. 'That's it, Sir. All sorted. Nothing to worry about.'

chapter twenty-eight

The taxi ride to the airport had been largely uneventful, though Harry, being shy and socially inexperienced, had kept mostly quiet during the journey. Maria, however, had been chatty and upbeat, and Harry couldn't help but admire her; after all, she was not really that much older than he was, yet she was so much more outgoing, so much more worldly wise. Harry hadn't been in the company of many attractive girls previously; in fact, Harry hadn't really been in the company of girls at all. Actually, he had to admit to himself, he hadn't really been in the company of anybody his own age apart from those whom he'd been at school with and even then they had teased and taunted him so he had tended kept himself largely to himself. A trait that had not altered over time. A trait that had not been helped by his mother's over-protectiveness. Even now, the silence in the cab had been broken on a couple of occasions by Harry's mother ringing his mobile, firstly begging him to reconsider and return home, and when that failed to ask him if he had packed his tablets and to make sure he kept her fully up to date with what was going on. After the third call, Harry turned his phone off and apologised to Maria, who simply shrugged.

As the rest of the journey progressed, Harry couldn't help imaging what was to follow. There was some apprehension, for sure, on arriving at the airport and checking in, but by the time he had hauled his case onto the weighing scales he could barely contain his mounting excitement.

Much to Maria's disgust, the plane had been delayed for thirty minutes. Harry hadn't minded at all; he had spent the extra time exploring the whole new world of the departure lounge and its myriad shops and outlets.

Finally on the plane, Harry sat next to Maria. She turned and smiled at him as the plane taxied along the runway.

'You must be pretty important,' she whispered in his ear.

'What? Important, me? You must be joking. Why do you say that?' Harry replied, somewhat taken aback.

'To be here in business class.'

'Oh,' said Harry, who, never having been on a plane before, didn't really know what she meant and thought that the spacious seating was the norm in aviation.

Maria saw the look of bewilderment on his face and realised that the naivety that Harry expressed was actually real, not put on for the effect of attracting attention or gaining sympathy, an act that she had encountered with so many men previously.

'Business class. Expensive. When the seatbelt sign goes off, go down to the back there' – she indicated to a curtain across the aisle at the toilets four rows back – 'and take a look behind the curtain.'

As the plane climbed and finally levelled out, Maria said no more.

The seatbelt sign dinged and went out.

'Go on,' she ordered.

Harry slipped out of his seatbelt, clambered past Maria, who was in the aisle seat, and made his way to the curtain.

Gingerly, he put his head through one side. The cabin beyond was indeed very different from the one in which he and Maria were travelling in. It was much bigger and there were three seats either side of the aisle, not the two that he and Maria had. The seats were smaller and the rows were closer together, but despite these apparent more cramped conditions, this cabin was virtually completely full, as opposed to his own, in which there were a fair number of empty seats. A passenger in the economy cabin glanced up from his newspaper and, seeing Harry's head protruding from the dividing curtain, fixed him with a disapproving look.

Harry quickly retreated and took his place beside Maria.

'Well?' she asked.

'It's not so comfortable in there,' Harry said in understatement.

'That's how most people travel. It's a lot cheaper, but believe it or not they still arrive at the same time we do.'

'Ha, ha,' replied Harry, detecting the note of sarcasm in her voice.

'I've never travelled business before,' admitted Maria.

'It's more expensive then?'

'Are you for real? Of course it is – miles more expensive. That's why I said, you must be important if UMBRA is paying for you and me to come to Basel business class.'

'You've really never been in this cabin before?' asked Harry.

'Mmmm...' Maria thought. 'Once, I was going to a conference with my boss, Professor Albrecht – you'll meet him when we get to Basel – we were travelling together. When we went to board the plane, he turned left towards the front and business class and, naturally, I followed him. We hadn't gone more than a few feet when he turned round, looked at me and asked where I was going. Right, he said, you should have turned right at the entrance, not left as he did. Cattle class, he said, that's where you are sitting. That, Harry is as close as I ever got to travelling business class before.'

'That professor of yours…'

'Professor Albrecht?'

'Yes,' Harry continued. 'He doesn't sound like a very nice man.'

'I couldn't possibly comment.' Maria smiled, making it obvious to Harry that she could and was going to.

'How is he a professor anyway?' asked Harry. 'I thought professors were all in universities.'

'Well, he was apparently a professor of computer studies for a while in Leipzig University, when he left, rightly or wrongly, he kept the title.'

'I get the impression,' said Harry, detecting Maria's tone, 'that you don't like him very much.'

'Look, he's my boss, don't you ever repeat anything I tell you.'

Harry nodded in affirmation.

'Yes, I don't really like him. He's quite overbearing and full of himself. He never gives anyone the credit they deserve. It has even been rumoured that he often steals people's ideas and passes them off as his own. Some people say that is how he got his current position in UMBRA. I'm not the only one who doesn't like him, but he's still the boss and we have to just get on with it.'

'So, will I not be working with you then?' Harry tried to keep any hint of disappointment out of his voice.

'It's up to Albrecht. Mr McNally sent me to meet you first simply because we are about the same age and he thought I was more likely to persuade you to come to Basel than Professor Albrecht.'

'Well, he got that right.' Harry smiled, then, realising what he'd said, he apologised.

'You don't need to apologise, Harry, it's been great to meet you… and to travel business class, of course.'

They both laughed.

chapter twenty-nine

A limousine was waiting for the pair when they arrived in
Basel.

Harry, by now, was quite frankly getting used to
travelling like this. And he could see that Maria was enjoying
herself too. The car swept out of the airport itself and into
the countryside beyond. Harry marvelled at the scenery, the
greenness of the grass in the lush fields with the amazing
backdrop of the mountains beyond. It wasn't long, though,
before a security guard was ushering the vehicle through the
heavy metal gates that marked the entrance to UMBRA's
headquarters.

Harry was immediately in awe of the vastness of the
complex. It wasn't tall, only four storeys at its maximum, but
it was spread over many acres, each building linked to the next
by tree-lined walkways.

After carefully weaving its way through the maze of
buildings, the car finally stopped. The chauffeur got out and
replaced his cap on his head before walking around the car to
open the back door in order to let his passengers alight. As
they did so, the driver stood formally, silent and motionless
beside the opened door. It was only when both Harry and

Maria were standing on the kerbside that he finally raised one arm in order to indicate which building was their final destination, at least for Harry's benefit, Maria already being familiar with the complex's layout.

The building that they set off for was, judging by the route taken, Harry surmised, near the centre of the complex, and looking at it, it was a little more ostentatious than most of the red brick and cladding edifices that surrounded it. They made their way towards, and then on and into, the building itself. A security guard, who had been seated behind a desk in the foyer, rose to his feet.

'Ah, Ms Moreau.'

Harry looked at Maria. He suddenly realised that hadn't actually known Maria's surname; she had just introduced herself as Maria.

'Mr McNally is expecting you.' The guard had spoken in perfect English, though he was clearly Swiss or even French, Harry couldn't tell which. The guard sat back down behind his desk and pressed a button in front of him.

'Ms Moreau and guest have arrived.' He spoke into the intercom. 'You know the way, I think, Ms Moreau.'

With that, he buzzed them in through the large heavy glass doors that were the true entrance to the building.

'Follow me, Harry.' Maria raced ahead towards the lifts at the end of the main hallway. Harry continued to look about, trying to take in the modern splendour of the building.

'Raymond's, sorry, I mean Mr McNally's office is on the top floor. He's the big boss.'

He was starting to get a bit nervous again. This was definitely outside his comfort zone. It seemed to Harry that the elevator whizzed up the floors at a breakneck speed, at least judging by the numbers on the small screen above his head. It finally slowed to a gentle stop. The doors opened.

Standing there was a familiar, tall, well-dressed man with a beaming smile and outstretched hand.

'Harry, great to see you again. You made it here alright then? Course you did, you're here, aren't you? Anyway, pleasant journey, I hope.'

'Yes, er… thanks. Mr McNally.' Harry felt his face flush and he shuffled his feet, embarrassed by the enthusiasm of the greeting.

'And you must be Maria Moreau, Professor Albrecht's told me all about you. His brightest star in the IT department.'

Given her rather strained relationship with her boss, Maria doubted that Albrecht had said such a thing.

'It was me that arranged for you to be the one that picked Harry up,' added Raymond unnecessarily.

'Yes, I know. Thanks,' mumbled Maria in return.

'Look, I've set up an initial brainstorming meeting so that we can swop ideas and what we each already know. You are welcome to stay and observe, Ms Moreau.'

Harry looked at Maria, who simply stared down at her shoes.

'This way.' Raymond indicated the open door to his office.

As they entered, the other occupants of the room looked round and rose slowly to their feet. Raymond introduced them one by one.

'This is Sarah, Dr Sarah Stephenson, our medical advisor.'

Sarah confidently took a pace forward and extended her hand for Harry to shake. Awkwardly and shyly, Harry tentatively grasped it, staring at the floor rather than at the older woman's face. Harry had always been socially awkward and being now thrust into a room of older strangers, he struggled to remain focused.

A tall, gangly man with severe features and early male pattern baldness, was next to step forward. He stood stiffly to attention and bowed his head ever so slightly whilst fixing Harry with a cold stare.

'Professor Hans Albrecht. Head of IT. We will be working together,' he announced formally.

'Yes,' Harry stuttered. 'Maria mentioned you.'

Albrecht turned his gaze to Maria, who now stood by Harry's side. 'All good, I hope?'

'Of course, of course,' Harry lied.

'This is Frank Kinney, my number two,' interrupted Raymond.

Frank Kinney smiled, just revealing a line of thin teeth between his barely parted lips.

Harry surmised that Frank Kinney wasn't particularly happy about being referred to as Raymond's 'number two'.

'The only person that is not here is Michelle Dubois. She's in charge of publicity. I didn't think we needed to bring her along just yet. We didn't want to overwhelm you at your first meeting with us, Harry.'

In truth, Harry did feel overwhelmed. He had never been good in company, and here he was in a major pharmaceutical factory, in a top executive's office surrounded by a group of professional people that he had never met before. Maria, sensing his discomfort, took his hand and led him to one of the waiting chairs.

When they were all seated, with Maria exiled to the back of the room, Raymond took charge. 'Right, let's discuss where we are, what we know and, perhaps more importantly what we don't know.'

He then continued, leaning slightly forward in his seat and addressing each of them in turn as he spoke. 'Erexat has been launched, we had, sorry, have, great hopes for it and this firm's future. But, as we now know, problems have come to light.'

Raymond sensed Harry's puzzlement. 'Sorry, Harry, that's

why you are here. There have been some reports of side effects, serious side effects, arising. But then you contacted me to tell me someone is selling our drug illegally, and I think that it is the illegal copy that is actually causing the side effects.'

'Umph,' interrupted Frank Kinney.

Raymond wheeled around and fixed Frank with a withering stare. 'Sorry, Frank, you have something to say?'

'Mmmm, okay then. What proof do we have that it's not our drug, that it's some form of copy of it? So far we only have this kid's word for that. How do we know he hasn't trumped the whole thing up as part of a teenage attention-seeking ploy?'

'Frank, please have some respect for our guest.'

'Your guest,' Frank continued, unabated.

'Sorry, Harry,' Raymond apologised.

'Don't worry,' said Harry. Then, looking straight at Frank Kinney and calling on all his reserves, he added, 'And I am not a teenager, I have turned twenty, and furthermore I have proof, as Mr McNally knows, that there is a scam going on here. I promised him I would help him get to the bottom of it. But, hey, if you don't want my help, I'll go home.' He started to rise to his feet but was restrained from doing so by Raymond, who placed his arm on Harry's.

'You are absolutely right, Harry, and I want you on board to help us resolve this.' He then turned back to Frank. 'If there are others here who don't want Harry's input, they can leave right now.' Although this remark was seemingly meant for everybody in the room, Raymond never took his eyes off Frank Kinney for a second.

Frank Kinney visibly backed off and slumped down in his seat.

'If that's resolved, can we proceed? Harry, I propose you work with Professor Albrecht.' He noticed Harry glance around at Maria. 'Oh yes, and of course Ms Moreau, in the IT department. You will have full access to all of our technology to try and track down any illegal website and hence the drug pirates.' Turning to the professor. 'That okay by you, Hans?'

By the expression on Professor Albrecht's face, he clearly did not relish handing over his department to a seemingly inexperienced young UMBRA worker like Harry. Though he affirmed, albeit reluctantly, but added, 'Under my supervision, of course.'

'Of course,' Raymond replied, and then added, 'and, naturally, with Maria's help as well.'

Harry smiled as he noted, with some pleasure, Professor Albrecht's face darken.

'Umph, waste of time, if you ask me.' Frank Kinney closed the meeting.

chapter thirty

After a fitful night's sleep, filled with anticipation, Harry was sitting in the breakfast room but only really toying with his breakfast when Maria arrived at his hotel to pick him up.

'Professor Albrecht sent me,' she explained, sitting down opposite him.

'I'm glad,' said Harry, looking up. A cursory nod to the waitress and Harry and Maria made their way to the waiting car.

It took only a few minutes to reach UMBRA headquarters. The hotel was so close by that Harry resolved to walk in each day. He felt that it would give him more time to compose himself.

Once through security, it took only a few minutes to reach their destination, an impressive two-storey building which stretched the entire length of the road on which they'd parked.

Maria opened the door, climbed out and bade Harry to follow her.

They pushed through the stiff glass doors, walked along a series of corridors and up a flight of stairs until finally arriving outside an office door which bore Professors Albrecht's name.

There was a small anteroom in which a slight middle-aged woman sat behind a desk and computer screen. She barely looked up as they entered. 'He's expecting you. Through there.'

Maria knocked the inner door tentatively.

'Come in, come in,' a voice replied impatiently.

Professor Albrecht remained seated as his two young guests entered. He barely glanced up from the pile of paperwork laid out on the desk in front of him. 'You took your time,' were his only words of greeting.

'Sorry, my fault,' uttered Harry in an attempt to deflect any criticism away from Maria.

Maria turned to him and smiled.

'That's as may be. But we have work to do, Mr Boyle. Maria, you can go – you are not needed at the present time.'

As Maria turned to leave, Harry started to make some protest, but Maria placed her hand on his arm to dissuade him from doing so.

'And close the door behind you,' Albrecht continued gruffly.

Professor Albrecht returned to his papers, ignoring the now alone and somewhat nervous figure of Harry, who stood in front of the older man's desk.

After a few minutes, Harry ventured to speak. 'When am I going to get started, Professor Albrecht?'

Albrecht's head remained down, still studying his paperwork. Finally he replied, 'Let's get a few things straight, young man.' He raised his head and fixed Harry with a cold stare. 'I am head of this department. It was not my idea to bring you here, but while you are here you will act in a simply advisory capacity. I, as is my rightful position, will lead this investigation.' A moment's silence, then, 'Is that clear?'

'As you wish,' Harry acquiesced. 'It was just that Mr McNally said—'

He was interrupted by the professor. 'I don't care what Mr McNally said – this is my department and while you are here you will do as I say. Clear?'

'If that's what you want.' Harry could now clearly see that Maria's description of her boss had not been wrong.

'I have allocated you a desk on the main floor and hopefully all the IT backup that you will need will be there. My secretary will take you over there now.' With that, he buzzed through on his intercom and asked his secretary to come in. 'Take Mr Boyle to the main office and show him his desk.'

No please or thank you, just the instruction, Harry noted. The secretary, however, did not appear at all fazed by his rudeness. Presumably she was used to her boss's gruff ways.

'Your job while you are here, Mr Boyle, is to infiltrate that pirate website, track the location of the holding area for the bogus drugs, or better still, the factory where they are being made. Understood?'

'But, but...' Harry tried to interject. 'There is a security system on the website, I tried, I tried—'

He wasn't allowed to finish his sentence or to explain his concerns. Albrecht rose to his feet and ushered them out of the office.

'Don't let him intimidate you,' the slight woman said as they made their way to what was to be Harry's place of work. 'His nose has just been put out of joint because Mr McNally overruled him by bringing you here.' These words did nothing to reassure Harry.

The secretary led him down the stairs and then down to and through what had been described as the main office. It was simply a long, relatively narrow room bereft of any redeeming features, rather it appeared more like a warehouse than an office, albeit an office lined by three rows of desks. Behind each desk Harry could just about discern the top of a bowed head, all the inmates appeared engrossed by their computer screens.

One or two did look up on Harry's arrival, more in curiosity than greeting. Harry walked silently down one of the rows to take his place behind the one empty desk in the room. There, he sat dejectedly, finally flicking on the computer in front of him. As it came to life, it became apparent that access to the internet was password protected. Neither Professor Albrecht nor his secretary had bothered to warn or prepare him.

He sat, head in his hands, for a few seconds. Then he started to look about him, taking in his surroundings and his fellow computer colleagues. As he glanced around, suddenly he saw a friendly wave and a smiling face two desks away.

'Maria,' he exclaimed.

Some of the bowed heads looked up, if only briefly, before returning to their tasks.

Maria made her way over to Harry's desk. She leant over Harry. 'Well, what did you think of Albrecht?'

'Mmmm... exactly as you described.'

'Told you. Anyway, ignore him. Let's solve this puzzle. Mind you, I saw that you did look a bit puzzled yourself when you sat down.'

Harry looked at her dejectedly. 'They didn't tell me that there is a security wall with computer access password protected before I can even get onto the internet, never mind track down that website that everybody is interested in.'

'Knowing Albrecht,' she replied, looking at the screen, 'it will be some type of test. One, I suspect, that he wants you to fail, so he can go back to McNally and say, "Told you so."'

'Okay, right. Let's show him.' Harry was now more determined than he had been at any time in this project to prove Albrecht wrong. And, he admitted quietly to himself, impress Maria. He bent over the keyboard and started to type in instructions.

'What are you doing?' asked Maria, transfixed by the speed of Harry's typing, often in response to prompts coming directly from the computer system.

'This system is, as most cooperate systems are, based on an IBM or UNIX operating system. Yes? Well, there are ways to easily bypass their security or password systems, for example through a backdoor.'

'A backdoor?'

'I thought you were an IT specialist?' queried Harry jokingly.

'Sorry, Harry, I'm a legit computer specialist, not a bandit like you, no offence.'

'No offence taken,' he replied, smiling up to her. 'A "backdoor" in a computer system, or it's sometimes called a "cryptosystem", which is usually some form of an algorithm, is a secret method of bypassing normal authentication or security controls.' Harry continued in full flow, losing Maria along the way despite her own knowledge of computer systems. 'They exist for a number of reasons, including by original design or from poor configuration. They may have been added by an authorised party to allow some legitimate access, or by an attacker for malicious reasons; but regardless of the motives for their existence, they create a vulnerability and most systems now contain them.' He leant closer over the keyboard, staring at the computer screen. 'So let's see.'

A few minutes passed, during which Harry continued to type frantically as the screen in front of him flickered wildly.

Finally, the screen opened up and lit up with the logo of UMBRA itself.

'We're in,' said Harry triumphantly.

'How did you do that?' asked Maria, amazed. 'When this system was set up, access was supposed impregnable.'

'I don't really know how I do it, I just can.'

Maria looked at him and laughed.

'Okay, so much for the intranet, now let's open the internet and go to work.' Harry moved the cursor onto the internet logo and clicked. 'Ahhh... no... no...' he exclaimed.

'What? Harry, what?'

'There are a couple of security questions to get past before it will let me in. Look.'

'And your point is, Harry?'

'Well, look, it's asking me some stupid questions like, "Who is your department head?" And, "What is your staff number?" I don't know the answers to those questions, but obviously given a bit of time, I can bypass them.' Then, thoughtfully, he mumbled, largely to himself, 'Maybe I could google the department head on my phone, but no, that won't give me a staff number – got to be careful, though, too many mistakes and it will block me out.'

'You may not know the answers, Harry, but I do. I work here, remember?'

'Great, let's go for it.'

chapter thirty-one

The next morning Raymond was sitting alone in his office. The phone rang. He answered it on the second ring.

'More trouble, I'm afraid,' Sarah Stephenson reported.

Raymond felt his shoulders drop. 'What this time?' he asked pensively.

'It's a bit worse this time,' she said, before adding unnecessarily, 'Sorry.'

'Just tell me.'

'There is a report again from the UK of more side effects. But this time two men were affected simultaneously.'

'Simultaneously?' queried Raymond, not understanding.

'Some sort of gay partner-swopping arrangement, apparently.'

'Mmm...'

'Two of the participants suffered heart attacks roughly at the same time. Good news is that thankfully both survived.'

'And the bad news?' asked Raymond tentatively.

'The bad news is that they both confirmed that they had taken Erexat, and worse...'

'Worse? What's worse?' groaned Raymond into the receiver.

'The authorities are on to it. It is a bit unusual for two people to have a heart attack at the same time and in the same place. So I expect we may be hearing from them soon.'

'Great, just great,' Raymond sighed.

As he replaced the receiver, he sat head bowed, deep in thought.

Several minutes passed, but he hadn't resolved anything in his head when the phone rang again. He snatched up the receiver, annoyed at his thoughts being interrupted.

'Hi, Raymond, it's Michelle, Michelle Dubois, from public relations, here.'

'Yes, Michelle, what can I do for you?' he replied somewhat disinterestedly.

'I thought you should know, I've had a reporter from one of the British dailies on the phone. He's asking about some side effects of Erexat. Apparently he'd heard on the grapevine that there had been some report of a recent incident. Do you know anything about any incident?'

Raymond was suddenly fully alert again. 'I am afraid, Michelle, that I do. Sarah Stephenson was just on the phone about two guys having heart attacks.'

Raymond was thinking fast – any negative publicity this close to the release of Erexat could result in its early demise. Who, after all, is going to risk prescribing or indeed taking a drug that the newspapers were flagging up as a danger to health?

'We need to stall him, Michelle. There is something going on here. We suspect that there is a pirate drug out there causing these problems, not our drug at all.'

'Can I tell him that?'

Raymond thought for a moment. 'Actually, probably best not. We don't yet have the proof and we are getting closer to tracking the fake drug manufacturers down. If we publish this now, they may well go to ground, we will never prove anything and the cloud will remain over Erexat for life.'

'So what do you suggest?' queried Michelle.

'I don't really know,' replied Raymond, trying to keep the exasperation out of his voice. 'Can you put him off publishing anything just yet? Tell him there may be some problems, that these are being investigated but at the same hint that there is a bigger story and offer him an exclusive if he holds off now.'

'I don't know—'

'Look, you are the PR expert, do whatever is necessary to hold him off at the moment. Okay?'

He slammed the phone down, regretting almost immediately the tone he had adopted with Michelle. This was not the way Raymond McNally dealt with his colleagues, not at all. It was, he realised, a reflection of the strain he was under.

He sat quietly at his desk, recalling the last two phone calls over and over in his head and trying to think of a way forward. Several minutes of quiet contemplation followed before he resolved to go and see if Harry had come up with anything that might bring them closer to finding the drug traffickers, stopping them and getting his drug and his career back on path.

*

Raymond found Harry and Maria sitting quietly side by side, deep in thought behind Harry's computer screen which illuminated both their faces. Harry supped pensively at a milky coffee.

'What's up?' Raymond asked as cheerily as he could.

'We're waiting,' Maria answered, looking up from her own coffee.

'Waiting? Waiting for what?' asked Raymond, intrigued.

'For one of them to switch their computer on,' said Harry shyly.

'Sorry, I don't understand.' Raymond sat down.

It was Maria who decided to take it upon herself to explain. 'Harry's got into the website again – we managed to bypass the security system that blocked Harry out before—'

'You bypassed the security...? Oh, never mind, I wouldn't understand anyway.' Raymond lapsed back into silence to hear the explanation.

'So Harry sent them a virus, a bit like a Trojan virus, but a bit more sophisticated.' She saw the puzzlement in Raymond's face. 'Don't worry about the technicalities, it simply means that right now we have access to their system.'

'So we can find out where they are based and then shut it down?'

Harry looked at Maria, who returned his smile and then replied, 'Yes... and no.'

'Yes and no?' Raymond was getting tetchy again.

'Yes, we can track where they are, when they turn their computer on. But no, we can't shut them down – not from here, anyhow. And, even if we could, they would know straight away that we had infiltrated their system and simply relocate.'

She was interrupted by Harry's scream. 'They've logged on. Quick, quick, switch the tracker on!'

There was a flurry of activity from the two computer operatives. A map came up on the screen, at first a map of most of Europe, but quickly it started to telescope in, firstly to western Europe then France and the UK, then just Britain, then England, finally narrowing down on London city and further scanning down into North London to finally place its red dot beside a single street in the borough of Enfield.

'Quick, switch to Google Maps,' ordered Maria excitedly.

A picture of a warehouse and storage area flashed onto

the screen with its formal address printed neatly below. Harry instantly grabbed a pen and paper and wrote the address down, fearing the screen might shut down as his had before.

'Gotcha!' he exclaimed loudly.

Raymond sat back in amazement, not quite sure how to put together just what had happened.

'So explain,' he asked.

Again it was Maria who did the talking, explaining quickly but precisely exactly what Harry had just achieved. He had pinpointed the website source and from the 3D picture it would appear to be a warehouse or factory outlet, which in turn may well be where the illegal drugs were in fact coming from. She handed the piece of paper that Harry had written the address down on to Raymond.

'What's all the fuss? I could hear it from down the corridor?' It was Frank Kinney who had appeared behind Raymond's shoulder.

Excitedly, Raymond explained Harry's findings. 'Looks like we've got them,' he added. 'Frank. You're in charge. I'm going to inform the UK authorities and get myself over to London to see things for myself and personally supervise the dismantlement of this outfit.'

chapter thirty-two

The plane to London was on time. Raymond ushered Harry into the seat beside him before taking Harry's laptop and stowing it carefully in the locker above their heads.

He turned to Harry. 'The British police have been informed by our security department, happily one of our top guys had previously worked in the Met, so it has all been taken very seriously indeed. One of their top men is meeting us at the airport. Have you got all the evidence, Harry?'

Harry had been sitting introspectively, a little overwhelmed by the speed at which Raymond had organised the trip and with being whisked off at a moment's notice.

'It's all on my laptop. I downloaded it before we left,' he replied, not turning to Raymond but remaining focused on the seat in front of him.

The flight was uneventful; they arrived shortly after they had managed to consume the plastic lunch the airline had provided. As they disembarked, Raymond pointed out two men standing stiffly at the exit door of the arrivals hall. They were looking officiously along the stream of passengers leaving the hall.

'Inspector Morrison?' asked Raymond as he approached the pair.

The older of the two replied in the affirmative, looking a little nonplussed at having been so easily identified as a policeman in the general throng of passengers and greeters.

'Mr McNally? Yes, and this is Sergeant Withers, he'll be working with me on this case.' He glanced suspiciously at Harry, who stood a foot or two behind Raymond, his head bowed, arms behind his back and silently shuffling his feet.

'Ah, this is my assistant, Harry Boyle. He has all the information you need to get on with things.'

The inspector looked Harry up and down, appearing even more sceptical.

Sensing the policeman's incredulity, especially given Harry's young age and his obvious reticence, Raymond reached for Harry's laptop case which hung by its strap loosely off his shoulder. At first, Harry withdrew involuntarily. Then he steadied himself and let the strap fall off his shoulder, and he handed the computer to Raymond.

'We've got all you need right here on Harry's laptop.' He proffered the computer to the older policeman.

The four transferred to a waiting police car and were whisked to nearest police station. All the while Harry, having regained his laptop, clung tightly on to it, his arms wrapped around the case as he sat in the back seat between the two policemen.

Arriving at their destination, Raymond and Harry were escorted to a small interview room behind the main desk. Raymond indicated to Harry to put the laptop down on the table and fire it up.

'Okay,' he said. 'Harry will take you through this. Basically there is a pirate company producing one of our drugs illegally—'

'What drug?' Sergeant Withers asked.

'A new one for erectile dysfunction, it's called Erexat,' Raymond replied matter-of-factly.

The two policemen glanced at each other, clearly trying to suppress a mutual laugh.

'This is no laughing matter.' Raymond was now overtly annoyed by the pair. 'People are being injured and some have even died because of the reckless actions of these illegal drug barons.'

'Sorry,' the inspector replied, somewhat taken aback by Raymond's forthrightness and his obvious sincerity and concern.

'Right, down to business then,' Raymond continued. 'Harry, show them what we've got.'

There followed a slow and painstaking couple of hours while Raymond tried to explain the intricacies of the illegal drug trade, its magnitude and its particular relevance to this case. As he did so, Harry flicked through his saved documents and details to confirm and highlight the issues discussed by Raymond.

Eventually, they rose.

'I think we understand now,' confirmed the inspector. Sergeant Withers nodded in agreement.

'So what can we do?' Raymond asked anxiously.

'You say you know the address where the drug is coming from?'

Harry and Raymond nodded simultaneously. Harry turned the computer screen around so that he once again was looking directly at the screen. He pressed a few buttons, then swivelled the laptop round again towards the policemen.

'There,' he announced triumphantly.

The two policemen leant in and took in the computer graphic. 'That's not far from here,' confirmed the sergeant.

The inspector looked up from the screen and turned to the sergeant. 'Right, get a warrant and we'll organise a raid.'

Sergeant Withers quickly went on his way, leaving the other three to, uncomfortably, await his return.

'Can we not get going?' asked Raymond impatiently. 'I don't want the perpetrators to get wind of what's going on and escape.'

'We have to do things by the book, Mr McNally. We need a warrant first before we can do anything.'

'How long will that take?' Raymond was clearly becoming more agitated by the potential delay.

'He'll be back directly, don't worry.' He made to get up and leave the small room himself. 'Do you want a cup of tea?'

Both Raymond and Harry declined.

An age seemed to pass before the two policemen returned.

'All organised. Told you it wouldn't take long.'

Raymond begged to differ but bit his tongue and kept silent.

'I've set up a unit to accompany us to the address you've indicated and we're ready to rock and roll.'

Raymond and Harry rose to accompany the inspector.

'Whoa,' he exclaimed. 'Where do you think you two are going?'

'We're coming with you,' Raymond replied.

'That, Mr McNally, would be most irregular.'

'I don't care. We're coming,' Raymond asserted.

The inspector realised that Raymond was not going to take no for an answer, so thought for a minute and then said, 'Okay, against my better judgement, you can come. But, and I mean this, you will remain in one of our vehicles until the building is secured. Is that clear?'

Reluctantly Raymond indicated his acquiescence.

*

It took another hour to put together the raiding party. The gloom of early evening was just settling on the party as they gathered. Raymond noted with some turpitude that the party contained armed officers. 'Just in case,' the inspector had told him. The party exited the police station in a mixture of police cars, vans and a detention vehicle with its small windows high up on its sides.

Raymond was transported in one of the unmarked police cars; he was sandwiched between the inspector and Sergeant Withers, who Raymond suspected had been briefed to keep an eye on him and not to let him interfere with the police work. Harry had remained in the police station; at least that was something that both the inspector and Raymond could agree on. Harry himself had not protested much in any case – he was not one for real-life action dramas.

On reaching their destination, the car pulled up behind a row of other police vehicles and the driver turned the engine off. All that remained was an eerie silence. Raymond looked around through the car's windows, which were slowly steaming up as the occupants waited for the signal to go. He took in the surrounding buildings and spaces. It appeared largely derelict with large open spaces strewn with tangled pieces of metal and general rubbish between a number of warehouses and storage sheds. Nothing moved. There were no lights in any of the buildings. The whole area seemed deserted.

'Is this the right place?' Raymond asked anxiously.

'Well,' the inspector replied gruffly, 'this is the address your boy indicated.'

Suddenly the peace was shattered by, 'Go, go, go,' which came crackling loudly over the radio.

The inspector leapt out of the car; the sergeant remained. Raymond could see the other policemen, many now donning bulletproof vests and carrying machine guns, disembarking from their vehicles and sprinting towards one of the large warehouses.

There followed distant shouts and a series of loud bangs.

'Tear gas,' the sergeant explained.

An eternity seemed to pass, but eventually the inspector opened Raymond's door and leant into the car.

'You need to see this,' he said as he led the way towards the warehouse.

'Did you catch them?' Raymond asked.

There was no reply.

As they entered the building, there were armed policeman stationed at every turn. The inspector led him through the entrance area of the large building, which in its time had acted as a sorting area before goods were distributed to different areas within the complex. Then down along a short corridor and up a rickety wooden staircase.

As they reached the top, Raymond could make out through the unlit gloom a large, empty space, devoid of life or activity but still containing a few desks at one end and a couple of large benches which stretched virtually the length of the building. On the desks there were a series of wooded cases, many of which were empty, but some contained bubble-wrapped packages. One of the armed policemen slung his rifle over his shoulder and tore open one of the packets. A number of smaller cardboard packs cascaded onto the floor and broke into individual smaller boxes.

Raymond bent down and picked one of these small boxes up. He recognised it immediately. It was a pack of twelve Erexat, or it was it?

The packaging looked cheap, the cardboard thin and the foil was of an inferior quality to that used by UMBRA.

He turned to the inspector. 'It looks like this is the right place. Where are all the people? Have you taken them away already?'

'Mmmm… 'fraid not.' The inspector looked glum. 'Place was empty when we got here. Looks like they left in a hurry, though, given all the gear that they seem to have just abandoned.'

'How? Why?' Raymond stumbled out.

'To me, they got a tip-off.'

'A tip-off?'

'Yes, a tip-off we were coming, and they scarpered quick as they could.'

'But, but…?' Raymond was confused. 'How were they tipped off? We only knew about this place this morning. That's only a matter of hours ago.' Silently, he mulled over the idea of the constant police delays and it rankled him.

'Wouldn't have been from our end, I can assure you, Mr McNally. We run a tight ship here.'

'What are you suggesting, Inspector?'

'I'm not suggesting anything, Mr McNally, but facts are facts, and somehow the people here got wind of our raid before it happened, and hey presto, they've disappeared into the ether.'

'I can't believe anybody from our end—'

'What about that boy of yours, your computer wizard? He was poking about on their website – could that have been picked up and warned them we were looking for them?' The inspector looked hard at Raymond.

Raymond then remembered what Harry had told him happened the first time he had tried to get into their website. They had detected his intrusion almost immediately and tracked him down within seconds. What if the same thing had happened again and the criminals had traced the source to UMBRA? Then of course they would have known they were rumbled and cleared out.

'Damn,' he swore quietly.

chapter thirty-three

Back in Basel, Raymond had called a board meeting to update his colleagues of events in London.

Initially all those around the conference table sat silently and listened to Raymond's report of events surrounding the raid of the warehouse. He told them about tracking its whereabouts and then contacting the local police and the subsequent raid.

'So it's all over?' asked a smiling Frank Kinney from the far end of the table.

'No. Unfortunately it turns out that this was only a distribution centre, not the factory for the drugs. We may have set things back for the culprits, but I fear we have not stopped them yet.'

Raymond told them about the findings within the distribution centre, including the suspicion that the manufacturer was based in India.

'And we know that, how?' Again it was Frank who spoke; this time he sounded cynical. The others held their silence.

At this point Raymond rose from his position at the head of the table and slowly opened the door to the conference room. From there he invited in a nervous-looking Harry, who shuffled shyly through the doorway and then positioned himself hidden largely behind Raymond.

Harry had already met some of those present but there were others who were unfamiliar to him. Raymond indicated to Harry to sit on the seat beside him at the table.

As Raymond himself sat down, he noted the surprise in many of his colleagues' faces, clearly wondering why Raymond was introducing this young, seeming socially inept individual to the higher echelons of UMBRA.

'This,' Raymond announced, 'is Harry Boyle. Our latest employee.'

'I'm sorry, Raymond,' Frank Kinney interjected. 'What exactly is going on here?'

Looking around, Raymond sensed that the others seemed to share Frank's sentiments.

'Harry,' he replied, 'is the one who managed to trace the culprits down to that warehouse, and he is going to help track the rest of them down, whoever and wherever they are.'

'Have you taken leave of your senses?' Frank had risen to his feet and leant forward with both arms outstretched and hands pressing firmly down on the table.

'I'm afraid I'm with Frank on this one,' added Hans Albrecht.

Most of the rest nodded in agreement or kept their eyes firmly on the floor.

'Look, Harry's tracked them once, and he can do it again. I know he can. Can't you, Harry?'

Harry looked unsure; he lacked Raymond's confidence and he didn't feel able to speak up and defend himself or Raymond.

'I've had enough of this,' and with that Frank Kinney stormed out of the meeting. Albrecht and a couple of others followed quickly.

Sarah Stephenson, Michelle Dubois and Brian Thompson did, however, remain. Important allies, Raymond concluded, but how long realistically could he retain their support?

Finally, it was Sarah Stephenson who spoke. 'So what exactly is Harry,' she smiled reassuringly at the increasingly fidgety guest, 'going to do?'

'When we raided the warehouse, it seemed that the perpetrators had been tipped off.'

'Why?'

'Because it was obvious that they had left in a hurry and they simply abandoned a lot of gear, knowing they hadn't time to remove it.'

'What sort of gear?' Sarah asked.

'Well, boxes of the fake Erexat for a start,' Raymond replied.

'Can we bring it in for analysis?' asked Brian the pharmacist.

'Already here, and ready for you to go to work.' Raymond was starting to feel a little more comfortable as the conversation was starting to go his way. 'But to my eye, at least, it is the same compound that we have already got from one of the victims.'

'So have we got anything new?' Michelle asked.

'Yes, we have. As the forgers left in such a hurry, they left behind quite a lot of useful evidence.'

'Like?' Sarah quizzed, as she and the others seemed to have become more optimistic and, indeed, supportive of Raymond's position.

'For a start, the drugs were found in bundles, and many of the bundles were still in the crates in which they had been transported to the warehouse. More importantly, many of these crates had markings and their original transportation details still attached.'

'So we can trace them?' Brian asked.

'Hopefully yes.'

'Any initial evidence of where they came from?'

'India.'

'Makes sense.' Brian reclined in his chair; the others turned to face him. 'India has a huge workforce, and moreover a skilled workforce. Many legit pharmaceutical companies get their drugs manufactured there – it's cheap, it's reliable and nobody ever asks where a drug was actually made anyway.'

'But India is a big place,' added Michelle Dubois.

'Ah, Michelle, the mistress of the bleeding obvious,' Brian responded tetchily.

Raymond fixed Brian with a disapproving stare. 'Please, let's keep to the subject. The transportation details that we have do seem to narrow things down a bit, but we have more to go on—'

'More?' Michelle had recovered from Brian's facetious remark and, whilst giving him a reproving glance, clearly wanted to know more.

'Yes, this is where Harry comes in.'

The remaining attendees swivelled around to look towards Harry, who by now had slunk off into a corner by the water dispenser.

'In the building,' Raymond continued unabated, 'we found a laptop – it was in the main office, forgotten in a drawer in one of the desks. I'm hoping Harry here, with his computer skills, can break into it and get more detail on the operation and, most importantly, the factory location. If we can get these details, maybe, just maybe, we can shut them down permanently.'

Sarah Stephenson turned again to Harry and, speaking softly, asked, 'And what do you say, Harry? Can you do it?'

'I… I think I can,' Harry replied nervously.

'Okay, everybody, let's break up now. I'll give you regular updates and we will all meet again soon.'

As the meeting broke up, Raymond reached for Harry's arm, keeping him seated at the table. He waited, though, till everybody had left and the door had closed behind them before addressing the younger man. 'Harry, they knew we were coming.'

'Who knew? What?' Harry looked confused.

'The people at the warehouse – they knew we were coming and they cleared off before we got there. Have you any idea how they did that?' Raymond took in Harry's worried expression as he spoke.

'No.' Harry shook his head firmly from side to side and added, 'Honest.'

'You told me the first time you broke into their system they detected you.'

'That's right, but—'

Raymond leant in towards Harry's frightened face. 'Could they have detected you again?'

'No. Definitely not. Ask Maria, she'll tell you. The tracer we used is state of the art. So far nobody's been able to detect its presence.' But then he added hesitatingly, 'At least as far as I know.'

'First time around you told me that these guys were pretty sophisticated in that they not only picked you up but actually got into your computer, isn't that right?'

'Yes, but this time we were extra careful, and with the high-tech equipment you have here I don't believe they could have...' But then he added, 'They couldn't have known we were on to them, could they?'

Raymond sat contemplatively for a few moments, then he decided to give Harry the benefit of the doubt, and anyway, he needed him – he doubted that anybody else in his workforce had the computer skills that Harry possessed to interrogate the laptop reclaimed from the warehouse.

'Okay, Harry, let's let bygones be bygones. Why don't you get to work on that laptop, but keep me informed all the way along, alright?'

'Sure thing, Mr McNally.' Harry got up to leave.

As Harry approached the exit, Raymond turned around in his seat. 'I need somebody, somebody reliable, to work with you, keep an eye on things, is that okay by you?'

Raymond could see that Harry was clearly taken aback by the suggestion of supervision; he was used to working in isolation.

Harry stopped, gave it a moment's thought, but, realising that he really didn't have an option, nodded his agreement.

'Professor Albrecht,' Raymond said thoughtfully, 'you and he don't really see eye to eye, do you?'

Harry didn't want to answer, but his demeanour gave away his acknowledgement of the statement made.

'So,' Raymond continued. 'So you will work with Maria. Is that okay by you?'

Harry smiled from ear to ear.

chapter thirty-four

Harry was determined to prove himself to Raymond. Raymond was probably the first adult that Harry had encountered that appeared to actually trust and, more importantly, respect him. He and Maria bent over the recovered laptop; they turned it on only to discover, as they had suspected, it was again password protected. Maria looked a little disappointed, but she knew from her previous experience that Harry possessed the skills to get around any security system.

'Look,' he explained, 'as we don't need to get into the operating system itself, all we need is access to the files – it is dead easy.'

Maria looked sceptical.

'Okay, watch,' Harry said as he bent down and reached into the satchel he had carried with him from home. 'Here's one I prepared earlier.'

He pulled out a CD and fed it into the CD drive of the computer.

'What are you doing, Harry?' Maria quizzed.

'Simple. At home, many years ago, I downloaded this Ubuntu file from the live .iso file for any Linux distribution.

It's probably the most popular file there is for this kind of problem. Mind you, you're really only supposed to use it if you forgot your own password.'

Harry booted up the computer from the CD and on the first menu that appeared was the prompt 'Try Ubuntu'. Harry chose the option.

'This file should allow me into the desktop. Yep, here we go.'

Harry started furiously pounding the keys. 'From here,' he explained, head down, engrossed in his endeavours, 'I should be able to access the hard drive by going to the places menu and choosing the Windows drive. Yesss… we're in,' he announced triumphantly.

'Look.' He turned to Maria and indicated the screen. 'I can now get into most files on the computer.'

Maria was impressed, but asked, 'Most files?'

'Well,' Harry replied a little despondently, 'if any files are encrypted I might have to work a bit harder, but I'm sure I can get into those too, given time.'

Maria nodded.

'Anyway,' Harry continued, 'for some files we need root access, but I can do this by opening up a terminal window.'

'A what?' asked Maria, who was become increasingly left behind by Harry's obvious enthusiasm for the task in hand.

'Don't worry about it.' Harry continued to punch the keys. 'It's pretty straightforward – all I need to do is go to applications, then accessories, then terminal, and hey presto!' He typed in an access code, but then a prompt requesting a password flashed up on the screen.

'So now what?' asked Maria.

'So now nothing.'

'What do you mean?'

'It's a diversionary prompt. No password is actually

required. Watch.' Harry pressed enter, leaving the password blank. The screen opened up before him, revealing its contents of files. He scrolled down the list.

'I can't actually see any encrypted files. They can't be as smart as they think they are. As far as I can see, we have full access.'

'Let's get Raymond in and see what we need to look at first.' Maria smiled, rising to her feet.

Reluctantly Harry nodded his agreement, engrossed as he was in the unfolding array of files on screen. Realistically he would have preferred to continue with only Maria for company, impressing her with his computer skills, but he knew that he was here for a reason, and Raymond was their boss, after all.

*

When Raymond finally arrived, the three of them sat huddled around the small laptop which Harry now balanced on his knees.

'So what have we got?' asked Raymond, his expression betraying his anxiety.

'Okay, so firstly I penetrated the computer's operating system, then used a widely available virus which can be used to break into and gain access to the files contained within the system.'

'Widely available? And legal?' queried Raymond.

Harry hesitated, blushed and then tried to hide his embarrassment by engaging the computer. 'Well. Not exactly.' He squirmed in his seat.

'What do you mean, not exactly? Not widely available? Or not legal?'

'Mmmm... it's not completely legit, but, but – okay,

everybody uses it. It's one of the most commonly used viruses for this purpose. I don't know anybody that's been done for using it.'

Raymond bent over the desk and raised his hand to his forehead. The ramifications of his firm being caught illegally infiltrating a private computer were not worth thinking about. If the press got hold of it, it would be a huge embarrassment for the company and curtains for himself within it. Then he looked for reassurance. 'Are you absolutely certain this is the right group we are looking for?'

'Hold on, give me time.' Harry pressed more keys, inspecting each file in turn for clues that might supply some evidence of the drug misuse.

'Whoa. Here we go,' he suddenly announced.

'What? What have you got?' Raymond moved his seat around to get a clearer view of the screen.

'Look, here is an order form for supply of Erexat. It's been saved in the documents file.'

'Great.' Raymond gave a sigh of relief. 'At last, something to go on.'

Harry read down the document then went to work pulling down file after file, as if searching for something.

'What are you looking for?' asked Maria, watching the computer screen intently.

'Hold on, hold on,' replied Harry distractedly. Finally he explained, 'The supply document clearly relates to email correspondence. I'm trying to track the email address or addresses used, maybe then I can break into them and get a better idea of exactly what's going on, and I guess from your perspective, Mr McNally, where it is all going on.'

'That would be helpful,' Raymond replied understatedly.

'What, the factory location?'

'No, no, not yet. Just the email address. If I can hack into that then we can look up old correspondence and maybe glean something from that. We have got to be careful, though,' Harry added cautiously.

'Careful? Why?'

'Because,' Maria interrupted, 'if we do get into their email provider and then their account, if they are using it they will see us scrolling around their emails and we're busted.'

'I'm in.' Harry had ignored the previous conversation and had battered on with his investigation. 'I have the email address, I'm on the server site and now all we need is their password.'

'How are you going to get that?' Raymond asked. He was genuinely interested now; he, like so many others, to their cost, had considered email a relatively secure method of correspondence.

'Piece of cake,' announced Harry, again reaching into his bag and producing what looked to be a simple USB plug. He plugged it into the side of the computer and sat back in his seat, placing his hands behind his head, still looking at the screen in front of him.

'What's happening?' Raymond asked.

Maria leant over and spoke softly in his ear. 'Actually, you probably don't want to know. What Harry's just plugged in is a unit that runs through all potential password combinations, going through millions in milliseconds. These devices are illegal worldwide. If I were you, I'd go and get a cup of coffee and come back when we do get the right combo, and just say you never saw us do this.'

Raymond did as his junior employee had suggested, returning about ten minutes later and even then taking the precaution of putting his head around the door first. 'How's it going?'

The two occupants of the small room were now both leaning forward, their noses inches from the computer screen.

Maria turned around to face her boss. 'I think Harry's got what you need.'

Raymond, as quickly as he could, with the remains of a mug of coffee still in his hand, recaptured his seat beside them. 'Tell me,' he commanded, firstly regaining and then reasserting his authority on proceedings.

'Harry has broken in to their email server—'

'You don't think they have detected you?' Raymond interrupted anxiously.

Harry replied, 'There's no activity on it at present, so I think we're okay. I am printing out the old emails so that we don't spend time on their site and risk exposure by trying to read them all now.' He paused, pressing another button. The printer whirred in the background, then he continued, 'There does seem to be a lot of correspondence with an address which, if I'm correct, has an Indian handle.'

'India. Yes, that makes sense. When we went through the stuff at the depot, there were boxes there which bore Indian addresses.'

'Harry, have you downloaded and printed them all out yet?' Maria asked anxiously. 'If we are on the right track, we don't want them to know we are on to them. Right, Mr McNally?' She turned to Raymond as she spoke. He nodded in affirmation.

'We are okay, trust me,' said Harry. 'Nearly there. I have downloaded the majority of the email file – it's quite big actually, a lot of correspondence. Probably not all relevant to our enquiries, but I don't want to miss anything.' He had added the 'our enquiries' with some pride; he felt, probably for the first time in his life, that he was doing something that was being respected by others outside his computer nerdy circle. The printing will take longer, obviously, but we can finish that after I pull out of the site. Done,' he announced.

chapter thirty-five

Raymond sat at the head of the conference table. He looked and felt exhausted; he had been up most of the night scrutinising the emails and printouts that Harry had provided.

'Sorry for calling you all in at such short notice, but there have been some developments.'

'Developments?' Frank Kinney leant forward over the table as he spoke.

'Yes. Important information has just come through. I believe we are close to tracking down the source of the counterfeit tablets.'

'Counterfeit tablets?' Some of the committee members looked at each other quizzically. 'What counterfeit tablets?'

Raymond had forgotten that not everybody was as well informed regarding the recent discoveries as himself and a couple of fellow committee members. He took time to explain Brian Thompson's findings from the analysis of the drug recovered from the Bakers and then the complex trail to the online sales of the drug and the tracking down of the possible source in India.

'This is terrible,' stated Sarah Stephenson from the far end of the table. 'What are we going to do about it?'

'Well, if it's in India, there's probably little we can do,' interjected Frank before Raymond could answer. 'I can contact Interpol and see what they can offer, but in my experience of counterfeit drugs, there is often little or nothing that can be done to stop production. The bandits just up and move once they get wind that we're on to them.'

'Let's try and be a bit more positive, eh, Frank? They don't know that we are on to them yet, so we do have some time.'

'Well, okay,' agreed Frank reluctantly, 'but we have to face the fact that this might be the end of Erexat, before it even got off the ground.'

Raymond couldn't help but feel that there was a certain degree of satisfaction in Frank's tone, as if he actually was enjoying seeing him fail in the post that Frank himself had coveted.

'I'll talk to the Indian authorities myself and try and get things moving as quickly as possible—'

As he spoke, Michelle Dubois spoke out. 'I'm afraid I'm with Frank on this.'

'What? Why?' queried Raymond.

'I'm afraid that there's been a development from my end also.' She paused and sat back to allow the interest in the room to build. 'Someone has leaked details to the press. I've been told that at least three of the nationals are going to run a story in the next day or two, if they can get a bit more info to go on.'

'Then it's more important than ever that we regard this as completely confidential among ourselves. We need time.'

'I doubt we have the time.,' Sstated Frank, leaning back in his seat.

*

Over the next few days, Raymond devoted the bulk of his time to contacting and negotiating with a variety of UK and internationally based police forces. With Harry having tracked down the perpetrators, Raymond had thought that arresting them and stopping the trade of the illegal drug would have been relatively straightforward. Not so. He had been made to leap through a variety of legal and bureaucratic hurdles before finally being told that it was not as straightforward as he had surmised. At least at the end of his negotiations he had gleaned the name of the head policeman in Delhi that had been briefed about the illegal trade, but results from this quarter remained painfully few and far between.

Given the information that Michelle had imparted at the meeting that the press were on to the story and the obvious conclusion of such a story appearing in the nationals vis-à-vis the demise or at least the severely restricted use of Erexat, there was little to prevent Raymond becoming increasingly frustrated and being suffused by an overwhelming feeling of impotence in his ability to prevent what was now seeming inevitable.

He paced up and down his office, trying to determine his next move. Finally, after a number of painful hours' deliberation and his blank refusal to see anybody in his office, he sat behind his desk and buzzed through to his secretary.

'Ruth, get me flight times to Delhi and set me up a meeting with the police inspector that's on the case there,' he barked into the intercom, immediately regretting the curtness of his tone.

'Chief Inspector Gupta?' came the somewhat sheepish reply.

'That's him.' And then belatedly, 'Thanks.' Then, 'Oh, and I'll need a visa.'

Raymond had come to the conclusion that as it was ultimately his job on the line, notwithstanding the inherent risk posed to himself and any other innocent individuals that he chose to involve, he resolved that he should now personally try to oversee the shutting down of the illegal trade in the drug that he bore ultimate responsibility for. It seemed the only way to do that was to go to Delhi and try to expedite proceedings there.

Having set things in motion, he sat back and relaxed a little in his chair and stared at the ceiling. Then he had another thought. Initially he struggled with the idea and tried to dismiss it, but the logic of it kept recurring. Finally he gave in and lifted the phone.

It rang for a few minutes unanswered, then, 'Hello?'

'Mr Murphy?'

'Who's this? What do you want?' He was clearly annoyed by the unrecognised telephone number.

'Sorry. Slab, it's me, Raymond, Raymond McNally from UMBRA.'

'What do you want?' came the growled reply.

'I have news for you.'

'What news?' There was still suspicion in his voice.

'Do you fancy a job? Come to Basel, I'll organise your flights and I'll tell you. I think I could do with your help in getting to the bottom of things, though.'

Slab was not used to job offers, let alone those from a high-ranking manager in a major pharmaceutical company. 'Who is this? Are you having a laugh?' came the gruff reply. 'Cause if you are...'

'Slab it's me, Raymond McNally. We met in my hotel room – well, I use the word "met" loosely. You sort of forced your way in. It was about your son and his premature death, you made me promise to keep you in the loop and see if we can't make those responsible pay for what they've done. Well, I think we might, after all, be able to do something, but I think I might need a man of your particular skillset on this one.'

'Skillset?'

'Don't worry, I'll explain when you get here. I'm going to put you back to my secretary; she'll arrange the flights.' Then, almost as an afterthought, 'Tell her you might be coming to India with me – she'll need your details for a visa.'

'India?!' Slab shouted incredulously.

*

As he left the office, he checked with Ruth that she had spoken to Slab and got all the necessary details from him.

'Yes, flight here's booked and I'm getting you flight times to Delhi. Online visa applications in progress. Mmmm… he does sound a little… little…?'

'Rough and ready?' added Raymond helpfully.

'Well, yes.'

'Don't worry about it – rough and ready may be just what is required.'

Ruth nodded but still appeared confused by her boss' choice of travelling companion.

'There may be another traveller, I'm just off to brief them now.' With that, he left the office, closing the door quietly behind him.

He found Harry and Maria where he'd last seen them, huddled together in a corner of the IT department, both glued to a single computer screen.

'Any progress?' he asked.

Both appeared startled by the unexpected interruption, having been so engrossed in their endeavours so as not to notice his approach.

'Not a lot. But at least they still don't seem to know we're on to them and are monitoring their communications.' It was Maria who spoke; Harry, recovering from Raymond's intervention, had returned his full attention to the computer screen.

Raymond explained to Maria and the top of Harry's head his decision to take control and travel to India himself to oversee things. 'And I would like one of you to come with me to keep on top of developments and to guide me to the factory itself.'

Harry now looked up, seemingly fascinated by the thought of a possible trip to India, even forsaking his interest in the screen, at least briefly.

'Sorry, Harry, not you. I was thinking of taking Maria along.'

'But why not me? I'm the one who got you the information in the first place,' moaned Harry.

'Well, that's exactly why I need you here. On top of things, Maria will keep in close contact with you and advise me as we go along. I'm going to send you home, Harry. I think it's for the best at the moment. I will, though, arrange for you to have full access to all UMBRA's IT programs, software, whatever you need. You will remain in charge of the IT side of things – you are more important to us behind a computer than trolling around India with us.'

Raymond had decided to stoke Harry's ego to persuade him to stay behind and allow Maria to travel in his stead. In truth, it was because Maria was an employee of UMBRA and therefore he could take responsibility for her. Harry was a loose cannon and, perhaps more pointedly, Raymond didn't feel he could cope with the wrath of Harry's mother should she find out that he'd taken him to India and exposed him to possible danger.

chapter thirty-six

A s Raymond, Slab and Maria disembarked the Swissair
Boeing 747 at Delhi airport to walk the short distance
from the plane to the terminal building, the heat hit them and
Raymond noted the growing beads of sweat that appeared to
trickle down from the top of Slab's bald head. He wiped his
forehead with his sleeve, but only after he had first removed
the increasingly inappropriate black leather jacket that he had
insisted on bringing.

Inside the terminal building there was the relief of air
conditioning which mitigated against, at least to a degree, the
stifling heat and humidity outside.

Although relief was palpable at the change in atmosphere,
the rivers of sweat now became even more noticeable. The trio
quickly moved to clear immigration and then on to retrieve
their bags from the luggage belt before finally clearing customs.

Exiting the terminal, Raymond spotted an attractive young
woman approaching them and offering a tentative wave.

'Mr McNally?' she enquired in perfect English but with
a soft southern Indian accent. As she spoke, she took in his
travelling companions, appearing increasingly quizzical at
their appearance. One was a small, slim, dark-haired girl, who

appeared to be in her late teens or early twenties, and the other was a large-set bald-headed man, clutching a leather jacket over his shoulder. The large man appeared uncomfortable, sweating profusely on his face and head and into the armpits of his crumpled cotton shirt. His face was red and he repeatedly wiped his forehead with his sleeve, puffing loudly as he did so.

'Yes,' Raymond proffered his hand. 'Detective Sergeant Banerjee, I presume.'

'Please, call me Amrita. DCI Gupta sent me to meet you.' She smiled a sparkling white smile, set in a perfect soft-skinned and unwrinkled face and with deep brown eyes that seemed to draw Raymond in.

'My car's in the car park. This way.' She indicated the covered walkway straight ahead and she moved towards it, beckoning the others to follow. The roof of the walkway offered a degree of protection from the glare of the sun. *An improvement*, Raymond thought, *from what would have been its purpose back home – dank and dismal rain.*

'This is Maria.' Raymond introduced the small, slim girl to the DS as they walked. 'She's our computer wizard. And this is Slab.' He indicated his large companion. 'He is…' He hesitated. 'He is…' He paused, trying to find the right word. 'Security.'

Slab glanced at him and smiled.

The small party of travellers, trailing their bags behind them, followed the young detective along the walkway and towards the car park.

Raymond moved up beside the young detective and talked to her while his companions looked about themselves, taking in the strangeness of their new surroundings. Apart from the heat and the humidity, there was a hustle and bustle in every direction with an incessant background wall of noise: people talking, calling one another and everything accompanied by a constant rumble of traffic beyond the airport perimeter fence.

Raymond stopped momentarily, and the detective sergeant did so too, turning to face him.

'Has DCI Gupta explained the nature of our mission?' he asked, but without waiting for an answer, he continued, 'The Metropolitan police at home have traced the illegal drug production to somewhere in Delhi. For them to come here was going to take an age to get permissions, etc., so we agreed that I come over and link up with you and your team directly. They mentioned that somebody on your team had already had a tip-off about some illegal drug factory?'

'Yes, that was me.' She turned her head as she spoke to face Raymond. 'That is why I was sent to meet you. Though…' she continued, a little despondently, Raymond thought, 'DCI Gupta is taking personal control of enquires – my role is just to meet and greet, I'm afraid.'

As they reached the car, Raymond was a little taken aback by its make and its appearance. It looked like an old-fashioned Morris Oxford, a car that Raymond remembered from black-and-white films of the fifties, those usually made in the old Elstree studios in London. By all accounts, Morris had stopped making such vehicles in and around the late 1950s, early sixties.

The car had a short, stubbly frontage with a curved bonnet supplemented by a steel radiator cage that stretched across most of the front of the width of vehicle and was surmounted by two large, rounded headlights. As with any of the cars Raymond recalled, it was a flat grey colour, and this one was showing its age with a number of scratches and bumps along the bodywork.

'Nice car,' observed Slab sarcastically.

'Standard police issue,' replied the detective sergeant, not rising to the bait. She was not so young nor so unworldly wise as to realise the general lack of appreciation of Indian cars.

'It is a Hindustan Ambassador, actually. We modelled them on the English Morris Oxford.'

Raymond nodded, justified in his earlier assumption.

'Though even we stopped making them a few years ago, but they remain very popular here in India. We tend to keep them running much longer than in your more disposable economies.'

She lifted up the boot cover for the party to stow away their luggage, but even though their bags were relatively modest, only two of the three could be wedged in. Slab made to throw his bag onto the back seat as he climbed awkwardly through the one small passenger door and edged behind the folded front seat. Maria clambered in beside him as Raymond pushed the rear of his seat back into its upright position.

'All okay in there?' Amrita asked, glancing in the rear-view mirror.

Raymond turned around in his seat to look at his companions. Slab took up the majority of the small rear seat, his bag took up more of the remaining space, and Maria appeared to be squashed up against the side panel and window.

'Where to?' he asked.

First stop was to be the Police Central Headquarters to meet the elusive DCI Gupta. But this was not before a memorable journey through Delhi's road system.

Leaving the airport, things seemed tranquil enough, but as the city approached, Raymond was shocked to see other cars overtaking theirs. Although they were driving on the left, as in the UK, cars were flying past on both sides of their vehicle and others seemed to be approaching virtually head on. Besides the four-wheeled vehicles, Sergeant Banerjee, who was gripping the steering wheel with a steely determination, was being repeatedly forced to swerve to avoid numerous scooters, motorbikes and bicycles on route. The cycles themselves were not the problem, but what was, was that they carried not only the rider, but also perhaps a passenger on the cross frame, or, if motorised, up to four or five other passengers hanging on for dear life. Alternatively, others were overloaded with massive bags piled high on the rider's back, the handle bars and the cross frame. Like the car drivers, the cyclists seemed to have no awareness of any highway code; they appeared from all sides and travelling in a multitude of different directions, even though they were now all on a relatively small road with only two lanes.

As they rounded one particularly sharp corner, they were confronted with a large Brahma bull being ushered along the road by its owner, who brandished a stick, waving it behind the large beast's buttocks.

Raymond glanced from side to side, taking in the pantomime going on around him, amazed at the skill with which Sergeant Banerjee, apparently without any thought or concern, simply manoeuvred around each and every obstacle and carried on their journey.

Arriving at the police headquarters, Raymond noted that even Slab, as he slowly and carefully extracted himself from the small car, appeared to be somewhat taken aback by the journey they had just endured.

To lighten the atmosphere, Raymond remarked, 'Is the traffic always like that?'

'Oh no,' came the reply. 'You should see it at rush hour.'

'Can't wait,' murmured Slab.

Led by Sergeant Banerjee, Raymond and his colleagues passed through the main body of the building and ascended two flights of stairs before stopping outside an office door surmounted with a plaque bearing DCI Gupta's name. Amrita Banerjee knocked the door tentatively.

'Come in, come in,' came back gruffly a voice from inside the office.

On entering, Amrita Banerjee attempted to introduce Raymond and the others, but was, Raymond noted, immediately and rudely interrupted by her boss.

'I know who our visitors are, Sergeant Banerjee,' he stated curtly. Then, with more politeness, he rose from his desk and came around it to shake Raymond's hand. 'Mr McNally, we have been expecting you. You are most welcome.'

Raymond observed the short, rather rotund figure of Amrita Banerjee's boss. He wore a khaki uniform that reminded Raymond of the TV series *It Ain't Half Hot Mum*. Raymond also noted what he thought was a very artificial smile of greeting as Gupta spoke.

They shook hands, and DCI Gupta, moving back behind his desk, indicated for them to sit in the group of chairs out at one side of the desk whilst he himself sat himself down, facing them from behind the desk. To Amrita Banerjee he offered a cursory wave, indicating for her to retreat to the back of the room where there were no chairs and she simply had to stand against the wall.

Raymond had taken an instant dislike to DCI Gupta and his curt manner, but he knew he had to hold his tongue; he was, after all, relying on this senior police officer's goodwill in the investigation to come.

'What has Sergeant Banerjee said so far?' Gupta asked.

Raymond felt the question was a barbed one, as Amrita had already explained that she had simply been tasked with meet and greet. It seemed to Raymond the DCI was almost testing his sergeant through Raymond.

'Absolutely nothing so far,' he replied noncommittedly. He glanced over at Sergeant Banerjee, who stood to attention at the back of the room.

She smiled discreetly in his direction.

The interview continued, with Raymond outlining the

information they had to date. He brought Maria in at intervals to explain the technological side of things as they arose.

'Basically, from what we can ascertain, there is a counterfeit drug mimicking ours being manufactured here in Delhi and being sold over the internet to unsuspecting patients.'

DCI Gupta spoke slowly. 'And this is based on? What? Emails found in a warehouse? Slim evidence, if you don't mind me saying so.'

'We think the evidence is sound, and... I believe you had an informer who reported something similar?'

'Who told you that?' Gupta shot a stare at his sergeant, who simply kept her gaze on the floor. 'A most unreliable man,' Gupta continued. 'Very untrustworthy. I don't think anything he said can be taken seriously.'

'But he's dead – why is he dead then?' Amrita Banerjee exclaimed, regaining her courage.

Gupta, startled by her intervention, intoned, 'Sergeant Banerjee, I think you should leave – these discussions are above your pay grade and none of your business. Please leave. Now.'

Amrita turned to leave, but Raymond stood up and, fixing the DCI with a hard stare, told him in no uncertain terms that he wished her to stay and furthermore to be part of the ongoing investigation.

'With respect, Mr McNally, who I allocate to this investigation is nothing to do with you. You cannot tell me how to run my police force.'

'Okay then. I'll talk to your superior officer.'

Gupta seemed to back down a bit. He clearly did not want to be usurped nor to lose control of this investigation.

'Alright then.' He spoke after a short pause for reflection. 'I will allow Sergeant Banerjee to continue in her role as a liaison officer with yourselves.'

Amrita Banerjee tried to suppress a small smile as her superior fixed her with a withering stare.

Following the audience with the chief inspector, Amrita Banerjee was instructed to escort their guests to their hotel in central Delhi, but not before DCI Gupta had taken her aside and made it clear in hushed but no uncertain terms that she was not to discuss any confidential police information with their visitors.

*

The hotel, as many in India are, was totally out of keeping with the crowded, dirty and frankly chaotic exterior that was downtown Delhi.

The Taj Ambassador was one of central Delhi's many top-rated hotels. As they entered the reception area, they were immersed in the cool fragrance of flowers drifting on the air-conditioned air.

The three looked about themselves, taking in the plush surroundings. White marble dominated the interior of the wide and spacious reception area. On either side of the entrance hall rose tall, rounded pillars again hewn from white marble. The only furniture in the hall were two stiff-backed chairs covered in a green and yellow velour; they stood either side of a small coffee table on which sat a large chess set, the figures in their starting positions. At the far end of the hall stood a uniformed man behind a long teak reception desk. He stood stiffly to attention but forced a beaming white smile as they approached.

'Mister McNally and friends? We have been expecting you.' He bowed slightly as he spoke. 'I have your room keys here.' He proffered them to each in turn. 'We have put you all on the same floor.'

'Thank you,' replied Raymond courteously on behalf of his team.

Amrita Banerjee offered her hand to Raymond. 'I'll leave you now to get settled in.'

'You'll be back?'

'Of course, of course, but it's getting late now and you must be tired. We will meet here in the morning, say 8am, and then we can begin our investigations.' She waved over her shoulder as she turned to leave.

Raymond watched her exit the building and climb into her faithful old car before driving off.

chapter thirty-seven

They had sat in the bar area for a while after Sergeant Banerjee's departure, but following their long flight, it wasn't long before Raymond and Maria's heads started to fall and drowsiness overcame them. They roused at the sound of a waiter dropping a tray and being chastised by his boss; at that point Raymond made his excuses and headed off to his bedroom and a night's sleep. Maria was quick to follow. Slab, however, seemed content to simply relax in the bar seat and sip at one of many whiskies he had lined up before him. Eventually, though, he too succumbed to sleep, albeit slouched in the chair on which he sat.

Raymond was in the bathroom when he heard his door handle being turned and the locked door rattle as someone tried to open it.

He put his head around the bathroom door. 'Yes,' he shouted. 'Who is it?'

'Room service,' came the reply.

Raymond made his way to the door, turned the key and reached for the door handle, but before he could open the door it was burst open by the two individuals on the other side of it. They pushed their way into the room, knocking Raymond backwards onto the bed.

One of the intruders then produced a gun and thrust it into Raymond's face.

'You are not wanted here,' the man with the gun breathed, pressing his face close to Raymond's whilst still pushing the gun hard into Raymond's temple.

Raymond heard himself say, 'Who are you? What do you want?' only to be replied to with the same mantra as before.

'You're not wanted here.'

There was a noise behind them in the doorway. Both men looked up, startled.

It was Maria. She had obviously heard the commotion in Raymond's room and had come to investigate.

'Maria, get away!' Raymond yelled. The words were no sooner out than he was struck across his face by the butt of the handgun. The blow was sufficiently hard that he lost consciousness almost immediately.

*

When he awoke, he was sprawled across the bed, a pool of blood on the bed cover where it had leaked from the wound on his head. The room was silent, the door still ajar. He had no idea how long he had been unconscious for – he guessed not long, but the intruders had gone.

Then he remembered Maria. He rushed to his feet and out of the bedroom and across to hers. Her door was open also, but there was no one inside. He searched around frantically, but the room was empty.

He ran to the lift. He pushed the button and paced back and forth, waiting for the lift to arrive. He paced and paced, tracking the lift's progress on the illuminated floor indicator above its doors.

It seemed to take an age, stopping at virtually every floor.

Finally losing patience, he ran back along the corridor to the fire exit door, pushed it roughly aside and made his way down the concrete steps two at a time.

Bursting out of the lobby, some customers turned around, shocked at his sudden entrance from an unexpected quarter and still with blood oozing from his head wound. He looked around the foyer. Nothing seemed out of place. As a uniformed hotel employee approached, probably to simply see that he was alright, Raymond spotted Slab reclining in the armchair that they had left him in, a number of empty tumblers on the table in front of him and him audibly snoring as his head lolled back on the headrest.

Raymond pushed aside the uniformed employee and raced over to the reposed figure. 'Slab, Slab, wake up!' He shook the giant of a man forcibly.

'Eh, what?' He rubbed his eyes and pushed himself up in the seat.

'Somebody broke into my room,' Raymond tried to explain. 'I think they have Maria.'

With that, he turned, scanned the foyer area and then made to run to the door leading to the garden and then to the exterior wall of the hotel and on to the outside city.

'Come on. Quick,' he shouted at Slab.

Slab made to get up, but he was still a bit befuddled from being aroused so abruptly from his sleep and also confused by Raymond's clear agitation. Nevertheless, he made to follow Raymond out through the hotel doors.

Raymond stopped on the hotel steps. All was quiet and serene in the garden; he could still discern the hustle and bustle from the outside street, but nothing seemed out of place. He sank to his knees. Slab came up behind him and stood, looking down on the forlorn figure.

'What's up?' he asked in as caring a voice as a Glaswegian hard man could muster.

'I think they've kidnapped Maria.'

'What? Who?' asked Slab incredulously.

'That's just it, I don't know.' Raymond's head slunk further onto his chest. He explained to Slab the events of the past hour or so and his supposition that it was to do with the investigation into the illegal drug trade, given that it was clear that the intruders' purpose was to warn him off.

'But we only just got here. How did they know…?' Slab scratched his head.

'There must be a leak somewhere,' Raymond postulated. 'We've got to find Maria.'

chapter thirty-eight

Having spent the last hour or so scouring the perimeter of the hotel and beyond, Raymond and Slab, both breathless from their efforts, stood facing each other at the hotel gate. Raymond leant with one hand on the gate pillar to steady himself as he panted.

'We've got to tell the police, somebody, they've taken her, Slab, they've got her,' he wheezed.

'But why?' asked the big man, both hands on his knees, trying to get a breath.

'They were warning me... us, off. That's all I know.' He fumbled in his pocket for his mobile phone and punched the numbers furiously. He dialled the number that Amrita Banerjee had given him for ease of contact.

When she answered, he barked the details of what had happened almost before she had a chance to speak.

Finally, the message imparted, she said, 'I'll be right over.'

It was fifteen minutes before the police sergeant, accompanied by a uniformed officer, arrived in the foyer of the hotel where Raymond and Slab sat, going over and over the detail of what had just happened.

'Sorry, the traffic,' she tried to explain.

Raymond was on his feet, ushering her to sit.

The uniformed officer stood to attention behind her seat as Raymond explained the details of the assault and Maria's kidnapping.

'How did they know? You have only just arrived,' she asked incredulously.

'Exactly what we have been trying to figure out,' Slab interjected.

'There must be a leak somewhere.' She looked thoughtfully at Raymond. 'Who at your factory knows you are here?' she asked.

'A few people… I don't know.' He scratched his head. 'I don't think anybody there could have anything to do with it. I refuse to believe it.'

He paced back and forth, trying to make sense of what had happened.

'We've got to keep an open mind, that's all I'm saying,' Amrita Banerjee added defensively while watching him walk up and down the small area at the side of the foyer in which they were sitting. She turned to her colleague. 'Radio it in, Reyansh.'

The uniformed officer, without speaking, turned and made his way back to his car to do as he was bid.

'Okay, leave this to us,' she added as she rose to follow her colleague. 'We will get her back, do not worry.'

Raymond watched her helplessly as she exited the building, not at all reassured.

Slab remained seated as Raymond started to pace the foyer again.

'What do you think we should do?' Slab finally asked, trying to regain Raymond's attention.

'I don't know, Slab, I just don't know.'

*

For the rest of the morning Raymond remained in his room. He lay on the bed, then he tried sitting at the window, but his attention was elsewhere; he couldn't settle, not till he knew that Maria was safe. Amrita Banerjee had detailed another uniformed officer to stand outside his room in order to deter any unwelcome visitors. *Closing the stable door after the horse has bolted*, thought Raymond, but he hadn't said as much to the police sergeant; he had simply nodded his gratitude at the time.

Hours seemed to pass with no news or developments. The sun was going down behind the domed roof of the temple that was just visible over the hotel's formidable exterior wall. Slab and he shared the view but also their concern for Maria. Raymond's eyes started to droop as he sat in the chair, observing the scene. He hadn't realised how tired he was.

Suddenly, he was disturbed by his mobile phone buzzing in his pocket. He had forgotten it was there. He pulled it out and looked at the screen.

Number withheld.

He pressed the green receive button.

'Yes?'

'Mr McNally?' A gruff Indian accent.

'Yes, that's me.'

'We have somebody here who wants to talk to you.'

Raymond heard the phone being moved around.

'Raymond, it's me,' a frightened voice shouted down the phone.

Raymond recognised the voice immediately. 'Maria? Where are you? What's happened to you?'

But before she could answer, the first male voice came on the line. 'Now you listen to me, Mr McNally, if you want to see you friend here again…'

'What, what do you want me to do? Is it money, is that it? My firm can pay, whatever—' he reasoned down the phone.

'It is much simpler than that, Mr McNally. We just want you and your other friend to go home. Nothing more, nothing less. If you do as we say, then this young lady here will be on the next plane home after yours. But if you choose not to listen, then she'll still be going home, but in a box. Do you understand me?' he growled.

'Loud and clear, whatever you say. Just don't hurt her, that's all,' Raymond pleaded.

The phone went dead.

Just at that moment the uniformed officer who had been standing outside and heard the voices leant around the door and asked, 'Is everything alright, Mr McNally?'

'Yes, yes, nothing for you to be concerned about.'

'I thought I heard your phone?'

'Oh, just the office, nothing special, nothing to worry about.'

Slab looked at him quizzically; clearly Raymond had chosen not to involve the police in this latest development.

As the officer withdrew, Slab asked, 'So? What was that all about?'

chapter thirty-nine

Maria struggled against the bindings on her wrists. They were too tight and kept her arms firmly tethered behind her back. She was seated on a cold, stony floor. The room was empty apart from some discarded cardboard boxes and old newspapers. It smelt of damp and decay. The only light came from a small square window high above her head.

She recalled with some trepidation the sight of Raymond bleeding on his bed and then the way she had been bundled out of the room, down the stairs and roughly thrust into the back of a waiting vehicle.

She surveyed the emptiness of the room and then pushed herself back into the wall behind her and tried to push herself up onto her feet, the only limbs that were not secured.

It took three attempts to get to her feet, and only then because she managed to grip and guide herself up the wall using her hands as much as her bonds would allow. She made her way across to the one door in the room. She swivelled around so she could grasp the handle. With some difficulty she was able to turn the handle and then to pull on the door to try to open it.

Try as she might, it would not open. It was firmly shut,

and as no key was evident it was obvious that it had been locked from the outside to keep her from escaping.

As she stood, now facing the door, tears welled up in her eyes and trickled down her face. She tried to recall more of the journey that had brought her to her present predicament. But she remembered very little of the journey through the streets of Delhi, pinned as she had been to the floor of the car and held there by two sets of her abductors' feet. But when they had pulled her roughly out of the car, she had seemed to be in a deserted yard; the sounds she could hear made her sure that she was still in the city, though where she had no idea.

Pulled across the courtyard, two large Indian men each holding tightly on to one of her arms, they thrust open a large door in a grey and decaying building and dragged her inside.

They crossed what appeared to be a large but empty factory floor. This area seemed to be cleaner and more recently used than the exterior of the building would have suggested. It was, however, devoid of any life. Maria noted abandoned desks, many with glass jars, measuring flasks or flameless Bunsen burners neatly arranged on their surfaces.

Leaving the spacious laboratory area, her captors opened another, though much smaller, inner door and pushed her down some stone steps and on into the small room that was now her cell.

She cried out for help, firstly towards the window high above her head and then at the door that prevented her escape.

She waited and listened. Although she could just make out the distant rumble of traffic in the roads beyond the factory, no one called out in response to her cries.

She tried again, as loudly as she could muster.

But again, no response.

She sank to her knees in despair and then flipped herself over to sit again, this time with her back to the door itself, trying to work out what was happening to her. Time passed; it seemed like an age alone in the dark and dismal room.

Suddenly she heard noises from beyond the door.

She called out.

She struggled to her feet and stood back from the door.

She heard a key turn and then the door opened.

To her dismay, she recognised the man who entered as one of her captors. He was a tall and, unlike so many of his countrymen, heavily set. His clothes were cheap, shabby and loose-fitting. He had made no attempt to conceal his face, seemingly confident that Maria would not get the opportunity to ever identify him to the authorities.

'What am I doing here?' she screamed into his face.

He pushed her roughly away without replying. She fell back against the wall and sank down it.

Another man entered the room; this one Maria did not recognise – he was smaller, bearded and more neatly dressed than the first man.

The first man then suddenly produced a knife from his waistband. He held it out in front of him.

Maria looked in terror at the knife; everything else blurred into the distance. The man held it tightly in his right hand. It was short-handled with a curved blade about nine inches long. The blade was well polished, and light from the small window above Maria's head glinted off it.

He moved forward towards her.

She pressed herself back against the wall, trying to get as far from the knife as was possible.

He grabbed her shoulder with his left hand, the knife now perilously close to Maria's face. Her eyes fixated upon it.

He pushed her roughly onto her side and then deftly cut the rope that secured her arms.

He stood up and looked down upon her.

Maria, released from the bonds, rubbed at her wrists, which were painful from the tightness of the bonds that up till a moment ago had pinned her wrists together.

The second jailor manoeuvred himself around the first. Maria then noticed for the first time that he was carrying a small tray. As he neared, he then leant down, placing the tray on the floor beside Maria.

She looked down at it quizzically.

It contained some bread, a cup of water and a bowl of some indistinguishable brown gloop.

Without a word, the two men then withdrew, keeping their eyes on Maria as they did so.

The door closed and a key turned, leaving Maria alone once again in the small room.

chapter forty

Raymond had summoned Slab to his room. Slab looked as tired as Raymond himself felt. The big man was unshaven and even more dishevelled in appearance than his norm. It was clear that he had been more affected by Maria's disappearance than he was likely to admit.

The two men sat facing each other, Raymond on the bed and Slab on the chair in front of the dressing table and mirror. Initially there was a silence between them. Raymond observed that the chair appeared too small to support the giant of a man, but it did so without complaint.

The somewhat comical appearance did little to lighten his spirits.

'We're going home,' Raymond suddenly announced.

'What? I don't understand.' Slab looked incredulous. 'What about Maria? We can't just abandon her here.'

'I don't think we have any other option,' Raymond replied, his eyes fixed on the floor. 'The kidnappers have made it clear that we are unwelcome here and unless we leave, Maria will remain a hostage or worse. They said that if we leave they will let her go.'

'And you trust them?' Slab was now on his feet, pacing back and forth, angrily pushing the chair aside.

'I think we have to. What else can we do?'

'We can try and track them down. If I could get my hands on them…' Slab looked more menacing than ever, Raymond thought as he watched him continuing to pace up and down, but now he pummelled his fists as he did so.

'We will have to rely on the local police,' Raymond conceded. 'They at least know the place and possibly the likely suspects.'

Slab looked far from convinced.

Raymond spent the rest of the day on the phone making the arrangements. Slab, on the other hand, just sat about in his room sulking.

Raymond knocked Slab's door. After a few minutes the door was opened slowly and cautiously by only a few inches. Slab's bald head then appeared in the gap between wall and door as he peered around the edge of the door suspiciously. Seeing it was Raymond standing there, he opened the door more widely and then turned and strode back into his room. Raymond followed him and watched Slab slowly lowering himself to sit on the edge of the bed.

'Okay, I've made all the arrangements. We are off this evening – a taxi will pick us up in about two hours to take us to the airport. Get packed and ready to go.'

Slab looked up at him.

Raymond could almost feel the ice in the stare that Slab portrayed.

'Look, I know you are not happy, but the way I see it, we have no other choice. Just trust me on this one, Slab. Okay?'

Slab remained silent, but his downcast look suggested his unwilling compliance with Raymond's wishes.

The taxi arrived right on time in front of the hotel foyer where Raymond and a disgruntled Slab stood, cases at their feet.

Raymond scanned the foyer. He was sure the kidnappers had placed somebody in the hotel to ensure their departure, and he wanted to make sure that they witnessed his and Slab's leaving.

At first he couldn't detect anything or anyone out of place. But then he spotted him, or at least he thought that he must be the observer: a moustached, greasy-haired man in a cheap suit was seated behind a pillar at the rear of the foyer. To all intents and purposes, he was waiting for a fellow guest and was reading a newspaper as he did so. Raymond, however, had caught him peering over the top of the paper and taking a definite interest in their departure.

Catching Raymond's gaze, the man immediately returned to reading his newspaper, but still did glance up occasionally at the pair as they passed their baggage to the hotel porter and the driver, and then followed them out of the cool of the hotel's air conditioning to the clinging heat of the exterior.

They climbed into the vehicle, Raymond in the front beside the driver and Slab squashed himself into the back seat.

Raymond instructed the driver, just loudly enough that the man who had been lurking in the foyer and had now followed them to the hotel doorway could hear the instruction to take them to the airport, international departures.

As they pulled away, Raymond looked down at the car's wing mirror and could just discern the observer turning around and talking into a mobile phone.

Arriving at the airport, there was the usual hustle and bustle; the driver deftly wound the car through the mass of people who, crossing the roads in front of them, seemed to have scant regard for their own lives, never mind the small children that many dragged behind them.

Stopping in front of the main terminal building, Raymond alighted from the vehicle and Slab slowly followed. They retrieved their luggage and Raymond pointed Slab towards the main entrance slightly beyond them. As he thanked the driver, Raymond noted another vehicle pull up some fifty yards short of their own. There were two men in the front and one in the back. Raymond recognised the front seat passenger as the man from the foyer.

Initially the three made no attempt to exit their car, rather they sat motionless, simply observing Raymond and Slab's movements as they pulled their cases towards the terminal entrance.

Only when the pair had reached the automatic doors and moved towards the check-in desks did two of the men alight the vehicle, leaving the driver behind the wheel. The two men then slowly made to follow Raymond and Slab through the terminal building.

Standing in the check-in queue, Raymond glanced around intermittently to see the pair who now stood beside one of the airport kiosks. One leant forward to light a cigarette from a match the other proffered. *The 'no smoking' rules had not yet reached India*, Raymond thought. The queue was long and their progress slow. Raymond kept quietly glancing around to watch the pair who in turn watched them.

It was only when they reached the check-in desk and Slab leant forward, placing his two massive forearms on the check-in desk and offering his ticket, did Raymond observe the two men turn and move off, clearly satisfied with the outcome and the imminent departure of the pair.

As Slab picked up his case and was about to place it on the weighing scale, Raymond suddenly moved forward and grabbed Slab's arm.

'Let's get out of here,' he said softly into Slab's ear.

'What…?' Slab turned, shocked by what he thought he had just heard Raymond say.

Raymond turned to the check-in assistant. 'Sorry, something's come up, we are not checking in right now.'

Slab glared at Raymond.

'Come on,' Raymond reiterated. 'Let's get out of here… Now.' He turned to leave, dragging his case behind him.

Slab, angry and unsure of what was going on, made to follow him.

They made their way quickly across the check-in area and then Raymond turned towards the back of the building, down a short corridor and towards an unmarked door leading to the outside.

Slab looked around. 'Where the fuck are we?' he stated, and then asked, almost as an afterthought, 'And what the fuck are we doing here anyway?'

'Trust me,' came the reply as Raymond continued to hurry along the corridor and then pushed the door ahead of him open, stepping outside onto a walkway beside a small slip road.

There ahead of them stood Detective Sergeant Amrita Banerjee.

She was standing beside the open door of an unmarked police car. She beckoned them towards her. 'Hurry,' she said, 'we need to leave now, before someone sees us.'

Raymond and Slab threw their cases into the boot of the car and dived into the empty back seat. Amrita Banerjee climbed into the driver's seat and started the engine.

'You weren't spotted?' she asked as she manoeuvred the car from its parked position and then out onto the roadway, accelerating past some other parked vehicles. 'You are sure no one saw you leave?' she asked again, glancing at the air through the rear-view mirror.

'We were being watched—' Raymond said, but before he could finish the sentence, Slab interrupted. 'We were being scooped? Who the—?'

'There were two guys – they followed us from the hotel and were hanging about in the check-in area. They didn't think I'd spotted them, but I guess they weren't the best undercover agents in the world.'

'Did they see you escaping?' Amrita Banerjee asked, an increasingly nervous tone sneaking into her voice.

'No, at least as far as I can be sure. When they saw us at the check-in desk and Slab putting his case on the weighing machine, they upped and left. I guess they thought their job was done.'

'And there was nobody else?'

'Not that I saw. How about you, Slab, did you spot anybody watching us?'

Slab clenched his fists and shook his head, still not quite grasping just what was going on.

'What about you, Amrita? Who else knows about this?'

'Absolutely nobody.'

'Not even your boss?'

'Especially not Chief Inspector Gupta. He and I don't see eye to eye on many things, and trust me, this would definitely be one of those.'

Through the mirror Amrita Banerjee observed Slab swinging around in his seat to face Raymond directly. 'Would somebody like to tell me exactly what the holy shite is going on?' he said, raising his fists a little above his thighs as if to emphasise his anger at not being included in any of the planning of this escape.

'Calm down, Slab, just a diversionary tactic, that's all.' Raymond tried to sound reassuring, despite facing an increasingly aggressive Slab McBride and the inner turmoil he himself was feeling.

The car sped along the small slip road, then up a ramp and out into the bright sunshine. People were still milling about outside the terminal building, but Raymond thought the crowd did seem to have diminished a bit, probably as the majority of flights had arrived or departed by now.

The policewoman accelerated away and headed for the motorway.

Raymond looked back, trying to spot the two men who had been following them. He let out an audible sigh of relief when he realised that he couldn't see any sign of them. He turned to face forward again just as other cars hooted as Amrita Banerjee eased her way out and off the slip road to join the rows of cars already making their way along the carriageway.

Raymond looked around at the traffic all around, fearful that his trackers might again be in one of the other cars and might spot them.

Slab read the signs on a stanchion above the motorway; they indicated that they were heading back into Delhi itself. He was still confused and angry and couldn't quite make out just what was occurring, so he now leant forward, gripping the back of the driver's seat.

'Can you tell me, please, what we are doing here?' he asked, fixing Amrita Banerjee's reflection in the driver's mirror with a menacing stare.

'You better tell him, Mr McNally,' she responded whilst weaving in and out of the traffic ahead.

'Okay, Slab, they told us to leave. You were unhappy to do so. Well, so was I. But if we didn't go, they had threatened to hurt Maria.'

'Okay?' Slab growled. 'I'm with you so far.'

'So Amrita and I hatched up this plan—'

'Plan?' Slab growled as he frowned, squashing his face into a grimace and bearing his teeth. He didn't like it that they hadn't trusted him enough to include him in any such plan.

Amrita Banerjee then spoke – helpfully, she hoped – speaking over her shoulder to Slab. 'We decided to make it look like you were leaving but for you to remain and stay undercover, at least for a while.'

'Nobody else knows,' Raymond added quickly, 'and they mustn't.'

'We thought,' Amrita Banerjee interjected, 'that by staying here you could help, for example by using your company's resources and your knowledge of Maria, to help locate her more quickly and, even more importantly, to track down the perpetrators.'

'Okay, I kinda get that.' Slab's anger seemed to be dissipating.

'Well,' the sergeant replied, head firmly facing forward as the traffic merged with another slip road and the queue ahead slowed. 'They want you gone. Obviously they must consider you a threat. We don't quite know what sort of threat, but a threat nonetheless. So if we can work out why they want you out of here, we can exploit that to try and solve our problem.'

'Mmmm…' growled Slab, not entirely convinced.

The car sped as quickly as possible through the crowded streets before pulling into a small side road and then into an even smaller alleyway.

Here Amrita Banerjee pulled the car to a halt, and, leaning forward and pointing upward, she turned to her two passengers and said, 'There's my flat, third floor. It's not much. But the best a young detective sergeant can afford these days. It will do for the time being.'

'Do for the time being?' repeated Slab.

'Yes, I'm sorry, Slab, not to include you in our deliberations,' Raymond interjected. 'Amrita has kindly offered to put us up in her place till we can sort things out.' Adding a little dejectedly, 'If we can sort things out.'

They disembarked the car, Raymond and the sergeant glanced about anxiously, trying to spot anyone that might have followed them. Slab just made do with heaving the luggage out the car.

They made their way towards the apartment block and entered it by a side door. On entering, they found themselves in a small, concrete, bare stairwell. Following the sergeant's lead, they went up the grey concrete stairway, Amrita had explained that the lift hadn't worked in living memory. She led the way, Raymond followed behind and Slab brought up the rear one suitcase in either hand.

Reaching the third floor, Amrita pushed open the door of the stairwell and turned left down a short, narrow corridor with doors on either side until she stopped outside one of the doors marked '308'. She pulled a key from her pocket, opened the door, then stood aside and ushered her two guests inside.

The apartment was compact. A small sitting area was combined with a tiny but functional kitchen. Three doors led off from the sitting area. One was ajar and revealed a bedroom, Amrita's, Raymond thought, observing some discarded clothes on the bed. The other doors led to a small bathroom, with just room for a shower but not a bathtub. The other door was closed, but Raymond guessed this was likely a second bedroom.

Amrita Banerjee moved towards the closed door and opened it widely. As Raymond had guessed, it was a guest bedroom, and seemingly his and Slab's for the duration of their stay.

The only furniture inside the room was a small wooden cupboard and two twin beds. A window on the far side of the room leaked a little shaft of light between its drawn curtains. Despite the attempt to exclude the direct sunlight, the room was unbearably hot. Raymond could feel the beads of sweat collecting across his forehead.

Amrita Banerjee, clearly immune to the temperature, strode across the room and edged between one of the twin beds and the far wall, reaching for the curtains to pull them open.

Light streamed into the room. Raymond and Slab blinked at the sudden transformation from gloom to full sunlight. Shielding his eyes, Raymond moved across towards the window as Amrita struggled with the catch to open it.

'Here, let me help.' He eased past her.

After a few tugs the window opened, and he fastened it in an open position. Street noise flooded into the room, accompanied by a light but welcome breeze. The breeze carried with it many of the smells of Delhi itself: sweet smells of cinnamon and other fragrant spices mixed with curries of various hues, but also the more unpleasant aromas of dirt and poverty, such was the dichotomy of this great city.

Slab sat down on the edge of one of the beds.

'Okay,' he growled, fixing his gaze on Raymond. 'What exactly is the plan?'

'Well,' Raymond deliberated, 'it's a sort of work in progress.'

'You mean you don't fucking know, do you?'

'I wouldn't exactly put it like that, Slab. Let's be a little more positive, eh? You didn't want to leave Maria behind; nor did I. So we're here now. The kidnappers think we've gone, but we're still here and we are going to work with Amrita to get her freed.' He looked at Amrita Banerjee for support.

'Exactly,' she said, but without much conviction.

chapter forty-one

Maria awoke; she was cold and stiff. Although her small cell had been unbearably hot during the day, the temperature had plummeted during the night. She had done her best to arrange the flattened card boxes into a makeshift mattress and covered herself as best she could with many of the newspapers that she had gathered from the floor around her. Try as she might, it was difficult to stop them shifting and falling off her body as she attempted to keep warm.

She had slept only fitfully, kept awake by the discomfort and the cold, but not least by the scratching of a rat, or worse, rats. She had glimpsed one of the creatures as it emerged from a crack in the wall at the far end of the room, making its way across the room, partially obscured by the gloom of the evening, to finish off the meal that her jailors had provided and that Maria had only picked at.

She watched the creature grab a piece of bread in its mouth and then scurry quickly back to its home behind the crack in the wall.

There had been other noises throughout the night, more scratching sans scurrying, which Maria had hoped was simply the lone rat making off with more of the leftovers. There were also intermittent sounds of talking coming from beyond the door, suggesting that some of her kidnappers were still outside, ensuring her continued captivity.

As light streamed in through the small window, the emptiness and squalor of the room in which she was held once again manifested itself to her. She felt unwell, she was tired from lack of sleep, but also she felt nauseous and her stomach was cramping. She called out, hoping to attract some attention from the guards.

Their conversation halted, but only momentarily before resuming once again.

She called out once more. 'Please help me, I am not well. Please.' She heard someone approach the door. A key turned and slowly the door opened. The man made sure she was not planning anything before he entered the room. Maria was huddled up against the far wall. She was pale and looked tired, and most of all, frightened. 'Please,' she said, wrapping her arms around her stomach. 'I think I am going to be sick, or worse. Please help me.'

The man slowly withdrew once again, closing the door behind him. Maria slumped onto her knees and, still clutching her stomach, wailed uncontrollably. The door eased open again and her jailor reappeared; he thrust a bucket towards her. When she didn't immediately take it from him, he dropped it noisily on the floor, turned and left, locking the door behind him.

Maria reached for the bucket and wretched uncontrollably into it, the meagre remnants of yesterday's meal being deposited into the dirty grey metallic bucket. Initially relieved, Maria collapsed back onto her makeshift bed and sobbed quietly to herself. Her stomach cramps, though, were increasing, and she knew there was worse to come. She reached for the bucket to keep it nearby.

Just in case.

chapter forty-two

Harry was alone again in his bedroom. He could hear his mother moving about downstairs, clinking plates and clunking cutlery as she tidied up after lunch. It was already dark and grey outside as the winter months drew in. Little light penetrated the small room; however, Harry remained oblivious of the gloom that surrounded him as he sat bent over the computer, his face illuminated by the screen in front of him.

He was fully aware that it was his own autistic tendencies that drove him to keep interrogating the computer, not able to let go of the task that Raymond had set him.

He had been disappointed not to be taken along to India with Raymond and the others, but he did understand Raymond's reasoning on the matter. He wasn't directly employed by UMBRA, they didn't need two IT geeks along and he was younger than the others. *Well, not all, to be fair*, he thought – Maria was around the same age.

He wondered how she was. He found, to his surprise, that he missed her company. He was even more surprised that he felt that way. Harry had been a loner all his life; he had few friends and certainly none that lasted.

Of course he also recognised that his mother would have lost the plot completely if Raymond had even suggested Harry should travel to India with them. She had been difficult enough about the trip to Basel.

So at home he remained, but he had been allowed to take the computer found at the raid home with him. Raymond had reasoned that if anyone could prise more information out of it, then Harry could.

He felt proud, probably for one of the first times in his life, that someone outside his family circle had actually had faith in him and entrusted him with a worthwhile task.

So with that he had sat for hours on end, probing the computer's hard drive, trying to extract any information that could in some way be useful to Raymond and his team.

He flicked endlessly through file after file, trying to find one that he had not previously opened and examined. He felt tired and yawned loudly; he had been at his task for a number of hours today alone, pausing only for a bowl of homemade vegetable soup and a cup of tea that his mother had brought him and insisted he consume.

As he examined file after file, he quickly came to realise that he was simply turning over information that he had already gleaned. Exasperated, he was about to give up when out of the blue a signal flashed up on the computer's email inbox. He had already accessed the emails and suspected, given that the owners must, by now, be aware that he was in possession of the computer, that it was simply junk mail.

He opened the email file. The message seemed to emanate from an overseas delivery company and simply stated: *Failed to deliver package.*

He opened the email. It was indeed a standard email from a delivery company which offered tracking of the object posted with them. There was no mention of its contents; it simply informed the recipient that an attempt had been made to deliver the package to the address given, which Harry immediately recognised as the distribution centre. But as no one had been there and the package required to be signed for, it had been returned to the delivery firm's local distribution centre in London and there awaited to be picked up and signed for.

Harry noted down the address and determined to fetch the package himself in the morning.

He slept fitfully that night, excited by the prospect of picking up the package and hopefully some new clue that he could pass on to Raymond and the team. He tossed and turned as he mulled over what the package might contain. Important files? More samples of the drug? Or another counterfeit drug the dealers had been working on?

*

Finally morning came. He was awoken by his mother calling him down for breakfast. He was surprised that he had slept. He must have drifted off, despite his inner turmoil. He didn't think that he had slept long, not from the fuzziness of his head.

He dressed quickly and raced down the stairs. He was aware of his mother emerging from the kitchen as he threw the front door open and fled down the garden path.

His mother reached the door a few seconds later but could only stand open-mouthed as Harry jogged down the street and managed to board a bus that was in the process of moving off.

chapter forty-three

While Slab sat in front of the television, flicking through seemingly endless TV channels in Amrita Banerjee's apartment, Raymond and Amrita Banerjee studied the reams of emails that Harry had forwarded and copied in the police department on. Most, while relevant to their investigation, were of no real help in identifying the perpetrators or in locating the factory where the drugs were being produced.

Amrita Banerjee propped her head up with her hand as she carefully studied each page in turn – most simply referred to quantities of Erexat, but some others clearly referred to apparent counterfeit drugs that the group were producing and prices of same. Others were just chat between the factory owners and their customers. Raymond sat beside her. He too studied the email attachments but was relying on the police sergeant to pick out the relevant ones.

When Amrita took a comfort break, Raymond continued to scroll down the emails. He studied each in turn, disregarding most. He felt for Amrita Banerjee, as clearly both of them by now were growing somewhat weary of reading information that didn't really help their cause. He was becoming increasingly pessimistic of actually finding something of relevance. Yawning, he opened up yet another email and glanced at the contents.

He was just about to discard the email, which had been an incoming one obviously from a supplier of some of the basic ingredients that counterfeiters had ordered. At first it simply appeared to be a short missive confirming that the required products were available and ready for shipment. The buyers could expect delivery within the next couple of days. As Raymond scrolled down though the correspondence, he quickly realised that the topmost email was one of a series of messages back and forth from the supplier to the purchaser. The messages were spread over a number of pages. Most of the dialogue was the purchaser detailing his or her needs and the supplier replying with availability, timescales and costs, but near the bottom of the dialogue the purchaser had revealed a delivery address for the products.

He read it over to himself one more time, then called excitedly to Amrita Banerjee. 'Have you heard of a place in Delhi called Tilak Ngar?'

'Why do you ask?' she replied as she returned from the bathroom, a puzzled expression on her face.

'This email.' He pointed at the screen. 'Look here.' 'This appears to be the delivery address of the base chemicals for the production of the drug they went on to sell.'

'Tilak Nagar.' Amrita mulled over the address. 'Yes, that makes sense.'

'What do you mean?' asked Raymond, hardly now able to contain his expectation.

'Tilak Nagar, it's in the Old City, just off Chandni Chowk—'

'Shandy, what?' Raymond asked impatiently.

'No, Chandni, Chandni Chowk,' Amrita replied curtly. 'Chandni Chowk is a boulevard that runs westward from the Red Fort. You've heard of the Red Fort?'

'Mmmm, yes, of course,' Raymond lied.

Amrita looked at him sceptically. 'Chandni Chowk is a wide road, and unlike other parts of the city, it actually has a divide running down the centre of the road to keep vehicles on the right, or should I say left, side of the road.'

'That's a novelty,' replied Raymond, smiling as he thought of the chaotic traffic systems he had already witnessed in this overcrowded city.

'More importantly,' Amrita continued, ignoring Raymond's jibe, 'it has a lot of quite large buildings on it and in the numerous side streets that branch off it, many of which, in places, overhang the sidewalk. It is possible that some of those might be large enough to house a drugs factory.'

'Possibly, yes,' Raymond mused. 'Any operation such as this doesn't necessarily need a lot of space. In the past many successful enterprises have originated simply out of somebody's kitchen.'

'Even more of relevance,' Amrita continued, 'along the length of and in the side streets off of Chandni Chowk, there are many arcades.'

'And Tilak Nagar?' Raymond asked again.

'Tilak Nagar is an area along the Chandni Chowk which is famous for its market.'

Raymond looked at her quizzically. 'So…?'

'So the Tilak Nagar market, like most others in Delhi, sells lots of different things, but…' She paused.

Raymond stared at her.

'But,' she continued, 'it is most famous for its chemical market.'

Amrita sat back contentedly and fixed Raymond with a self-satisfied look.

Raymond took a moment to think things through.

'A chemical market? Of course, of course, that makes

perfect sense. If the factory is there, then they could access many of the ingredients that they needed, right there on their doorstep; only then would they have to order in those that weren't immediately available.'

He got to his feet and paced back and forth across the room.

Slab seemed to sense the change in atmosphere; he put down the TV remote and turned to face Amrita and Raymond. 'What's going on?'

'I think we have a breakthrough, Slab,' Raymond confirmed. 'We might have found the factory where the drug is being made. So what should we do next?' Raymond was thinking out loud.

Amrita remained silent, thinking over the options.

Slab just stared at them.

Finally, Amrita spoke. 'I think I should inform Inspector Gupta,' she said.

'But shouldn't we just follow this up ourselves?' pleaded Raymond.

Slab kept silent.

'I thought of that,' said Amrita Banerjee. 'But what realistically can we do? There are only the three of us – you have already been threatened. I think that realistically we have done all we can at present.'

Reluctantly, Raymond was forced to agree. Even with Slab's presence they wouldn't stand a chance against a gang of drug dealers.

'Okay, do it,' he said.

Amrita lifted the phone, dialled the number of police headquarters and asked to be put through to DCI Gupta.

Raymond watched as she waited to be put through to her boss.

After several minutes he seemed to come online. Raymond

could hear his disgruntled voice asking Amrita where she was and what she was up to.

'Sir, Sir...' She tried to interrupt his flow. 'I have important information. I think I know where the counterfeiters' factory is.' She paused.

There was further dialogue from DCI Gupta's end, though Raymond couldn't make out what was being said.

'I don't think how I came across the address is important at the moment, Sir. What is important is that we act quickly and try to seal off the area and take down the factory ASAP.'

Further conversation ensued, with Amrita Banerjee pleading her case, but apparently being repeatedly rebuffed by her superior officer.

Finally DCI Gupta rang off and Amrita slowly replaced the telephone receiver. She turned to Raymond and the increasingly incredulous Slab. 'He won't act, at least not until I report directly to him and explain where the information came from.'

'What? Where?'

'I'll have to go to headquarters and see him. I'll keep you out of it. As far as everybody's concerned, you are back in Switzerland. I'll say that I was just copied in to the emails from UMBRA for information and to keep the investigation alive. As far as anybody knows I just came across the address almost by accident as I pursued my enquiries.'

'I can't say I'm happy,' replied Raymond. 'But if he is insisting that you see him, you better go and get things moving as fast as you can. We'll keep our heads down here and wait for you to come back and let us know what's happened.'

Amrita got to her feet and, without glancing round at her fellow conspirators, turned and made her way out of the apartment.

Raymond and Slab sat quietly, not speaking.

Finally it was who Slab broke the silence. 'I don't trust that Gupta chap,' he growled.

'Couldn't just be that you don't like anyone in authority in general, or the police in particular, Slab?'

Slab contemplated what Raymond had said. 'I suppose that could be part of it. But I still don't trust that Gupta chap.'

'I think I know what you mean, Slab. But what can the two of us do? Maybe we should just leave it to the authorities and not try to interfere.' He paused, but then, turning to look out the window, 'Though maybe, just maybe...'

'Maybe, what?' asked Slab, rising to his feet.

'Maybe, rather than just sit here and wait, we could go and have a quick recce of the area before the cops get there.'

'I'm in,' asserted Slab, just glad to actually get doing something practical. He switched off the television and made for the door.

'Hold on. Hold on, Slab,' Raymond shouted after him. 'We can't just go there. They'll spot you, I mean us, a mile off. We'll need to disguise ourselves, and we need a plan.'

Slab returned to the room and sat back down, glancing menacingly around.

chapter forty-four

They had borrowed some typical Indian clothes by bribing a couple of members of an Indian family that lived next door to Amrita. They then slipped out a back door leading onto a small alleyway in order to avoid any chance of being observed. Raymond led the way; Slab followed a few steps behind, constantly looking over his shoulder to ensure that no one followed.

At the end of the alleyway they stepped out onto a main street. It was noisy and bustling, with people pushing past each other in order to make headway. Cars and tuk-tuks buzzed by centimetres from the pedestrians, their horns constantly sounding and their drivers shouting instructions to one another or an unfortunate pedestrian who got too close.

Despite the local garb, Slab still drew puzzled expressions. He was of a very different shape to the generally thin and gaunt local population. The garments were ill-fitting, stretched to capacity as they were by his bulky frame. Overall he gave a not very credible, if somewhat ridiculous, impersonation of a native. His turban was tightly bound around his head, but his pale Glaswegian features were hard to disguise. Raymond decided not to pass comment; he at least seemed to blend in and had slipped through the crowds without apparent recognition or query.

Hailing a passing tuk-tuk, they jumped in. The driver turned and stared quizzically at Slab as he manoeuvred himself awkwardly into the seat in the confined space of the small vehicle.

The driver turned back and assumed his usual driving position when Slab, now seated, returned his stare, accompanied by a look of malevolence.

'Where to, boss?' the driver asked without turning around once more.

'Take us to the Tilak Nagar area off the Chandni Chowk,' Raymond barked, annoyed that the driver, by the tone of his question, clearly had recognised that they were not of local origin.

'Yes, yes, Sir. I know where that is.' He spoke with a typical Delhi dialect, putting an emphasis on almost every individual word in turn. 'Any particular reason, Sir, why you want to go there?'

'Just want to meet up with somebody, that's all,' Raymond replied impatiently, making it clear to the driver that no further explanation would be forthcoming.

The tuk-tuk sped through the congested streets, driver and customers conversing no more. The driver, though, yelled and gesticulated at much of the traffic around him as he weaved his way towards their destination.

After no more than fifteen minutes, Raymond and Slab were extracting themselves from the small taxi. Raymond paid the driver and added a generous tip, which he hoped the driver would accept as a token to move away and not mention his two strange passengers to anyone else. They then made their way through the melee of people moving back and forth, most carrying bundles, some on their head. Many of the bundles appeared impossibly large and to be defying gravity.

Finally, Raymond stopped. Slab, not paying attention, being drawn to the sights and sounds around him, collided into the back of Raymond.

'Sorry, pal,' he grunted.

'Pay attention, Slab,' said Raymond, shaking himself free. 'Look, I think that's the building.' He pointed to a two-storey building with a rickety wooden staircase climbing up the outside. Most of the windows were boarded up and the building looked to be in poor state of repair. Despite its dilapidated appearance, there appeared to be a man standing guard at the front entrance. He leant back on the wall behind him. He was wearing a clean white linen suit and shiny black leather shoes. His black greased-back hair and reflective sun glasses completed the look of someone out of place in the backstreet in which he found himself.

There was no sign of any police activity.

The guard inclined his head as he lit a cigarette, then, blowing smoke from his mouth after inhaling the first lungful, he glanced up and down the street, looking for intruders.

Raymond pressed himself back against the wall of a house behind him and, outstretching his arm, pushed Slab back too. He raised his right index finger to his lips to tell Slab to remain silent.

They remained motionless as they watched the guard pull himself up from his slouched position against the wall and then pace back and forth, surveying the surrounding district. Suddenly he turned and made for the door itself. He shouted something up an inner staircase; it looked as if someone had called to him and he was replying. Then, in a bound, he was through the door and was scaling the staircase within.

Raymond signalled to Slab to remain where he was whilst he started to ease himself along the wall and closer to the target building.

He stopped – a number of men, including the guard, were emerging from the house. Each seemed to be carrying a bundle of some sort.

Raymond cursed under his breath. Where was Gupta and the police raid?

Raymond signalled to Slab to back off and the two of them retreated down the street, finally turning left into a small quiet alleyway.

'I think they are clearing out,' muttered Raymond.

Slab nodded his agreement. 'Want me to go in and get them?' he asked, a clear threatening tone to his voice.

'No, let me ring Amrita and see what's going on,' he replied through gritted teeth.

Raymond pulled out his mobile phone and punched in the number of Amrita Banerjee's mobile.

It took several minutes for her to answer.

'What's happening your end?' he barked down the phone.

'I'm sorry, Raymond,' came the reply. 'DCI Gupta won't do anything till he is certain of the facts. He says he's sent somebody down to have a look at the place and then, and only then, will he organise a raid.'

'Well, we haven't seen anybody sneaking around trying to reconnoitre the place.'

'What do you mean, you haven't seen anybody? Please tell me you are not down there?'

'We couldn't just sit around. Anyway, can you please try and persuade Gupta to act? It looks like most of the gang are fleeing the nest.'

'Okay, okay, I'll do my best. But please be careful, don't do anything foolish. It will be me that will get the blame.'

'Okay, okay, but please just get him to get a move on.'

Raymond did feel sorry for Amrita. She was, he surmised,

between a rock and a hard place, caught between Raymond and her somewhat intransigent boss.

It was a further hour before Raymond and Slab heard the sound of approaching police sirens. Raymond put down the cup of coffee that he had been sipping slowly at, as he and Slab had sat and waited patiently in a nearby café after Amrita Banerjee had pleaded with them not to approach the building but to wait for her arrival.

Two marked police vans swung around the corner at the far end of the building, screeched to a halt, the vans' back doors swung open and a group of heavily armed men wearing body armour jumped out and ran towards the building. They stopped, taking cover at the front entrance, then one of the group signalled them forwards and the others brushed past, rushing through the doorway and up the staircase.

A lot of shouting and banging of doors followed before one of those who had entered the building re-emerged and waved to those remaining outside that it was safe to enter. It was only then that Raymond spotted Amrita Banerjee and her boss getting out of an unmarked vehicle further down the road.

Raymond stood up and was about to make his way towards them. It was Amrita who spotted him first and tried to quietly signal to him with flicks of her head to try and make him disappear into the now assembled and watching crowd, but DCI Gupta seemed to sense his colleague's unease and followed her gaze, spotting Raymond, made all the more obvious by the hulking figure of Slab who now followed him.

'What is he doing here?' He turned to confront Amrita. 'You told me they had left India.'

'I thought they had,' she lied.

'Well, clearly they haven't.' Gupta was beside himself with rage, but he at least superficially suppressed the anger he felt at being duped and, forcing a smile, turned to face the pair, who by now had nearly reach them.

'Mr McNally and Mr... Mr...?'

'McBride,' added Raymond.

'Mmmm, yes. McBride. Quite so.' The police chief turned towards Slab, who nodded in greeting. 'And to what do we owe this pleasure?' he asked. 'I was led to believe that you had left our pleasant land.' He turned his gaze to glare disapprovingly at his sergeant.

Raymond picked up on the body language and countered. 'Amrita knew nothing of this. It was entirely our own idea.' He inclined his head towards Slab, including him in the conspiracy theory.

Slab nodded in agreement, though not quite sure why he did so. Raymond continued, 'We were told that if we left, Maria would be released. We just wanted to make sure that that did actually happen. But it hasn't, has it?'

Gupta was forced to concede the fact.

'So if she is still held captive, we just felt we had to stay and try to help in any way that we could.'

'This is most irregular,' Gupta interrupted. 'I should have been informed.' Again he glanced down at Amrita suspiciously.

In return she simply shrugged her shoulders and forced a weak smile.

'Well, as we're here, can we see what you've found?'

Gupta was about to protest, but Raymond had already turned to make his way through the open doorway. Gupta's protest was blocked, as was his progress by the large frame of Slab, who moved himself between the DCI and Raymond before himself turning around and following Raymond up the stairway.

On reaching the room above, Raymond looked around, trying take everything in before Gupta had a chance to have him evicted.

Police were swarming everywhere over the small interior. There was a single desk at the far end of the room and a couple of cupboards; both appeared empty as their doors hung open, having already been accessed by the police. Otherwise, apart from a few discarded plastic sacks, the room appeared empty.

'Looks like we were too late.' Gupta's voice echoed behind the pair as the DCI entered the room.

Raymond continued to prowl around the room. He tore open a few of the plastic sacks, but there was nothing but household rubbish within. He prowled around the room, looking for any hidden entrance or door that might conceal something of greater importance to the investigation and, more importantly, for any evidence that Maria had been held here.

There was none.

As he moved around the confined space, pushing aside some of the police officers as he did so, it became apparent to him that this was not what they were looking for.

'This isn't it,' he announced to no one in particular.

'What do you mean?' asked Gupta, becoming increasingly agitated at Raymond's presence and interference.

'Can't you see?' Raymond gesticulated around the room, exasperation in his voice. 'This place is much too small to house a drug-producing factory; it's probably just office space somewhere to collate and process orders. Look around you – there are no benches, no pipettes, ovens or even Bunsen burners. There are no traces of any chemicals. Surely you are not going to suggest that they moved all of that before they did a flit?'

Gupta swallowed hard. 'Let's just leave it to the professionals, okay?' He turned to leave.

Raymond threw his hands up in exasperation.

He looked at Amrita, who had remained standing motionless, watching the departure of her boss.

Finally he said to her despairingly, 'We are no further on, are we?'

chapter forty-five

Brian Thompson was alone in the laboratory; it was late in the evening and everyone else had long since departed for home. He had toiled throughout the day trying to break down and analyse the tablets that Raymond had collected from the victims' families. Initial inspection had revealed that all the tablets were entirely similar in appearance, weight and markings, suggesting that they emanated from a single source – it would be too much of a coincidence otherwise. There were important differences in appearance from UMBRA's own product: they were a slightly different size and the markings were different. But these were not things, he suspected, that the average consumer would pick up on or be worried about.

For a number of hours he had painstakingly performed a number of chemical analytical techniques to try to break down and identify the various elements in the counterfeit drug's make-up in order to identify if there were any important differences from their own agent. He trolled through the latest results from the chromatography he had performed, studying carefully and comparing those of the original UMBRA drug and the counterfeit agent. Immediately he noted a misalignment in a single area between the two samples. Not trusting the result, as any good scientist would, he went back and re-ran the test. Several minutes later he compared the two new analyses. Same result – a discrepancy between the two.

'Got you,' he announced to himself.

Now all he had to do was identify the rogue agent or agents within the counterfeit drug.

He slid the wheeled office chair on which he sat across to a nearby bench. He prepared a solution of the tablet and inserted it into the mass spectrometer. As Brian knew, the spectrometer would turn the atoms that made up the compound into ions, which it would then separate by passing them, firstly through an electric field and then through a magnetic field, so that all the individual parts would then fan out into a spectrum. Each area of the spectrum would be like an individual fingerprint helping to identify the culprit.

Eventually, supping on a cup of coffee to ward off tiredness and following the repeated testing and further painstaking analysis of the drug's chemical make-up, he was finally able to lean back in his chair, nearly falling off it in the process due to the stiffness in his limbs, and smile contentedly to himself.

'So that's the problem.' He whistled to himself.

He checked his watch; to his surprise it was 4am. The time had flown by unnoticed as he had been totally absorbed by his detective work.

He mentally tried to work out the time in India. He recalled that there was a five (or was it six?) hour difference. He was a bit befuddled; the tiredness he felt was only now really starting to kick in. Anyway, he reasoned India's time was ahead of the UK, so it would be well into the morning out there.

He lifted the receiver from the telephone attached to wall near the laboratory entrance and dialled Raymond's mobile number slowly and carefully so as not to make a mistake in his current state of mind.

After only a couple of rings, Raymond answered a little warily.

Brian reasoned that the number he was ringing from was not one that Raymond, nor his phone, would immediately recognise.

'Raymond? Hi, it's Brian.'

'Brian?' Raymond replied, still a note of equivocation in his voice. Then, after a few seconds' silence, 'Sorry, sorry, Brian, of course. You took me a little by surprise. I wasn't really expecting a call from you.'

'Sorry to take you by surprise,' Brian continued. 'How are things going out there?'

'Don't ask. I thought we had something, but it turned out to be very little and now we are being made to feel that we have outstayed our welcome. Anyway, what can I do for you?'

Brian could barely hold back his excitement and was once again fully awake. Given Raymond's bad fortune, he realised that what he had found may help lift his spirits too.

'A bit of good news, I hope.'

'Good news? I could certainly do with some.'

'I think I have identified the problem with the rogue drugs.'

'Go ahead.' It was Raymond's turn to wake up.

'Well,' Brian continued quickly. 'I ran some – well, actually many – different tests…' He went on to start to detail the types of investigative procedures that he had undertaken, only to be interrupted by an increasingly impatient Raymond.

'Okay, okay, Brian. So what's the bottom line?'

'Yeah, sorry, just got a bit carried away. After the analyses I can confidently say that the chemical make-up of the active ingredients in the original and the counterfeit drugs are absolutely identical.'

Raymond could feel his shoulders starting to slump. 'And that's the good news?' he asked dejectedly.

'No, no, wait you haven't heard it all. The active ingredients may be the same, but the fillers are definitely different.'

'Fillers, fillers, what do you mean?'

'The filler is what we mix with the active ingredients to bind then together and to harden the whole into a tablet.'

'Okay, I'm with you so far.'

'Well, the filler is usually an inert substance, usually a plant extract or the like. Cellulose is probably the commonest used.'

'Yes?' Raymond was growing impatient again.

'Okay, so the analysis I ran revealed that, yes, there was a plant extract filler, but it wasn't the one we use and, and, more importantly, it is not inert.'

Raymond sat forward, now listening intently to what Brian was trying to say.

'The counterfeiters appear to have used a different plant extract altogether – for some reason they have used an extract from a plant called *Ephedra Sinica*, probably simply because of its availability. It grows mainly in South West Asia, but many other places as well – it is called Asmania in Hindi. It's a shrub which, uncultivated, reaches about one metre high…'

'Please, Brian, less of the horticulture. Get to the point.'

'The point is,' Brian replied, a little tetchy at having been interrupted in full flow and trying to demonstrate the research he had carried out on his boss's behalf. 'The point is ephedra, ephedra.'

'What are you going on about?' It was Raymond's turn to be a bit tetchy.

'Ephedra… Ephedrine, don't you see? That's where it comes from… This plant.' Brian couldn't keep the smugness out of his voice, so proud was he at having made the discovery.

'Ephedrine, you mean the basis of amphetamine?'

'Amphetamines, crystal meth, MDMA or ecstasy, as we know it. It turns out that amphetamine derivatives from this plant ephedra have been used for medicinal purposes for centuries.'

'So the counterfeiters have included this compound in their product? By mistake?' Raymond queried.

'Well, it's certainly there. Whether by mistake or design I couldn't say.'

'You mean they could have included it deliberately?'

'Well, it's a theory.'

'Why on earth would they do that?' Raymond asked disbelievingly.

'The amphetamine group of drugs lift spirits, in extreme cases cause euphoria. So that might heighten the sexual experience and, of course, amphetamines can be quite addictive.'

'Both reasons why the customer might come back for more?'

'Exactly,' confirmed Brian.

'However,' he continued, 'it could simply have been that the plant was easy to obtain in India and equally easy to process. Especially given the risks.'

'Of course, of course,' Raymond added. 'That would explain everything. Amphetamine-type drugs raise blood pressure, cause cardiac arrhythmias, both of which can lead to heart attacks or strokes! Well done, Brian, that's the answer. Well done!'

'I'm going to report my findings to the Committee for Safety of Medicines, the General Medical Council and, of course, the police. It may take a bit of heat off UMBRA.'

'That's great, Brian, go ahead, but I still worry that if we can't stop this drug on the ground our problems are only likely to continue. We can inform all the authorities we can think of, but there is still public opinion to consider – who's going to risk taking Erexat if we can't be absolutely sure that it's safe?'

Brian rang off and Raymond paced up and down, trying to make sense of this latest information and how best to react to it.

chapter forty-six

Maria sat dejectedly, back against the wall, her feet and legs tucked up to her body, her arms wrapped tightly around them. It had been a long, cold night. It had been quiet through the night-time hours, but now she could hear some noise coming from the other side of the locked door. There appeared to be a number of people beyond the door moving about and exchanging greetings in Hindi. She herself was feeling more and more unwell. She was having intermittent bouts of explosive diarrhoea and she felt nauseous now most of the time. Her mouth felt dry and she licked her lips to try to moisten them and relieve some of the soreness from the cracks that appeared within them. There was little relief to be gained, as her tongue was as dry as her lips. She tried to raise herself up but was surprised at how weak she had become. It had been days since she had been able to keep any food down, and now even the sight or smell of it made her stomach churn. Even the water that her jailers had left made her feel ill; it had a peculiar smell and was not the crystal-clear liquid that she was used to at home. She suspected that water to be the cause of her stomach problems and hence her downward spiral into malnutrition.

The door opened and one of her jailers stepped into the gloomy space of the room. He looked towards Maria, having just scanned the room to ensure no intruders or traps to aid her escape. Maria remained seated on the floor, unable or unwilling to rise. She looked up at him with bloodshot eyes, eyes which would have been tearful if it were not for the dehydration that overwhelmed her.

Seeing her pitifully weak state, the man sank down onto his hunkers beside her; he gripped her chin in one hand while reaching behind him to remove a small bottle from where it was attached to his belt below the small of his back.

He forced her head back and raised the water bottle to her lips. Water spilled down her chin and onto her stained and dirty clothes. She spluttered and choked on the warm liquid. Then she felt the nausea rising and she vomited what little she had down her jailer's shirt.

He threw her aside and leapt to his feet, pawing at the wet mess on the front of the shirt. He said something to Maria that she couldn't understand, though its intent was clear from the menace on his face.

He turned and called to another man who was lurking behind the door. After a few moments this other man appeared. At first, he just stood in the doorway; Maria couldn't make out his features other than that he was a tall, rather rotund figure as she blinked at the man silhouetted by the light coming from the room behind and steaming into the gloom of her prison cell.

The second man stepped further into the room and she could now make out his features more clearly; he was bald but with a small black moustache and a round face. Under normal circumstances Maria would have found his appearance a little comical, almost a caricature of an Indian stereotype. But this man was no gentleman. He waved the first man aside and then lowered himself to Maria's level. He positioned his face directly facing hers and moved it threateningly to within a couple of inches. Maria tried to pull back, but the wall behind prevented her.

Through gritted teeth, he spoke to her in perfect English. 'We – that is, you and I – are having some trouble with your friends.'

Maria stared up at him.

'We told them to leave India. If they did, then we would set you free.'

Maria didn't say anything.

'We told them we'd free you, but I have now found out that they are still here.'

The other man shuffled his feet behind the larger man and kept his gaze on the wall above Maria.

'If they don't leave, it will be all the worse for you. Do you understand what I'm saying?' There was a vehemence to his tone.

Maria nodded her understanding.

The large man reached behind him to retrieve something from his back pocket.

Maria winced and tried to draw back, fearing he was about to pull out a knife or worse.

Slowly the man brought his hand back around.

Maria closed her eyes.

'Open your eyes,' he shouted.

As she did as she was bid, he showed her what he now held in his clenched fist.

It was a mobile phone.

Maria heaved a sigh of relief.

'I want you to ring your boss. I want you to tell him that you are okay, but he and his colleague, that ugly brute of a man, must pack up and leave. Leave right now and not come back. Otherwise it will be the worse for you. Tell them if they want to see you alive again then they must go, and go now.' He spat the last words; Maria felt some of the spittle hit her face and she grimaced.

Slowly and reluctantly, she took the phone.

'I've put the number in already – all you need to do is press connect. No funny business, okay?'

Maria wondered how he had got Raymond's number, but she did as she was told.

After a few rings the call was answered.

'Raymond?' she uttered in a creaking voice.

'Maria? Maria? Is that you?'

'Yes. Yes,' she replied, choking back tears.

'Where are you? Can we come and get you? What's happened to you?' Raymond spoke quickly; he had so many questions to ask.

'I'm still a prisoner – you have to help me. I'm not well. They say they'll let me go if you leave India.'

At that moment the large man reached for the phone, releasing it from Maria's grasp. He placed a handkerchief over the microphone to disguise his voice and then spoke. 'She's here. She's with us and she's safe. At the moment. You didn't do as we told you, Mr McNally. You have one more chance. Leave or you won't see your pretty young friend here ever again.'

'How did you find out that we—'

But the sentence wasn't finished as the large man had cut him off and had then risen to his feet to tower over Maria once more. 'Let's hope he gets the message this time.' He glared down at the forlorn figure of his prisoner.

Maria looked up at him and then vomited over his shiny black shoes.

chapter forty-seven

Harry had ignored his mother's calls as he had bounded down the road. The bus was just about to pull away from the stop when he had jumped on board. He moved slowly down the moving vehicle, clutching the backs of seats to steady himself. As he made his way to the back of the bus, he could see his mother standing at the gate of their house, looking forlornly at the rear of the bus now making its way along the street.

As he took his seat near the back of the bus, he reached into the inside pocket of his anorak and retrieved the email printout he had brought with him. He studied the address again and then, opening up his mobile, punched it into Google Maps. Harry hadn't really done much solo travelling; his mother, fearful of a seizure occurring in public, had always insisted on accompanying him or driving him herself where he needed to go. In reality it had been years since Harry had had a seizure, and in all likelihood he had grown out of the propensity for them to occur. His neurologist had confirmed as much and had even suggested coming off the medication. This, though, had been strongly resisted by his mother. She had reasoned that Harry himself wasn't aware when he had an attack, yet she had witnessed them in the past and under no circumstances did she wish to take the risk of them starting up again.

Google Maps flagged the destination and suggested a number of possible routes. He choose the shortest bus option, rather than the underground, which he hated, because of the crowds and a feeling of claustrophobia. This option was a journey of approximately fifty-seven minutes with three different buses to catch and a final walk of about six minutes. Harry had confidence that, despite his lack of experience, this would be a walk (or rather a bus ride) in the park.

Alighting the third of the three buses, he again consulted Google Maps for his final directions on foot.

As he rounded the corner, there was the delivery firm's storage depot ahead of him. Clearly it had been built and sited, as it was on the edge of the city, for the convenience of parking and manoeuvring of the delivery vans, many of which, Harry noted, were parked up against the far wall, their work done for the day. The storage facility also boasted a number of visitor's parking bays for people who had missed the arrival of their package to drive in and pick them up. The centre, though, did not really though cater for walk-in clients such as Harry as he puffed his way across the forecourt.

He heaved the heavy wooden door that was the entrance to the building itself open and made his way to the counter across the short hallway. There was nobody behind the counter until, after a few minutes, one of the employees stuck his head around the partition that divided the area behind the counter from the larger sorting office behind.

'Be with you in a minute,' he announced before retreating behind the partition once more.

It was in fact several minutes before he reappeared, wiping a few drops of tea from his upper lip.

'What can I do for you, Sir?' he asked, looking Harry up and down.

Harry's insecurity kicked in; he thought the man behind the desk was viewing him suspiciously probably because of his youthful and rather dishevelled appearance. He strengthened his resolve and stepped forward to the counter, producing the email from his pocket. 'My boss sent me down to pick this packet up. The factory was closed when the driver tried to deliver it, so we got this email.'

The postal worker took the email from Harry and read its contents slowly. He looked again at Harry, who simply smiled in reply.

The man behind the counter examined the email again, then he shrugged his shoulders, turned around and then disappeared behind the partition once more.

Several more minutes past before the man reappeared once more. In his hands he held a small box or container; it measured about twelve inches high, a further twelve inches across and was about eighteen inches long. It was heavily parcelled in brown paper. Paper which bore several postage and other marks. Harry could make out the delivery address as that of the distribution centre that they had raided earlier.

'You'll have to sign for it, and I'll need some ID.'

Harry had predicted this. Of course because of his epilepsy he hadn't yet got a driving licence which most people used as ID, but he had had the foresight to bring his passport, one that he had obtained some years back in the hope of a holiday abroad, a holiday that never materialised. 'Too hot, no proper food and full of foreigners,' his mother had explained. So it was that every year the two of them had always just visited relatives in Blackpool and others in Southport. However, the passport had been necessary on his trip to Basel and was, therefore, no longer a virgin.

The man behind the counter examined the passport carefully, looking down at the picture therein and then back up at Harry. Finally, apparently satisfied, he pushed a sheet of paper over the counter to Harry and asked him to sign.

With some relief Harry snatched at the pen that was offered and quickly signed the document, pushing it back to the other man.

The parcel was then gratefully received into Harry's arms and he turned to leave.

'When will that office reopen?' the man behind the counter asked before Harry was out the door.

'I'm not sure,' was the mumbled reply.

'It's just that we get a lot of parcels for them.' His voice trailed off as Harry strode back across the car park.

*

His mother appeared to be out when Harry returned home. He hoped that she wasn't out looking for him. It wouldn't be the first time that she had come after him when he had left the house without her permission. There had been innumerable times when she had embarrassed him in front of his friends and peers and he had had to slink off home under her watchful eye.

Harry checked each room in turn in case she was sitting in one quietly awaiting his return and then to question him about his whereabouts.

No, she was definitely out.

He let out a sigh of relief; the last thing he wanted right now was an interrogation from his mother. Besides, he was impatient to examine the package that he'd just picked up.

He mounted the stairs, two by two, and pushed open his bedroom door. Placing the parcel carefully on his desk, he shoved the door tightly shut. He couldn't lock it; his mother had forbidden any form of lock or bolt – 'In case you have a seizure in the night.'

Sitting down at the desk, he started to examine his prize in more detail.

There was the distribution centre's address handwritten and emblazoned across the front. There was another address, this one also handwritten but in smaller print on the surface underneath the parcel, taking it that the delivery address was the top. The package had been crudely secured, with layers of Sellotape binding down the plain brown paper packaging.

Harry tore at the paper covering, ripping it off bit by bit as it came apart from the rows of Sellotape. He tossed the paper packaging into his wastepaper bin. Inside was a simple cardboard box, again tightly sealed with Sellotape. He tore off the Sellotape, which at first resisted his attempts to remove it but then split and allowed Harry to access the box's contents.

He placed the box back on the desk and peered within.

Inside were tightly and neatly packed rows upon rows of medicine boxes. All bore the name 'Erexat' and looked extremely genuine, though, as Harry now knew, this was not the case. He pulled out a box and examined it. There was no indication from where it came; indeed, it actually stated UMBRA's address on the packaging.

Harry sat back in his seat and stared at the box and its contents. He started to wonder how it had got through customs with all the checks they were purported to have. But then he reasoned that was why it had to have been delivered by a private delivery firm and not the routine postal system, where checks were more stringent, especially for international parcels. A private firm would offer more flexibility, and even if they were confronted with border sniffer dogs, they would have been trained to detect illegal narcotic-type drugs, not pharmacological agents such as Erexat.

He lifted the box, turned it around and then upside down, so that some of the remaining medicine boxes spilled out onto the floor.

'Damn,' he said as he reached down to replace them.

His expletive had been as much for the lack of any other markings that could help identify the source as for the spilled packages.

He heard the front door open.

'Harry, is that you up there? I'm home.'

'Yes, Mum, just doing a little research on my computer.'

'That damn computer. How many times have I told you not to spend so much time on it?'

'Yes, Mum,' he replied, at the same time gathering up the box and its contents and stuffing them into a cupboard before covering them with discarded clothes.

'Come down and talk to me. I want to know where you went and what you've been up to since you ran off this morning.'

Harry swore under his breath and tried to think of a viable excuse.

He was still thinking as he descended the stairs. His mother was standing at the bottom, looking up at him expectantly as she removed her coat.

'So?' she asked.

Harry quickly formulated a response that he thought she might buy into. 'I just decided, at the last minute, to go to the library and do some background research into the drugs market.'

Seeing the look on his mother's face, he quickly added, 'I mean the pharmaceutical industry, not, obviously, illegal drugs.'

'Obviously.' His mother regarded him sceptically but appeared to accept his explanation.

At least no more was said on the subject.

'I'm going to make us some lunch. Clear up whatever mess you've made up there and then come down and give me a hand.'

'Right, Mum, no problem.' Harry turned and retreated up the stairs.

Over lunch they sat at either end of the small kitchen table. His lunch comprised of a bowls of soup accompanied by a simple ham sandwich; Harry's mother noticed Harry's faraway look. In truth, his mood was one of disappointment rather than anything else – disappointment at not having extracted any really useful information from the package he had intercepted.

Suddenly, he remembered, and in doing so stood up so quickly that he knocked his chair over to his mother's obvious surprise and alarm.

'What the...?'

She never got to finish the question, as Harry had already left the kitchen and was halfway up the stairs.

He dived into his bedroom and knelt down, scrabbling under his desk for his wastepaper basket. Reaching it with his fingertips, he grasped roughly for it and pulled it out into the light of the bedroom.

On top of the pile of discarded papers, food wrappers and paper cups was the brown sheet of wrapping paper, curled up into a ball as he had discarded it minutes earlier. He quickly retrieved it from the pile and attempted to flatten it back out again. Then he turned it over and leant forward to examine the second smaller address that had been scrawled on the underside of the package. He squinted to make out the writing, which was virtually illegible and clearly in a foreign hand. The letters had been formed in an alien manner to that taught in English schools.

He reached over the desktop for a pen and his writing pad and then carefully attempted to transcribe the address onto a sheet of paper.

Slowly the address seemed to reveal itself to him. Excitedly he noted that it appeared to be the return address in case the package didn't reach its intended destination for any reason. It was evident that the parcel had started its journey in India – Delhi, in fact. Harry could barely contain his excitement as he realised that the address in front of him must be the actual address of the factory where the drugs were being made, before being packaged up and sent on to distribution centres like the one here in London.

He struggled with the street and regional details, as they were unknown to him, but he did his best to transcribe them into readable English as he could.

He could hear his mother coming up the stairs.

'Not now, Mum, I'm busy, please.'

He heard her turn around and retreat back down the stairs. He had no doubt he would face a grilling later.

But that was later. What was he to do now? He had the address of the factory in Delhi, but he didn't have Raymond's phone number. He wasn't even sure if his mobile phone would work out there. He slumped down on the bed and looked at the address again.

2955 Kinari Bazar
Katra Shah N Shah
Chandni Chowk
Delhi 110006
INDIA

Obviously it meant nothing to him, but he strongly suspected it would be helpful to Raymond and his team, if it was indeed the factory.

He sat deep in thought until he finally came up with an idea. He reached for his mobile and tapped in the numbers. His call was answered on the second ring. *Swiss efficiency*, he thought.

'Er, hi,' he mumbled. 'Can you put me through to Raymond McNally's office, please?'

'Mister McNally is not available, I'm afraid.' The operator spoke quietly and assuredly.

'I know, I know,' Harry stuttered. 'He's out of the country. But I just need to speak to somebody in his office or department that could contact him for me.'

'Putting you through,' came the reply without any further discussion.

Another few rings, longer this time, until finally the call was answered. 'Hello, Frank Kinney.'

'Mr Kinney. Hi. You probably don't remember me, my name's Harry Boyle, Mr McNally has had me working for him.'

'Yes? I am aware of that fact,' came the reply.

'I know that he's in India trying to track down some counterfeit drug producers.'

'I'm aware of that fact also, Mr Boyle. What is it that you want?' Irritation clearly apparent in his voice.

'You do work for him?' Harry asked.

'I work with him, if that's what you mean?' Frank Kinney replied again, a little tetchily.

'Can you get hold of him for me, do you think?'

'And why would I want to do that?'

'I have some important information for him, it's an address, one I think he's been trying to locate.'

'And what is this address?' Frank Kinney spoke now a little more intently, as if he was paying more attention at last, it seemed to Harry.

Harry read out the address, trying to pronounce the names of the streets as best he could.

'Hold on, give that to me again. Slowly, this time, so that I can write it down.'

Harry repeated the address.

Finally Frank Kinney came back on the line. 'Okay, Harry, isn't it? Listen to me. Don't pass that address on to anybody else – not at the moment, anyway. It could be dangerous. I will contact Raymond myself and pass your information on to him. Leave it with me. Okay?'

'Shouldn't I just talk to—'

'Leave things entirely to me,' Frank Kinney interrupted forcefully.

Then he rang off.

Harry sat dejectedly on his bed, not entirely satisfied with the outcome of the conversation.

chapter forty-eight

Rahul Patel sat behind the large mahogany desk, his arms extended and hands outstretched and resting on the expensive green leather covering. He surveyed the large office space that surrounded him. Over the years, as his wealth had increased, he had made a point of not being bashful about it. Around the walls hung a number of original and expensive paintings; some were youthful, but some were antique, even ancient, one dating back, he had been assured, to the eighteenth century. To be honest, he had to admit, the older ones didn't really fit in with the rest of the décor, which was more modern in design, consisting largely of glass and chrome, but it was the undoubtable fact that he had spent many hundreds of thousands of rupees to acquire them that impressed him most and warranted their display.

The plush décor of the office contrasted greatly with the unfortunate wretch that knelt on the floor on the opposite side of the desk from him. The man was held down by two larger men standing on either side of him.

'Please, Mr Patel, a simple misunderstanding, please.'

Rahul Patel leant forward and fixed the kneeling man with a stare. 'It was on your recommendation that we employed the informer Amit Saagar. Was it not?'

The prisoner clasped both hands in a pleading position; tears welled up in his eyes. He had heard what had happened to his friend Amit Saagar and he knew of Rahul Patel's reputation.

'Please, Mr Patel, he was a friend. His wife was my wife's sister. He was out of work and she asked me to help find him a job,' he wailed loudly. 'I didn't know that he had talked to the police. He seemed a genuine sort of a man.' The tears ran down his cheeks.

'We run a tight organisation here and across Delhi – we do not need unnecessary police interference. Do you understand?'

The man nodded vigorously.

His two guards avoided their boss's eye and simply looked down to the back of their captive's head.

'We run a perfectly legitimate agricultural chemical industry here in Delhi, do we not?'

The kneeling man again nodded, even more vigorously.

'You have worked with us for a few years now, haven't you? Do you have any reason to suspect anything is illegal with our operation?'

The man nodded, then shook his head, trying to answer both questions at once.

'So why do you think your friend Mr Saagar contacted the police?'

'I have no idea.' He paused then continued, 'It was only after you sent him to work in that other place...' His voice trailed off.

'What other place?' Rahul Patel looked hard at the man. 'Oh, you mean our other factory?'

'Yes, yes... It was when you heard that he had been to university to study pharmacy that you moved him. Don't you remember?'

Patel thought for a moment before remembering that it was true. He himself had hoped to make better use of Saagar's skillset rather than confine him simply within his agricultural chemicals empire.

'And you knew nothing of his covert activities with the police?'

'Of course not, of course not. I am but a humble servant.' He bowed over, his head touching the floor. 'Please believe me.'

Rahul Patel thought for a few minutes as the unfortunate man sobbed loudly on the other side of the desk.

Finally he addressed one of the guards. 'Rohit. Get him out of here.' Then, to the prisoner, 'You, you, go back to work where we can keep an eye on you. If I hear anything further about you which might harm the organisation, it will be all the worse for you. Do you understand me?'

'Thank you, thank you, boss.' He rose to his feet, wiped his face and was promptly marched out of the office.

Rahul Patel took out a handkerchief and carefully wiped the sides of his mouth. He hated the way that saliva gathered there when he was angry with someone. But he had more weighty matters to attend to and was glad to have dismissed the entourage. He reached for the telephone on his desk.

He looked up the number and dialled it.

It was answered quickly.

'Mr Patel?' the voice at the other end queried. The caller's number had obviously registered on the recipient's mobile screen. 'What can I do for you?'

'I think we have a problem.'

'A problem? What do you mean?'

'Mr McNally and his team haven't gone home, have they? Despite my explicit orders to you to get them out of India.'

There was silence at the end of the phone.

'So, DCI Gupta, what is your next move?'

'We still have the girl. I'm confident that they will go sooner or later.'

'I don't share your confidence, I'm afraid.'

'So what do you want me to do?' The voice at the other end betrayed some apprehension at the expected answer.

'I am going to close the factory down. At least temporarily.'

'Close it down? Why?'

'I have heard that it may only be a matter of time before you will be asked to close it down officially.'

'I haven't heard anything.' Gupta sounded disbelieving.

'Trust me. I have received some worrying information regarding a breach of security.'

'What about the girl?' Gupta asked.

'Get rid of her.'

'Get rid of her? How?'

'That is entirely up to you, Inspector.'

Rahul Patel heard Gupta sigh and then put the phone down. He hoped that Gupta was up to the job. However, if he wasn't, he knew a man, or men, who would be.

chapter forty-nine

Raymond, Slab and Amrita sat in Amrita's front room and tried to work out what to do next.

'They seem to know every move we make,' Raymond argued. 'They know we stayed on in India and now I'm really worried for Maria's safety.'

'There must be a leak somewhere,' Amrita interjected before he could continue.

'We need a plan,' he said. '...And we need to keep it to ourselves.'

Slab had been quiet; he sat on one of the cushioned high-backed chairs and stared at his feet. Now he looked up, more interested in the conversation.

'We are under real pressure to leave,' Raymond summarised.

'Maybe you should,' Amrita stated.

Now it was Slab's turn to interrupt. 'These kind of people. There's absolutely no guarantee that even if we were to leave, they would free her. I would'na,' he added. 'She's too valuable as a tool with which to manipulate you.'

'I know, I know you're right, Slab, but they seem to know everything we're up to and we seem to have reached an impasse anyway.'

'Is there anything more we can do to try to get more information to try and get ahead of the game?' Amrita asked.

'It's a long shot, but we did leave Harry with that computer and access to all our files – he might have come up with something more.'

Raymond rose to his feet and retrieved his mobile from his jacket which was hanging over the back of another chair.

Amrita and Slab watched him as he dialled the number and raised the phone to his ear.

'Hello, Mrs Boyle. It's Raymond, Raymond McNally here.' Then he added, 'I'm ringing from India.'

After a moment's hesitation, she replied, 'He's here, but I'm very worried about him. He has been very agitated – he didn't sleep last night. I heard him pacing about his room into the small hours. With his condition, lack of sleep is very dangerous. His consultant told him so.' She paused, but then added, 'I wish he hadn't got involved with you.'

As she spoke, Raymond detected footsteps coming quickly down a set of stairs and then approaching the phone.

'Is that Mr McNally? It is, isn't it? Mother, give me the phone, I need to speak to him.'

There were some muffled sounds; his mother had clearly covered the mouthpiece with her hand whilst she remonstrated with her son.

Harry seemed to win the battle, as his voice came on the line. 'You got my message, then?' he asked.

Puzzled by the question, Raymond hesitated and then answered, 'What message?'

'I rang your office. They said they'd contact you.'

'No, I never heard anything, but to be fair we have been moving around a lot and there hasn't always been phone coverage. What did you want, anyway?'

'I think I've got the address of the factory that you've been looking for,' Harry replied excitedly.

'What?!' Raymond exclaimed, glancing around at his compatriots and signalling his excitement to them at the revelation. 'How...? How, did you get it?'

Harry went on to try and explain to Raymond about the package, its retrieval from the depot and the return address on it. He reached into his pocket to pull out the piece of paper with the address on it. He retrieved it and was about to read the address to Raymond when he felt it. At first he tried to dismiss it. But the sensation grew and became more powerful. It was like a 'déjà vu', an 'I've been here before' feeling. He recognised it immediately.

'No, no!' he exclaimed.

'What is it, Harry?' Raymond asked, concerned by the interruption.

There came no reply.

Raymond then heard a clunk as the receiver hit the floor, followed by a louder but lower-pitched thump.

He heard Harry's mother scream in the background.

He could hear her footsteps approaching, but they were muffled by a grunting noise, as if someone was struggling to breathe accompanied by a rhythmical banging as if something was repeatedly striking the floor, over and over again, seconds apart.

'Harry, Harry, you'll be okay, you'll be alright,' his mother wailed as the rhythmical noise in the background slowly seemed to abate.

Raymond yelled into the mouthpiece, 'Harry? Mrs Boyle? What's going on?'

There was no reply. But he could hear heavy breathing not far from the fallen receiver and what sounded like Harry's mother sobbing.

He waited a few moments before calling out again. 'Harry? Mrs Boyle.'

He heard the receiver being picked up. It was Harry's mother. 'I knew this would happen. Harry's had a fit, a big one. Grand mal, they call it. I knew this would happen. He hasn't been sleeping, he's been so agitated about meeting you and being involved in... whatever you're involved in. It's been ages since he had a fit – we thought he'd grown out of it. But here we are, back to square one, and it's your fault.'

Raymond was a little taken aback by the turn of events and more so by Harry's mother clear anger at the effect on Harry's wellbeing.

'Is he going to be alright?' Raymond was genuinely concerned.

A few more minutes passed before Mrs Boyle had regained her composure and felt able to talk to Raymond again.

'Don't worry. I've seen these attacks many times before. It's frightening when it happens, but it's usually over quickly. He'll need to sleep, though. He is usually tired and a bit muddled afterwards. Sometimes he bites his tongue in the attack and that's quite sore, but I've checked and he hasn't done it this time, thank goodness.'

'I'm so, so sorry Mrs Boyle. We never wanted this to happen. Harry was just so keen to help, and to be honest we couldn't have managed without him.'

'I know. I'm sorry too – it isn't your fault, I know that.' Her tone had softened. 'He was just so excited about passing on the address he'd found.'

'Do you know the address, Mrs Boyle?' Raymond felt a little callous asking her when her son had just collapsed, but he reasoned time was of the essence.

'No, I don't.' Her tone had hardened a little. 'But it's here beside him – he had written it down.'

'I'm really sorry to ask, but it is really important, Harry knew that. Can you read it out to me? Would that be possible?'

'Hold on. I'll just place him in the recovery position. He needs to be on his side till he comes round properly, otherwise his tongue can fall back and he could choke on it.'

Raymond heard shuffling noises as Harry's mother positioned him safely.

Then she came back on the line. 'I've got it. Oh my goodness, there are some funny words in this address.'

'Just do your best, Mrs Boyle,' Raymond pleaded. 'Spell out any words you can't pronounce.' He signalled to Amrita to give him her notepad and a pencil.

Harry's mother struggled through the contents of the sheet of paper as best she could. Then Raymond read them back and made any corrections that she indicated.

'Okay, I think we've got it,' he concluded. 'How's Harry?'

'He seems to be coming around. I better get to him. He's often a bit confused, but all it takes is somebody there to reassure him and tell him what's happened.'

'Thank you so much, Mrs Boyle. We are in your, and Harry's, debt. Please, please give him our best and tell him I'll come and see him as soon as I get back.'

'Goodbye, Mr McNally.'

The line went dead.

chapter fifty

Amrita Banerjee studied the sheet of paper that Raymond had given her. On it he had scribbled the address that Harry's mother had dictated to him.

'I know where this is,' she said, still looking at the page. 'It's actually not that far from the offices that we raided earlier. See,' she pointed to the address, 'it's off the Chandni Chowk, the main roadway that we went down to find the other place.'

'Makes sense,' added Raymond. 'Easy to keep tabs on what was going on in the factory.'

Slab rose to his feet and looked back and forth between the two of them.

It was Amrita who grabbed the initiative. 'They may not know we have this—'

'Yet,' interrupted Raymond. 'If past proceedings are anything to go by, then they may already know.'

'I know – I'm not waiting for clearance this time.' She lifted the telephone receiver and hurriedly barked some orders down it, concluding the conversation with, 'Just go. Now. We have no time to lose.'

'Who were you talking to?'

'Remember the armed response team that helped us last time?'

'Yes?'

'Well, I have a friend who is one of the captains of it. He owes me a favour. I just called it in.' She smiled contentedly. 'They are on their way to your address as we speak.'

'We had better go too,' replied Raymond, reaching for his jacket.

The three quickly exited the building and broke into a jog as they reached the street. Amrita Banerjee lead the way, closely followed by Raymond and Slab, who lopped along behind them.

'It's not far,' she shouted over her shoulder. 'No point in taking the car, quicker on foot.'

Raymond had to agree; having now experienced Delhi's chaotic traffic, he had no doubt on foot would get them there a lot faster.

*

As they arrived outside the address that Harry had identified, Raymond could hear police sirens approaching fast. He stopped and, leaning forward, hands on knees, he tried to catch his breath.

Slab arriving a few seconds later, pointed at the two-storey, slightly dilapidated building in front of them and asked, 'This it?'

Raymond nodded his affirmation.

Slab made to push past them and make for the building's front entrance, but Raymond grabbed him by the arm to restrain him. Slabs bulky and muscular frame nearly pulled Raymond over, but the big man stopped and, turning around, fixed him with an angry stare.

'These bastards owe me,' he growled.

'I know, Slab, I know. But listen.' He raised his hand to cup his ear to emphasise the statement. 'The troops are on their way. Let's let them go in first. We don't know what's waiting for us in there. There is no point in you rushing in and getting shot or stabbed, is there? That's not going to avenge your son, is it?'

Slab seemed to relax; he realised the truth in what Raymond was saying. He stood as if rooted to the spot, then he slowly turned his head back to look at the building in question. As he did so, he caught sight of a group of Indian nationals pushing and shoving past each other, some carrying bundles, others empty-handed as they appeared to be ushered out of the building and towards the street by two more smartly dressed men, who were gesticulating and shouting at the fleeing workers.

Slab made to move forward again, but as he did so he was halted in his tracks by the sight of at least four police squad cars and two troop carrier-type vans hurtling down the street towards the factory.

The cars and vans skidded to a halt, and an army of police officers jumped out. The group of workers who were trying to escape were immediately halted in their tracks and pushed up against a wall by the arriving law enforcement officers.

The two men who had been at the rear of the fleeing workers, and had appeared to be directing operations, stopped in their tracks on spying the arriving police. Initially they appeared uncertain as to what to do, but then they turned on their heels and fled back into the factory.

Raymond looked about; none of the police seemed to have spotted the two fugitives in the melee outside the factory gates. He was about to shout at them when, out of the corner of his eye, he detected some rapid movement. He turned only to see Amrita, closely followed by Slab, charging towards the factory entrance in pursuit of the remaining two perpetrators.

'Shit,' he exclaimed, but then turned to follow them.

Inside the factory it was quiet apart from the sound of rapid footsteps crossing the floor above as Raymond, still breathing heavily from the earlier run, had paused to take in the surroundings.

There was no doubt, as he looked around, that this was a chemical factory. All the instrumentation that he recognised from his own career in pharmaceuticals was there spread out in front of him in the large open-plan space of the building. In one corner stood a series of crates. He moved slowly over to take a closer look.

He prised open the lid one of the crates, one that stood on top of just one other. Behind these two were a number of higher piles of crates that stretched nearly to the ceiling and across the breadth of the room.

He peered into the now-open container. It was stuffed full of small medicine boxes, all very similar to UMBRA's own Erexat containers.

'All ready for export,' he whispered to himself, and then involuntarily broke into a smile as he realised that, finally, his quest for the source of the counterfeit tablets was over. This was it. He was in the right place.

As he stood looking down into the crate, he heard a noise behind him. He turned quickly. It was Amrita Banerjee pushing one of the miscreants ahead of her; he had his arms tethered behind his back, held there by a pair of handcuffs. Behind this pair emerged a very sorry-looking man whom Raymond immediately recognised as the other of the two men who had tried to flee, but it was clear that he too was going nowhere as the he was being held by the collar and even partially lifted off the ground by the considerable bulk of Slab, who stood just behind him. Raymond also noted that the unfortunate man had droplets of blood dripping from his nose and mouth, and had been limping quite badly as Slab ushered him along.

'Thanks for your help,' Amrita Banerjee directed sarcastically at Raymond.

'Sorry, I got distracted. Look.' He pointed at the pile of crates in front of him and then lifted out some of the tablet boxes to show her.

There was a loud banging behind them. They all turned simultaneously towards it. Police were flooding into the factory, shouting and banging their shields with their batons, a tactic Raymond had seen on news programmes previously; he had understood it was a tactic to confuse and disorientate rioters or others to be arrested.

The police officers stopped when they spotted the small group huddled together ahead of them. Then one man stepped forward from the rest; he pulled off his helmet and, moving his baton from his right to his left hand, he then outstretched his right in greeting and smiled. 'Amrita.' he exclaimed. 'Good to see you.'

'Thanks for coming, Aarav,' she replied. 'I think we are in the right place.' She gesticulated towards the pile of crates behind her.

'Glad to be of assistance.' He smiled at Amrita as he and two others moved forward to arrest the two captives. They replaced Amrita's handcuffs with plastic ties and then Aarav handed the cuffs back to Amrita.

'Yours, I believe?'

'Thanks again, Aarav. Good job.' She flashed a winning smile in his direction.

Raymond felt a pang of jealousy for the way she had looked at her fellow police officer.

'What's wrong with you?' Amrita asked, catching Raymond's scowling expression.

Raymond winced at being found out.

'You should be happy. It looks like this time we got them. Somehow they had always been one step ahead of us. Again it looked like they were already preparing to clear out before we got here, but this time they were only half a step ahead and we've got them.' She clenched her fist and punched the air in triumph.

Raymond laughed, and he even thought that he detected a small smile emerge at the side of Slab's mouth.

As they congratulated one another, there was a shout from upstairs.

Amrita turned and lead the way up the stairs to find out who was calling and why.

As they walked down the corridor towards the rear of the building, they could hear footsteps ahead of them as other police officers made their way towards the caller from the other direction.

The man who had shouted was standing in the doorway of a small room off the corridor. He was looking into the room and barely noticed Amrita's and the others' arrival.

'Looks like a prison cell,' he said, as much to himself as to them as they stood silently behind him, gazing into the small, dimly lit room.

As Raymond took in the room, he had to agree – and an unpleasant, dirty and dingy cell at that. In the half-light he could make out a discarded water bottle lying in a corner and pieces of decaying food, often surrounded by small piles of vomit and worse, scattered across the floor.

'Maria,' Amrita and Raymond uttered simultaneously.

But there was no sign of her.

chapter fifty-one

Maria put her arms out either side of herself just to try and steady herself as she was thrown from side to side as the car travelled along, braking or swerving intermittently and expectantly. The car boot in which she had been thrown by her captors was small and dark, yet with the vehicle's jolting manoeuvres her head and body were repeatedly bounced against the car's bodywork. She felt sick because of the erratic movements, but also because of her treatment while captive.

As the car moved along, Maria guessed from the erratic movements and the noises outside that they were travelling through the streets of Delhi. Occasionally she could hear the driver talking to another in the car's interior. The words were muffled, but she could make out some of the sounds, which appeared to be in Hindi. The two men's conversation was frequently interrupted by shouting, either from the driver or from more distant voices outside on the roadway. The car horn and those of others sounded frequently.

It was less than an hour ago that the door to her cell had been flung open and as light had streamed into the little dark room, Maria had squinted at the figure standing in the doorway. With the light behind him, she couldn't make out his features, but from the outline of his frame it was obviously her regular jailor, not the rescue that she hoped for.

'Get up,' the man had ordered.

Maria had been sitting on the floor, her back resting against the wall; she tried to struggle to her feet, but she was weakened by her period in captivity. She put her hands on the floor to try to lever herself up in order to assist her legs, which felt heavy and weak.

Impatient with her efforts, her jailor had stepped forward and, putting his arm under hers, he tried to lift her to her feet. Being only partially successful in mobilising her, he called out and a second man appeared at the doorway; this second man was unknown to Maria – she didn't think he had been down here before. This second man grabbed her other arm and between them they hoisted her up.

They part carried, part frog-marched her out of the small room and up a short flight of stairs. They then dragged her down a short hallway. They stopped at a door that led to the outside, and whilst one supported her, the other opened the door and looked around to check that there were no onlookers.

Satisfied he wedged the door open and then returned to support Maria as the three of them made their way through the door to emerge into the heat and light of the building's exterior.

Maria tried to shield her eyes as the bright sun burnt into them, but the men's grip on her arms prevented her from doing so.

They pulled her down a small path, her feet trailing the ground behind her. Reaching the car, they had opened the boot and thrown her roughly in.

A number of minutes passed; Maria guessed they were securing the building once more before they left. Then the car had been kicked into life and started to move.

It seemed like hours in the confines of the boot, but in reality it was probably only fifteen or twenty minutes that the car had travelled through the streets before coming to a halt. A few more minutes passed, then Maria could hear the two men talking again and then one got out and she heard him walking around to the back of the car.

The boot lid was flung open and the man grabbed her arm and pulled her forcefully out. She had no time to get her legs down and so she ended in a crumpled heap on the roadway behind the car. The assailant then let go of her arm, slammed the boot lid shut and then moved off quickly to jump through the open passenger door just as the car started to move off.

Maria watched as he shut the door as the car sped off down the small street. She felt dizzy and weak, and she slumped down on the roadway. There she lay, closing her eyes as much from the relief of being free as from her weakened and frail state.

When she opened her eyes again a few minutes later, she was aware of a small crowd that had gathered around her. She stared up through bloodshot eyes into their inquisitive faces. One woman then bent down and put a rolled-up piece of material that she had bought earlier under Maria's head, then she shouted something that Maria couldn't make out to one of the other bystanders. The man she shouted at turned, pushed his way through the crowd and then disappeared down the road.

Maria struggled to keep awake, weakened as she was by dehydration and malnutrition. It seemed, though, that despite her efforts, she kept lapsing into short periods of semi- or complete unconsciousness.

The next thing that Maria was aware of was being rushed along the street in a wheeled stretcher pushed by two uniformed men. They then lifted both her and the stretcher into the back of a waiting ambulance before setting off, sirens blaring, through the crowded streets.

chapter fifty-two

It was a few days later that Raymond, Slab and Amrita stood around Maria's hospital bed.

A doctor clutching a set of notes approached from the nursing station at the bottom of the ward. He offered a perfunctory greeting and then opened the file and read it for a few moments, flicking from page to page.

Finally, he lifted his head and addressed Maria directly. 'How are you feeling today?'

'Much better, thanks,' she replied.

He turned to Raymond. 'Are you her father?' he asked.

Raymond smiled, though he was taken aback a little; he hadn't considered himself old enough to be her father. Out of the corner of his eye he caught Amrita Banerjee stifling a laugh.

'No, no. Just a friend. We travelled to India together.' Then, realising what he had said was open to misinterpretation, he added, 'We are business colleagues. We were here on business.'

The doctor looked a bit sceptical but seemed to accept Raymond's explanation.

'How is she, Doc? When can we take her home?'

The doctor reverted his attention to Maria and addressed

her directly rather than Raymond. 'Well, young lady, you've done very well. I think that it is time to let you go home.'

Maria raised both hands in a sign of celebration.

'You were quite ill when you arrived. You had gastroenteritis and were severely dehydrated. You probably don't even remember arriving here?'

Maria shook her head to indicate that she did indeed have little or no recollection of being brought into the hospital.

'So,' he continued, 'if I discharge you, you must take it easy for at least the next few days. Agreed?'

Maria nodded.

'We have a suite booked in the Majestic hotel,' Raymond interceded. 'We will take good care of her.'

'You will need to bring some new clothes in for her,' the doctor added. 'Her own had to be burnt, such was the state they were in.'

'I can get some from her case at the hotel,' Slab offered, demonstrating a caring side that Raymond had not previously witnessed from the big man.

The doctor turned to leave and strode back to the nursing station.

'That's great news,' Raymond confirmed.

Maria couldn't contain her excitement at escaping from the noisy and crowed hospital ward. She was grateful for what they had done for her, but as she had improved she became increasingly aware of the environment around her. The hospital had been built by the British during their period of control; it had then probably have been a comfortable place to recuperate. Now it was chaotic to say the least; there were probably at least three times the number of patients it had originally been designed for. Nurses rushed about, constantly cleaning up messes extruded by patients who were clearly very ill. Hardly a day had gone by when Maria hadn't witnessed a death on the ward, with weeping relatives, and after their departure, the body, under a flimsy sheet, then being wheeled past the end of her bed on the way to the mortuary.

Amrita, who had remained silent and stood a little behind Raymond, pushed forward and addressed Maria directly. 'If you are well enough, could you come down to the station and make a formal statement? We need to document what exactly happened to you, from what you can remember, and, more importantly, to see if we can identify the culprits.'

'I don't really know if I can be of any help. Things are a bit muddled. I know there were at least two of them, but I really don't know if I could pick them out.'

'Don't worry.' Amrita placed her hand on Maria's arm to reassure her. 'Anything you do remember will help in our investigation.' Then she added, 'It doesn't have to be today – we'll get you out of here and get you settled in the hotel with Raymond and Slab. Possibly tomorrow? I'll come and get you myself.'

Maria, after a moment's thought, nodded her agreement.

Half an hour later, Slab was wheeling Maria out through the front entrance of the hospital and then lifted her into the back seat of a waiting taxi.

Amrita leant into the car. 'See you tomorrow then?'

'We'll get her there,' Raymond confirmed.

chapter fifty-three

The following morning, Maria sat in Amrita's office. Raymond and Slab sat in the corridor outside, waiting to take her back to the hotel. Amrita and another officer sat across the desk from Maria. Amrita tried to coax Maria through the events of her kidnapping.

She could remember being kidnapped from the hotel and transported to what turned out, from what Raymond had informed her last night in the hotel, to be the drug factory. She recalled being locked in the small room and then getting ill; after that things became blurred and difficult to recall.

With some prompting she remembered some details of her jailers and tried her best to describe one. 'The one that was there mostly, he was not tall – about 1.7 metres tall. He was Indian, obviously,' she added. 'He had a beard and small scar across his cheek.'

'Which cheek?' the second officer asked.

Maria appeared a little confused and tried to think back. 'His left – no, his right, definitely his right.'

'What was he wearing?'

'Just normal clothes. I didn't notice anything unusual about them.'

Amrita and the other officer looked at one another, recognising that it was going to be nigh on impossible to identify the culprit from Maria's sketchy description.

'He had small hands and was wearing at least two rings,' she added hopefully. 'He grabbed me to make me drink, you see.'

Amrita smiled, but she knew this added little more to the outline Maria had already provided.

'You said there was a second man?'

'He only came once. He seemed to be in charge.'

'Can you describe him?'

'Actually, although he only came the once, I got a better look at him. The other man was in and out quickly; this second guy was the one who forced me to ring Raymond. So I do remember him a bit better.'

'Go on,' Amrita said hopefully, leaning forward on the desk.

'He was a big man. Tall, but overweight. He was smartly dressed, unlike the other man. He had the phone in his pocket.'

'What about his appearance?' Amrita tried to keep Maria focused.

'I remember that he appeared a bit comical-looking.'

'What do you mean?'

'He had one of those moustaches, the one that curls up at either end. It made his face appear funny – we don't have those sort moustaches much in Europe anymore. Not since the British Empire, I guess.'

Again Amrita and her colleague exchanged glances. Although such facial appendages were uncommon where Maria lived, they were still familiar here, particularly among some of the upper classes in India.

Just as Amrita was about to close the interview, there was a commotion outside. Inspector Gupta had arrived and found his progress to his office blocked by an unfortunate office boy who had tripped and deposited a pile of paperwork in front of his door.

Gupta was remonstrating with him.

Maria also glanced around at the sudden interruption.

She froze. Her gaze fixed on the larger man.

Slowly she turned to face her interrogators once more.

Amrita saw the shocked expression on her face. 'What's wrong, Maria?'

For a moment Maria couldn't speak, then she slowly turned around again to face the two police officers. She leant forward so that her face was close to theirs.

'That's him,' she exclaimed. 'That's the second man.'

'You are sure?' Amrita asked incredulously. 'You are absolutely sure?'

'Absolutely,' Maria replied assertively.

chapter fifty-four

Back in Basel a couple of days later, Raymond called a board meeting to update them on the progress made in India. He had invited Harry over from London, and he and Maria sat side by side at the back of the room, slightly removed from the main conference table. Professor Hans Albrecht looked somewhat displeased at having one of his junior IT employees present at the meeting. He was also somewhat annoyed at the praise she was receiving, not only from Raymond but from the rest of the team as well. Though none were completely sure why she and the somewhat bashful and embarrassed young man beside her were at such a high-powered committee meeting in the first place.

Raymond introduced Harry as a recent addition to the IT staff and thanked him for all his good work, especially in locating Maria after she had been taken prisoner. Professor Albrecht stared daggers at the young pair, again not having been consulted over this recent appointment.

Raymond concluded their introduction with the words, 'We have to look to the future, and I believe these young people are the future.'

Albrecht choked on the glass of water he'd raised to his lips.

Raymond stood up and walked around the room while explaining in detail the recognition of the counterfeit tablets and the results of his investigations. 'With the help of my colleagues,' he indicated towards Harry and Maria, 'we located the local distribution point, and it led us to India. Where, after some mishaps, we, with the help of the local police force, finally found the factory that was producing the fake drugs. A local police officer has been arrested in relation to a cover-up of the operation.'

He went on to update them on the progress that had been made since their return home.

Amrita Banerjee had rung him only a few hours ago to brief him of the progress made. Gupta had been arrested. Initially he had denied any involvement, but an examination of his phone records and his bank accounts had proven conclusive, at which point he had conceded and turned state evidence in, in the hope mitigating some of the charges against him. He was fully aware how a police officer of his standing might fare in an Indian prison. In return for full disclosure, he had negotiated a dishonourable discharge from the police service, a loss of pension rights and a guilty plea to a lesser charge of aiding and abetting, which he was assured by those prosecuting would result in simply a fine and a number of hours' community service. Amrita had added that she would ensure that it would be as many hours of community service as possible, in as unpleasant place as she could find.

In return for the lesser prosecution Gupta had given extensive details of the counterfeit drug operation and had even hinted at similar operations in other regions of India. There were ongoing enquires and a number of raids had already taken place.

DCI Gupta had also named a man, a wealthy industrialist and owner of an agrochemical plant, as the drug overlord and brains behind the whole operation. Being a wealthy man, this Rahul Patel, when arrested, had immediately contacted and engaged the services of one of Delhi's top defence lawyers. With the lawyer on board, he was currently resisting all efforts to make him confess to any involvement. Amrita had told Raymond that despite his money and legal team, she was confident of implicating this Rahul Patel in the scam. A number of trained police officers were currently turning over his home and offices and accessing his emails and bank accounts.

What he didn't share with the committee was that Sergeant Banerjee had asked if Raymond could return to Delhi for any forthcoming trial. Without hesitation he had agreed to do so. In truth, he quite looked forward to meeting her again, this time in less trying circumstances.

Following his update, Raymond introduced the final new member of the board. 'Ladies and gentlemen, this is Catherine Stoker.' He indicated a young lady who had sat shyly beside him during the early part of the meeting and whom most present had mistaken as his secretary, there simply to take notes. 'Catherine, despite her benign appearance, is in fact a corporate lawyer of some repute. I think we are lucky to engage her services at this time. There is, I think you'll agree, bound to be some fallout from this whole affair, so I have employed Catherine here to keep the stories, particularly those in the press, fair and honest, with the threat of legal sanctions otherwise.'

The new UMBRA corporate lawyer smiled and bowed her head.

'So, colleagues, there you have it. While early sales have been hit, and hit hard, by the presence of the fake Erexat, I think we can now move on. The drug production and distribution points have been neutralised, and I am led to believe that all the head honchos in India are now under lock and key. So let's see what we can do to get our sales back up there.'

Assuming the meeting was over, some of the assembled team rose to leave. But Raymond had remained on his feet. 'There is, however,' he added.

Everyone sat back down.

'There is one loose end,' he added, looking around the room. 'During our investigations, it became clear that there had to be an internal leak, one emanating from our headquarters here in Basel.' He paused for effect.

The committee members looked disbelieving, glancing from one to the other. 'Impossible,' he heard someone mutter.

'I missed it at first, but the clues were there,' he continued. Then, turning to Brian Thompson, 'Brian, you informed me about the problem with the fake drug – why it was dangerous was because the counterfeiters had used the wrong filler.'

'Exactly that,' Brian confirmed.

'And that's what we acted on. But what I missed at the time was the other bit of information.'

'Other bit of information?' Brian struggled to remember.

'Yes. The filler was wrong... But the active ingredients were exactly those of our own drug.'

'Yes, I did report that, but...' A look of sudden understanding spread over his face. 'I see what you mean.' Some of the others around the table looked inquisitively towards the pharmacist. 'You mean, how were the active ingredients *exactly* the same as our own if they didn't have access to our formula?'

'Precisely.' Raymond glanced around the room. 'So the formulae must have come from here. The drug was too new for us to share it with any of our subsidiaries as yet.'

'So the next question is – who had access to the formulae?' Without waiting for an answer, Raymond continued, 'Well, obviously we all did, plus, I suppose, some of the manufacturing team, but I think we can rule them out.

'When I thought about it, when we were in India the criminals always seemed to be one step ahead of us. Of course in retrospect some of the information could have come from Gupta, but not all of it. And where was he getting his information from?

'No. I'm sorry to say, somebody in this room has to be responsible for this whole debacle.'

The committee were stunned into silence.

'So then I thought,' Raymond started to pace the room again, 'who would benefit most from the failure of Erexat?'

He paused; everybody looked at him expectantly.

Then, moving slowly behind Frank Kinney, he announced, 'That would be you, Frank, wouldn't it?'

Frank Kinney rose to his feet, protesting his innocence.

'I beat you to the job – you were always resentful of that and tried to undermine me at every opportunity. My failure would be your success.'

'Really, you cannot be serious.' Frank looked around the room for support.

There was none immediately forthcoming; most assembled there realised the truth of what Raymond had just said.

'Then, Frank, there is the little matter of Harry's phone call.'

'Phone call?' somebody asked.

'Harry located the factory site. I was in India and he didn't have a contact number for me, so he rang here and he talked to somebody here. Somebody who said that they would pass the information on to me.'

He turned to Harry. 'Who did you talk to, Harry?'

'It was him.' He pointed to Frank Kinney.

'That's precisely why I invited you along to the meeting today, Harry, thank you.'

'So, Frank, Harry gave you the location of the drug factory for you to pass on to me. But you didn't, did you? Can you explain why not?'

Frank looked flustered but replied, 'Okay, I admit it was me who took the call. I can't deny it, can I? Phone records will probably confirm it. But, look, you were in India, I couldn't get hold of you. You must have been somewhere out of phone signal range or something.'

'You didn't leave a message?'

'No, I thought I'd get hold of you later. Then I must have forgotten or something. Anyway, who is this kid? It could just have been a hoax or something.'

'But it wasn't, was it, Frank?

Frank fell silent.

'I might have believed you, Frank. After all, you have been a trusted employee of this company for longer than I have, but that was probably one reason you felt resentful of being passed over. Here was a chance to bury me and make some money into the bargain. It was you who sold the formulae to Patel and you who tipped off him and his compatriots whenever we got close. Why not just admit it, Frank?'

Frank said nothing, but he shook his head from side to side vigorously whilst looking around the table once more for support.

It seemed that everyone in the room was now avoiding his gaze.

'Anyway, Frank, you don't have to confess – we have all the evidence we need.'

Frank Kinney looked up at him with malevolence in his eyes.

Yes, Frank. As you have learnt, Harry there is a bit of a computer whiz kid. With Maria's help and my permission we have scrutinised your emails, phone records and bank records. I'm afraid the evidence is pretty damning, Frank.'

Frank Kinney visibly slumped in his chair; he buried his head in his hands.

Raymond stepped back towards his seat at the head of the table and pressed the intercom button. 'Slab, will you come in now, please?'

The door opened and was immediately filled with the wide frame of Slab McBride.

'Frank, meet one of our new security officers. He will escort you out and take care of you until the police arrive.'

He turned to Slab. 'Slab, meet the man who was responsible for the drug your son took. Could you escort him outside and explain the consequences of his actions to him? You have about ten minutes until the police arrive.'

Slab picked Frank Kinney up by his collar and bundled him out of the room.

'That, ladies and gentlemen, I think concludes the meeting.'

They all rose to leave, still incredulous at the turn of events they had just witnessed.

Raymond walked slowly over to where Maria and Harry had remained seated. 'Good job, you guys.'

He shook each by the hand in turn. 'Welcome to the firm, Harry. I have no doubt that you will be an asset.'

'An asset?' Harry looked incredulous. 'Up to now in most people's eyes I'm just another nobody.'

'In my opinion,' Maria added, smiling at him.

'Nobody,… is perfect.'